Fire in Broken Water

Also by Lakota Grace

The Pegasus Quincy Mystery Series
Death in Ghost City
Blood in Tavasci Marsh
Fire in Broken Water
Peril in Silver Nightshade
Silence in West Fork

FIRE
IN
BROKEN
WATER

by

LAKOTA GRACE

Version 1.0 – February, 2018

Published by Lakota Grace at CreateSpace

ISBN: 9781980243090

Discover other titles by Lakota Grace at www.LakotaGrace.com.

DEDICATION

To two of the best beta readers out there, Linda Henden and Kay Henden (who also writes, using the pen names Allyn and Ellen Keigh). These two have kept me out of the weeds, spotted all of the trees in the forest I've missed, and waved me off those disastrous detours. Thanks, guys!

CHAPTER ONE

The radio crackled to life. "Dispute in progress, lethal weapons involved."

My partner, Shepherd Malone, grabbed the mic and claimed it for us. We took the Middle Verde Valley exit off I-17, heading toward the river. Turning left, we bounced along a dirt road for about a mile, through gray-green hills of mesquite and catclaw acacia trees.

The spring bloom had faded and dust blanketed the sparse leaves. Heat waves shimmered at the end of the valley. I squinted at the cloudless June skies and hoped for rain. It was the age-old problem here in the Southwest—we needed the water, just not too much of it all at once.

My name is Peg Quincy and in addition to being a newly appointed sheriff's deputy, I'm a volunteer Family Liaison Officer, a FLO. I'm usually one step behind the firemen and the EMTs, smoothing the way for those in need. I gather information for the law, too, when a tragedy involves murder. I hoped this current call wouldn't involve that.

The dirt track leveled out into a graded gravel throughway. On either side of us, the desert scrub made way for fields of manicured grass, bounded by a white-painted fence. In one pasture a herd of thoroughbred horses grazed, some with frisking colts. Money here. We passed under an arch labeled "Spine Horse Ranch" and beneath that in smaller letters, "Black Onyx at stud."

At the small gatehouse, Shepherd lowered his window. "What seems to be the problem?" he asked the security guard.

"The ranch manager, Gil Streicker, told me to call you. We got a trespasser down by the first barn." He pointed to a deep-red wooden structure with a peaked roof.

Shepherd pulled into a parking area and we got out.

My stomach tightened as I readied for what lay ahead. Even in our quiet rural community, violence was often only a step away. The problem could be a homeless person with a psychotic break, a domestic dispute, or a burglary in progress.

We rushed past the corner of the barn to see a stout, middle-aged woman dressed in overalls, her long, black hair pulled into a knot. She held a pitchfork and jabbed threateningly toward the tall man standing in front of her.

"Damn you, Gil Streicker, I'll make you wish you were never born." Her voice was strong, and she accented each word with a push of her pitchfork.

"Yeah, well tell that miserable cripple brother of yours to stay the hell off our property."

"He's just claiming what's ours," she said. "You're stealing our water."

"*Your* water. Prove it," the man yelled.

She tilted the pitchfork closer to his waist, the tips of its sharp tines gleaming in the sunlight. "You stay away from what's ours or I'll kill you!" she exclaimed.

The ranch manager backed a step and his boot heel stubbed against the barn wall, halting farther retreat. Sweat gleamed on his forehead, and his hand dropped to a revolver on his hip.

"Get back, Serena. So help me if you don't, I'll—"

My partner drew down his weapon and I clasped mine as well.

"That's enough folks." Shepherd's deep voice cut through the conflict. "Miss, drop that pitchfork and step away."

She hesitated.

"Drop it, *now.*"

7

She released the pitchfork, and it tumbled to the ground.

"Sir, hands in the air," Shepherd ordered.

The man did so, and I breathed out the breath I'd been holding. If we'd gotten here minutes later, this dispute could have turned deadly. And it might still not be over.

"Peg?" Shepherd gestured toward the man's gun, a six-shooter. I walked over and drew it from his holster. I emptied the bullets and dropped them in my pocket. I checked the gun's chamber and then stuck the empty gun in my waistband for safekeeping.

"I need my gun back," Streicker protested. "I keep it handy for varmints."

"You'll get it back when we figure out what's going on here," I said.

Gil Streicker was a man in his early forties. He wore a sweat-stained cowboy hat, a denim shirt, and faded blue jeans. The jeans settled around his lanky hips like they'd been molded there. He was taller than me, too. At my six-foot height, I notice these things.

Shepherd holstered his own weapon and propped the pitchfork against the barn, away from Serena. "Now, folks, time to calm down a bit. Peg, take Mr. Streicker over there and get his story. Serena, let's you and I walk in this direction." He took her arm and led her away.

Standard policy. Separate disputants to get both sides of the story. But Shepherd called the woman by her first name. Did he know her? Not surprising. Shepherd, close to retirement, had called this rural valley home for most of his life. I'd only moved here recently from Tennessee and was still learning this western environment.

The ranch manager huffed a breath and held out his hand. "Call me Gil."

I took it in a solid handshake.

"Why don't we sit over there?" I pointed to a picnic table under the shade of a big cottonwood tree. The air was cooler in the shade, a light breeze rustling the leaves. A gray-and-white barn cat brushed against my leg and then drifted away.

Gil Streicker scowled, ready to make his case. He was breathing heavily, too, and I understood. Confronting an angry woman, an *armed* angry woman, could get the juices flowing better than a cliff side of rattlesnakes.

"Take a breath, Mr. Streicker, and tell me exactly what is going on here."

He shifted his attention to me, gave me a direct blue-eyed stare. "Peg—can I call you Peg?"

The man radiated unexpected sexuality, a physical heat perhaps heightened by the recent argument.

"Sure glad you showed up when you did," he said. "I might have had to *hurt* that woman." He touched my arm.

Standard approach for an alpha male—make first contact.

I leaned back out of reach and lowered my voice an octave. "You can call me Deputy Quincy."

He shrugged. "Serena Battle's brother—" Here, he turned and spat on the ground in disgust. "—destroyed our irrigation ditch. Cost a bundle to repair it. I sent my man over there with a bill and she tore it up. Now, this. She has no right to threaten us. Next time either one of that clan shows a face around here, I'll..."

"You'll what?"

"Never mind." He gained control of himself with obvious effort. "I know you're just doing your job." He gave a rueful grin and hitched at his trousers. The man was determined to be his own version of charming.

I wasn't impressed. "Serena and her brother live close?"

"Work this run-down plot of land south of us," Gil said. "We use the same irrigation ditch. With this drought, water has been scarce. Serena claims we been taking more than our share."

"Have you?"

He blustered. "You saw the pastures coming in. Maintaining that grassland for our horses takes water." He swept a hand of dismissal. "Hell, Serena's just growing a few vegetables down at her place. What does she need that much water for?"

I tried to remain neutral, but it was hard. My family came from farming background. They didn't have a lot of money either, but they were hard workers and honest as a clear shaft of water.

"So you're stealing it."

"That's what she *says*. Anyway, if she thinks something's wrong she can always sue us."

His easy manner seemed to indicate she wouldn't. Lawyers can eat up a lot of money in a hurry. On that battleground, this expansive ranch property probably had already won.

"You own this ranch?" I asked. He seemed overly involved and I wanted to check.

"No, not yet." He gave me a peculiar smile. "I'm the ranch manager."

"Then I'd like to talk to the owner."

"That would be Heinrich Spine. Let's see if he's available."

He rose in a loose-limbed way and strode toward the barn, perhaps assuming I wouldn't keep up with him. No problem. I matched him stride for stride.

The earthy scent of big animals filled the dim barn. We passed several empty stalls, and then one containing a magnificent black stallion. Big, with a long flowing mane. He hung his head over the door, his alert ears tracking our progress toward him. Gil paused to stroke the horse's cheek, caressing it gently like he might a woman's face.

We entered an office at the end of the building, and Gil waved to a girl behind the desk. She looked to be about twenty and had brown hair slicked back in an unbecoming ponytail. The pungent odor of stable manure drifted from her clothing.

"Gil, are you all right?" She looked up at him with shining eyes.

"I'm fine, honey, nothing for you to worry about. Call the main house and see if Heinrich is accepting visitors."

She talked on the phone for a few moments. Then she hung up and addressed Gil, ignoring me. "I'm sorry. The nurse says he's sleeping. He's not feeling well." Her voice had a little-girl tentativeness, as if she were seeking approval from him.

Gil flashed her a smile and turned to me. "Sorry, Peg. That meeting will have to wait for another day." He raised his hands, palms up, in a see-how-reasonable-we-are gesture.

The hair on the back of my neck rose. "Sooner or later, I'll have to speak with him. This matter needs to be resolved."

Gil shrugged, conversation over. As we left the barn, he bumped into me and I felt a secondary rush of heat.

At the end of the drive, Gil took my hand. Held it. Gazed into my eyes for a long moment, his invitation clear. Then he dropped my fingers and held out his own palm, all business. "You've got something that belongs to me."

I gave Gil back his revolver. "Don't be threatening people with that again or we'll have to..."

"Got to protect what's mine," he said, unrepentant. He wriggled his fingers in a give-me motion.

"I'll leave the ammunition at the gatehouse." I straightened, my voice formal.

Gil turned on his heel and left me standing there feeling as if I'd gone ten rounds in a welterweight boxing ring. The man was a primal animal, no doubt about it. And what did that make me?

Serena Battle had left by the time I reached the squad car.

"What did you think of our resident Lothario?" Shepherd asked.

"Heavy."

He chuckled. "Thought you might appreciate the experience. Brighten your morning."

"You didn't arrest Ms. Battle?"

"No cause. She's got enough on her hands with her brother, Hank. She promised to stay away from the ranch."

"And you believed her?" I asked.

"I've known Serena for years. Her daddy and I went deer hunting every fall until that stroke killed him. She'll keep her word."

"An arrest would emphasize the seriousness of what she's done..."

"Peg!" His tone held warning.

Shepherd didn't like to be second-guessed by anybody, least of all a junior partner. I was still finding my way on the uncertain ground of our working relationship.

We stopped by the gatehouse, and I surrendered the bullets, warm from their stay in my pocket. Then we jounced along the dirt road, back to I-17 to resume our regular patrol.

Shepherd was quiet for a while and I asked his thoughts.

"Considering Serena Battle."

"Feisty lady," I commented.

"She's had to be, ever since her pa died. She's sole guardian for her brother."

"Guardian?"

"Accident." He touched his head. "No motorcycle helmet."

In four words my partner summarized a life gone terribly wrong. I hoped it never happened to me that sudden. But being a cop, it could. Part of the risk that we took every day.

"What's with this water feud of theirs, anyway?"

"Serena might actually have a case," he said.

Shepherd let a sedan come up behind us and then slowed the patrol car to three miles under the speed limit. Sometimes he played games like this. Cars would follow behind the squad car like obedient ducklings, not risking a pass. Kept them honest, Shepherd said.

He shifted his attention back to the subject of our conversation. "In Arizona, water rights transfer with the property. And that land has been in Serena's family for generations. Since they used the water first, she'd have senior rights to the Spine Ranch, even though it flowed through there first."

"You warned her about trespassing. Think she'll stay away?" I asked.

"She better. Gil's a charmer, but that ranch is his life. He'd not hesitate to take drastic measures."

"He good at what he does?"

"The best. A wizard at handling horses. Heard they started a dressage program for their Friesian stock. You see the stallion?"

"That black in the stable?"

He nodded. "Nothing prettier on a misty morning than to watch that big stud running across the meadow, mane and tail a-flying."

A late-model red Porsche Carrera passed us going about ninety.

Shepherd flipped the light bar and sirens, and we rammed to speed. The driver spurted ahead for a moment and I thought we'd have a chase. Then he turned on his blinker, edged to the side of the road, and stopped.

"Cover me," Shepherd said, getting out of the squad car. "And call in the plate."

I did. The plate was clear, but the guy was giving Shepherd lip about something. Shepherd took the license and registration and walked back for me to check those, too.

"Trouble?" I asked.

"Nothing I can't handle."

But after he returned the documents to the car, Shepherd had the guy get out and do some sobriety tests. The man walked the line nice and straight, hit his nose with his finger, eyes closed.

Would my partner pull him in anyway? Always a judgment call. After more discussion, he wrote out the ticket, tore it off the pad, and gave it to the driver. Then Shepherd walked back to the squad car.

"Made our quota for the day on that one," he said. "Guy was high on something or just bullheaded. Maybe the size of that fine will quiet him down some. Hope so."

Shepherd was breathing hard from the adrenaline rush. I understood. Sometimes a routine traffic stop turned into more. This time it didn't.

The red sports car signaled properly and merged into the traffic lane, keeping to the speed limit as we passed him.

"Can't place that guy," Shepherd said. "But I've seen him before, someplace."

Often a life-defining event isn't clear until you look back on it later.

We'd just had two.

CHAPTER TWO

The next morning Shepherd waited for me in the station parking lot when I drove up. "More trouble at the Spine Ranch," he said. "They just called it in."

I transferred to his squad car and buckled up. He squealed out of the lot.

"The water problems again?" I asked.

"No. Fire in the stables."

A horseman's worst fear. Horses weren't the smartest of animals in an emergency. Even if stable hands led the horses out, sometimes the animals bolted back into the chaos of the fire, seeking the safety of their stall. I remembered the black stallion. Had they got him out in time?

Shepherd punched the patrol car to speed on the freeway. It didn't take long before we'd turned onto the rutted dirt road leading to the Spine Ranch. Then we slowed, eating dust from the fire department's pumper truck ahead of us. When we pulled into the ranch entrance, smoke billowed into the sky, and a ranch hand banged a palm on the hood of the squad car, stopping us.

"This way," he yelled, pointing to an open area.

Shepherd parked the car, and we followed the man at a jog. My cheeks burned from the searing wind. I coughed as debris from the fire fouled the air. The stable was fully engulfed in flames, and beyond, a herd of horses bunched nervously in a nearby paddock.

The stallion was there. They'd saved him, at least. He lifted his large black head in a challenge bugle. The mares around him fanned and then pushed together, wide eyes intent on the fire. Somewhere a dog barked. The smoke billowed in rough, white clouds when the water attacked it.

I tripped over a jumble of hoses crisscrossing the ground like a spider web torn asunder.

Shepherd grabbed my arm to steady me. "Slow down," he cautioned. "Firemen got it under control."

Streams of water arced into the center of the inferno. Flames crackled as water hissed into steam. A nearing siren signaled the arrival of another engine company. A fire like this could explode in our dry summer weather, igniting tinder-dry brush into a raging wildfire.

An oily black cloud burst upward, and the intense light from the fire blinded me. A timber crashed to the ground with an explosion of sparks. My foot slipped in the mud created from the defensive sheets of water, and my eyes smarted as we neared the fire.

"This way!" Shepherd pointed to one side of the barn where three first responders huddled over a still human shape on the ground. Gorge rose in my throat. Was there a fatality?

They had oxygen out, and one man was doing CPR. I remembered that course at the police academy, practicing until my arms ached on a rubber dummy. Here, an actual life was held in the balance.

Thump, thump, thump, then rest and breathe in. The man was unresponsive, with the cherry-red cheeks of carbon monoxide poisoning. One of the EMTs looked up at our approach. I tilted my chin in a mute question, and he shook his head. The prone man was probably already gone. But they'd try. They always tried.

The warble of an ambulance pierced my perception.

The young woman from the office yesterday rushed up to us. Her dark hair hung in tangled ropes, her eyes reddened by the ash filling the air.

"You called it in?" Shepherd asked.

She nodded. "Gil's hurt!" She pointed to the man on the ground. "The roof collapsed. I couldn't reach him." Tears mixed with soot on her cheeks, and she brushed them away in frustration.

"The heat drove me back."

A shiver ran through me in spite of the super-heated air. Gil Streicker! I'd questioned that man less than twenty-four hours ago, under this very cottonwood tree whose blackened leaves now drifted down in a fiery shower.

A firefighter sent a fierce stream of water cascading over the tree, and the fire hissed in defiance through the withered limbs. A beam in the barn collapsed with a muffled whump.

The young woman took one unsteady step forward.

"We got the horses out," she said. "But when I turned around, Gil ran back in. Then he was gone. Gone!"

I put an arm around her shoulder to hold her upright. Her expression was confused and her skin icy cold. She was shocking out.

"Someplace quieter we can talk?" I asked, wanting to remove her to a place of safety.

She waved vaguely at a big house shimmering through the haze. "The kitchen."

Shepherd looked at me. "Go with her. I'll watch over things here."

I didn't argue. I moved toward the house with the girl, leaving the searing fire-edged world behind.

An angular Hispanic woman in a maid's uniform greeted us at the back door. The kitchen was a cool sanctuary after the smoky hurricane outside.

The woman put both arms around the girl and held her close, murmuring softly. The girl leaned into the embrace for a moment and then jerked back.

"Daisy, our barn cat—she might be hurt!" she said in jerky breaths.

Then she broke from the woman's embrace and whirled back toward the door. "He's dead," she wailed. "Gil's dead!"

I intercepted her before she could leave. "Come, sit here for a moment."

I took her arm and steered her to a kitchen chair. She slumped into it, weeping.

The woman who had embraced the girl extended her hand to me. "I'm Rosa Morales." She touched the girl's shoulder.

"*Pobrecita,* my poor little one."

Then she went to the kitchen sink, filled a glass with water, and set it on the oak table in front of the young woman. She gestured toward the glass to ask if I wanted one, and I shook my head. Then she silently left the room.

The young woman's fingers shook as she grasped the glass with both hands and gulped the water. She set the glass on the table, almost spilling it. Then she straightened, sniffing loudly, and wiped her nose on her sleeve. Slow awareness returned to her eyes.

I reached into my pocket for a notebook. "What's your full name, Miss?"

"I'm Amanda—Amanda Riordan." She raked shaky fingers through her matted hair. "I was upstairs when the fire started, trying to quiet my grandfather. He's old, gets upset by things he doesn't understand."

That would be Heinrich Spine, the ranch owner. That meant his young woman was more than an employee. I made a scribbled note. "Then what happened?"

"I smelled the smoke and ran down." Amanda Riordan's eyes filled with tears, and she snatched a handful of tissues from the box on the counter. Dark smears of soot streaked her cheeks as she swiped at her tears. "I called the fire department. But it wasn't enough!"

I waited a moment, letting her settle. "Any idea how the fire might have started?"

"Anything can set off fires in a barn," Amanda said, her voice raspy from the smoke. "Moldy hay. Or a careless cigarette. Smoking isn't allowed in the stables, but Heinrich smokes wherever he wants to. He and Gil often fought about it."

"Your grandfather," I prompted.

"Doctor Spine, world-famous German chemist." Her tone turned bitter. "His steel-trap mind snares everybody."

"Does that everybody include you?" I asked. It was almost as though she used her dislike as a buffer against this moment that was too heavy with smoke and death.

"Sometimes," Amanda admitted. "The family moved back here about three years ago to take care of Heinrich. Frankly, I don't think he's really that sick—he just wants the attention."

"You all live here in this house?" I asked.

Amanda nodded. "There's three of us—Heinrich, my mom, and me—oh, and Fancy, grandfather's nurse." Strength came back into her voice with the recitation of facts. "My dad doesn't live here. He's a doctor, but he and Mom are separated, sort of." Her dirty fingers traced the grain of the oak table, leaving ugly blotches of ash and mud.

I turned a page in the notebook and continued writing.

"Gil shouldn't even have been out there," Amanda said. "He was ill."

"Sick?"

"Vomiting, couldn't keep anything down. But it seemed to cycle. He'd be fine one minute, the next minute, really sick. I wanted him to go into the emergency room, but he brushed me off. Flu, he said." She jerked upright. "How is he? I have to go to him!"

"They are doing everything for him they can. Stay here with me." I touched her hand, trying to gentle the agitation that seemed to cycle through her body. I watched her closely as I asked the next question. "Was the fire accidental, then?"

"I suppose so." Her face turned doubtful. "But it shouldn't have spread like that. We put in a new sprinkler system last month. The water turn-on valve links to rate-of-temperature detectors. The sprinklers should have stopped the fire the moment it started. Gil was so proud of that system..."

"What was he like, your ranch manager?" I interrupted. My speech had shifted to past tense, anticipating the loss ahead. Amanda didn't follow my lead. On one level, she seemed to acknowledge the possible death and yet on another, fiercely denied it.

"Good with horses. The best."

Her eyes held shock and loss. And grief as well. Gil Streicker might have been good with horses, but he'd made a conquest here, too.

"Does Gil have any family, anybody who should be notified of his accident?"

"Nobody here. He's got a daughter back east. Her address might be in the files somewhere..." She shivered again, arms crossed tight to her chest. She seemed to drift in and out, losing awareness.

"When can I speak with your grandfather?" I asked.

"I'll call upstairs and see if he is up for visitors."

She spoke briefly to someone on the phone. Then she rose from her chair, her back stiff. "Come on. Let's get this over with."

We passed from the kitchen into a hallway filled with Pre-Columbian art, cloistered in deep alcoves, and from there into a huge living room. Thick adobe walls muffled the sounds from fire crews outside, and light filtered through curtains made of black and white Mexican serapes. The room sat heavy, masculine-hard at the edges, with outsized leather furniture and Western oil paintings.

A broad stairway banistered in wrought iron led to the second floor. At the top of the stairs, tall double oak doors blocked our way. Amanda Riordan knocked once and then walked in. I followed close behind. We entered a library lined with floor-to-ceiling bookshelves: some purchased-in-sets classics, combined with a mixture of old chemistry texts and books with German titles.

Dr. Heinrich Spine sat in a raised chair by the window, a cane by his side. His clothes hung loosely on a frame wasted by illness, his thinning gray hair plastered into a rigid comb-over. He had parted the curtains with one hand, looking down at the fire scene below. As we entered, he glanced up. His body showed the brittleness of advanced age but his eyes held a fiery intelligence.

His nurse sat in a shadowed corner, her body still to the point of invisibility. A tallish, middle-aged woman, pale in complexion. She was dressed in a dull mauve-colored shirtwaist and crepe-soled shoes, her graying hair pulled back in a severe bun. What was her name—Fancy?

"I wondered when you would bother to attend to my needs." Dr. Spine's querulous voice formed Germanic vowels with guttural preciseness.

"Heinrich, this is Deputy Quincy," Amanda began.

"*Doctor* Spine, please, since you cannot bear to call me grandfather. I can see the police uniform."

"Sit," he ordered me, gesturing to a wooden chair near him. "I cannot look up to that tallness."

A bony forefinger jabbed at the windowpane. "The smell of smoke awoke me. Then I heard the fire engines. Inform me what is going on down there. Is the fire contained?"

19

"Mostly," I said, "but your ranch manager, Gil Streicker, may have lost his life."

"A tragedy." His tone was perfunctory. "And the horses?"

"Safe," Amanda said.

"And you assisted in their rescue? I would expect that of you, at least."

Amanda's lips compressed into a tight line.

"Any reason why the alarm system in the stable would be inoperative?" I asked Dr. Spine.

"Absolutely not, if everyone did what they were paid to do." He slammed his cane against the chair leg as if striking someone. The sound of wood hitting wood jarred the stillness of the room.

"But they may all be incompetent, just as you have proved yourself to be, granddaughter." His voice was harsh, unforgiving.

The old man's fingers restlessly explored the table next to him. "Fancy, my cigarettes."

The nurse rose, extracted a pack from her uniform pocket. She lit one and handed it to him. When she passed me to return to her corner seat, a purplish birthmark on her right cheek flared. She angled her head, pulling the disfigurement into the shadows as she resumed a position of readiness nearby.

Heinrich held the lit cigarette in his mouth without smoking, the fumes curling upward. When the ash grew to an inch in length, the nurse picked up a thick crystal ashtray from the side table, waiting.

When he removed the cigarette from his mouth with shaking fingers, she followed under his hand with the ashtray, waiting for the ash to drop. When it did, Heinrich replaced the cigarette in the corner of his mouth, and the nurse retreated once more.

"And your mother, Amanda? Why is she not here?"

High heels clattered in the hallway, and a woman in her late forties entered the room. A Prussian blue silk dress draped her fashion-gaunt figure, and her face had the smoothness of cosmetic surgery.

"Father! You know you can't smoke like that..."

"Bad Heinrich!" He mocked her tone.

He waved the lighted cigarette in the nurse's direction. "Put it out, Fancy."

She lifted it from his fingers and stabbed it out in the ashtray. Her hands were red with nails bitten to the quick. Heinrich hadn't bothered to introduce the nurse to me. It must have slipped his steel-trap mind.

The slender woman turned to Amanda. "There's a smudge on your cheek."

Amanda jerked back from her mother's touch. "Gil is dead," she said dully. "I just know it."

"I'm sure that's not the case." The mother's hand waved in dismissal. "I saw the ambulance out there. They'll take care of it."

Some folks react to stress by minimizing events, by distancing. I tried to give Amanda's mother the benefit of the doubt.

"You don't understand. I loved him!" Amanda raised an anguished fist to her mouth and then pivoted and ran from the room.

"Please excuse my daughter's ill manners. The excitement must have distressed her." The woman brushed platinum locks away from her eyes with a nervous gesture and extended her hand. "I'm Marguerite Spine-Riordan."

I explained that the arson team would be investigating.

"That is not necessary. The fire was accidental." Heinrich's tone was harsh, daring me to contradict him.

"And you know that because?" My own voice turned strident. A man had possibly died here, and other than Amanda, nobody seemed to give a damn.

Calm down, Peg, I cautioned myself, taking a breath. "Gil Streicker was your manager. Any family that you know of?"

"None," Heinrich said, contradicting Amanda's earlier statement. "If he's dead, I suppose we'll arrange for cremation and burial." His voice was emotionless.

Like trash you have no further use for. I swallowed hard.

I gave Heinrich and Marguerite my cards so that they could contact me as the official family liaison officer assigned to the case. Then I offered one to the nurse, Fancy. She took it without comment and placed it on the table next to the pack of cigarettes.

Were Gil Streicker's injuries fatal? A niggle of suspicion started in the back of my brain. If so, we'd need to investigate. I'd make sure it was a very *thorough* investigation, before I'd let this family go back to business as usual.

I met Shepherd in the yard, and we walked back to the squad car.

"Dead?" I asked.

He nodded and settled himself on the passenger side, while I buckled up to drive. I rammed into gear and applied pressure to the gas pedal, needing to release some tension. The back tires spit gravel as we left the parking area.

"Whoa! Take it easy," he said. "What did you find out from the ranch owner?"

"He's an old man with too much money wielding too much control over his daughter and granddaughter."

"But any evidence of foul play?" Shepherd pushed a little.

"It could be a case of misjudgment," I admitted reluctantly, "if the man was overcome by the fumes when he ran back into a burning barn."

Shepherd grunted. "Won't know until the ME's report. Don't forget to follow up on that autopsy. Make sure they put this body at the head of the line."

That order was Shepherd's need to boss me around. Even with the current budget restraints, he never let me forget who was senior in the office.

"On it," I said.

He shifted into teaching mode. "Ever been through an arson investigation? You might want to follow the guy around tomorrow. Learn something."

"Good idea."

I jumped at his suggestion. I hated autopsies. The smell of my first one cost me my lunch. Didn't want to repeat that performance anytime soon. Shadowing a guy with a clipboard, instead, sifting through ashes suited me just fine.

***

At the end of our shift, Shepherd let me off at the sheriff's carpool where I picked up my Jetta for the climb up the hill to my apartment in Mingus. I was almost there when the check-engine light signaled an ominous red. Anxiety tightened my gut.

My car was twelve years old with over 200K on the speedometer. But it was a *Volkswagen*. They lasted forever, didn't they? I pulled to the side of the road and switched off the ignition to let it cool.

While I waited, I dialed the medical examiner's office and asked to speak to Dr. Sidney Morrison, my contact there. Solemn Sidney, we called him, because the dead fascinated him much more than the living. He loved conundrums. Maybe I could tempt him with this one.

"Heard about this interesting case," he said when I got him on the phone. "You'd love it. This guy gets drunk, pulls out his six-shooter. Pops off at one of those tall saguaro cactus in his backyard—one, two, three. Never guess what happened..."

I knew the story, but I didn't want to ruin his fun. "What?"

"Damn cactus fell over on him, killed him on the spot. Death by cactus. They lowered him very carefully into the old pine box."

I chuckled at the punch line. How to win friends and influence medical examiners. Then, "Hey, Sidney, I need a favor."

"Name it."

"Man by the name of Streicker, killed in a fire today."

"Got him lying on a slab here like a nice piece of rib-eye, medium rare."

Bile rose at the image. "Could you do the autopsy soon? Run the full tox screen on him."

"We always do the usual drug tests—meth, heroin, alcohol— but you're asking for more. You suspect something?"

Perhaps it was Amanda's report that Gil had been sick, or maybe my dislike of Heinrich Spine raised my suspicions. But whatever the reason, I wanted to make doubly sure Gil Streicker had died of natural causes. "We want the *full* tox screen," I confirmed.

Sidney was silent, and then said, "You mean the Marsh test for heavy metal poisoning? Led Zeppelin time! Who do I bill it to?"

"The sheriff's office here in Mingus."

So what if Shepherd objected. My partner was on his way to retirement anyway. Then I'd be in charge of the office again—that is, if the budget ever came through.

I hung up and tried the ignition. The Jetta started smoothly, no red light this time. I pulled the car onto the road and drove up the switchbacks to Mingus. Probably just a loose connection. I put the car's well-being in the same "think-about-it-later" bin as I did the future of my job with the sheriff's department.

It was almost dark when I pulled into the drive next to the old building that held my studio apartment. Reckless announced my arrival with a deep bay. When I opened the door, he planted huge red paws on my chest in proper coonhound greeting. Then he dashed down the steps and into the side yard to relieve himself.

Not easy on the big dog, shut up here by himself. I'd accepted the responsibility of caring for him because a man I'd sent to prison asked me to. The hound was a nuisance, but he was company, somebody who welcomed me home at night after a long shift.

Waiting for him, I noticed something taped to the front window. I took a closer look, thinking it might be a notification of a service call.

"Eviction Notice," the paper declared. "You have ten days to vacate this property."

What the hell? It wasn't much of a place—I was subletting from the bank that had gotten it from an estate sale. But eviction? That didn't make sense. I paid the rent on time, most months, usually.

I'd held my irritation in check for hours. First that miserable old man at the Spine Ranch, then being subjected to Shepherd's bossing all day, and the car troubles. Now this! I kicked at the front door frame. Its solid oak didn't budge, but I felt my toe wince from the impact.

I hobbled inside in pain and tossed the notice on the entry table. If they wanted me out, they'd just have to send somebody from the sheriff's office to evict me. Ha! I *was* somebody from the sheriff's office.

I grabbed the notice again and squinted at it in the hall light. Ten days' notice. That was over a week. I'd call the bank in the morning and find out what they wanted. I limped up the interior stairs to the apartment, Reckless tripping on my heels.

Later that night, I listened to the coyotes announcing the full moon in the hills around me. Priorities. That was what Shepherd drilled into my head. Put the important things first. Right now I had to solve the mystery surrounding Gil Streicker's death. And that would start with my first arson investigation in the morning.

CHAPTER THREE

Reckless got me up at dawn. After a quick run up mountain paths to keep us both in shape, I showered and readied for work. I dropped the dog at HT's house so that my grandfather could babysit him and hiked up to the Mingus sheriff's office at the top of the hill.

Mingus, nestled in the Black Mountains, had been a copper mining town at the turn of the century. Now it was an artists' colony and tourist destination, with 400 good citizens needing law and order.

Shepherd was in early, working on a crossword puzzle in his office. That routine hadn't changed. But since the budget cuts, my former assistant, Ben Yazzie, had elected to take a sabbatical and enrolled at Yavapai College, studying for his viticulture degree.

Ben was half-Italian, half-Navajo and depending on the day, he was either learning herb lore in his quest to become a Shaman or fighting with his uncle over his Italian roots. But either way, the degree in growing grapes seemed a good fit for him. Ben told me he was going to be the best wine-grape grower in Arizona, and I believed him.

These days, he pounded away at research on his computer rather than playing video games in the reception area. I missed him and his famous Blue Mountain Coffee. I didn't like change, and my life seemed full of it lately.

I grabbed a bottle of water from the refrigerator and wandered into Shepherd's office. The room was hot, even for this early on a summer day. I peered at the wall thermostat. No wonder! It was set at 85 degrees.

I reached for the dial, and Shepherd scowled at me. "Don't touch that. Need to conserve energy, spend less." He peered with disapproval at the bottle in my hand. "Enjoy that. I'm not ordering any more. Too expensive."

"You okay, Shepherd?" I asked. It was unusual for him to be grouchy this early in the day.

He fidgeted in his seat and scowled at me. "I've got to attend a hearing on that Porsche driver we nailed the other day. He's contesting the ticket."

That explained it. Nothing crankier than my partner facing a court date. Shepherd was meticulous about his paperwork, and nothing was less controversial than a motorist—especially a sports car driver—claiming he wasn't speeding when he was.

As a result, nine times out of ten the judge ruled in Shepherd's favor. Nuisance hearings were a waste of the court's time, too. But Shepherd hated getting up in front of people. He told me he'd had the problem since third grade when he threw up all over a new pair of shoes the day that the teacher forced him to recite the Gettysburg Address.

And his nervousness had worsened with age. Anytime the man was near a witness box, he broke into a cold sweat. I'd once mentioned there were counselors who could help him get over his anxiety, and he just glared at me.

On the other hand, perhaps this would be a cut-and-dried testimony. I didn't like that Porsche driver either, and not just because his car was red and expensive.

I offered to attend the hearing with Shepherd, but he waved me away. "Nah, I'll be fine," he said. "Drop me off at the courthouse on your way to play chimney sweep."

***

The charred smell of burned lumber hung in the air as I parked my Jetta near the fire site at the Spine Ranch. Ash from the fire and muck from the firefighters' hoses had turned the area into a quagmire. I ducked under the sheriff's barrier tape and approached the arson investigator.

He was a tall lanky man wearing a yellow hard hat. He tapped a clipboard nervously against his leg as he waited for me.

"Shepherd told me you'd be coming. How's the old bastard doing?"

He handed me another hard hat with a disapproving stare. "Thought he'd have told you to wear old clothes. Fire makes a mess of uniforms."

"I'll manage. What're you looking for?" I asked, trying to be sociable. "They send you the photographs from yesterday?"

"I don't need those pictures," he snapped. "I take my own."

"And then you'll be looking over insurance records and financials to see if there's a motive for setting the fire?"

"Shepherd didn't tell me you were a *rookie*." He peered at me with disdain. "I only determine *cause,* not motive. I leave the law enforcement to the experts."

His tone indicated I wasn't included in that category. The guy must have had a fight with the missus before he left home. He'd cut himself shaving, too. A tatter of Kleenex stuck to his chin.

He saw me staring and plucked it off. "Let's get started. Don't touch anything. Burn sites are unstable. Liable to come down on your head."

I clamped my mouth shut and followed meekly behind. First, he walked around the outside of the entire burned structure. Checking for perimeter damage?

He saw me crane a look at his clipboard and sighed. "All right," he said. "I'm getting a sense of how effective the ranch's fire protection was."

"How'd they do?"

"Not too bad," he admitted grudgingly. "They're on well water here, so they've run a filtered line from that pond over there. See the dry hydrant? And their electrical box is set away from the front exit. Good. Means it wouldn't be the first thing to go up in smoke with a fire." He made a check on his clipboard.

"Two exits, front and back." He crossed another item off his list and then peered into the barn. "The center aisle is wide enough for two horses and handlers at a time. Probably why they got all the horses out—get away from that!"

I jumped back as a timber crashed to the floor. I didn't touch the thing; I swear it moved all by itself. I swiped at my sweaty forehead and left a smear of soot.

"I'm going inside the barn. Follow in my footsteps," he barked.

Half the stable had disintegrated into blackened rubble, but the fire left a small arch of timbers standing by the back entrance. I brushed away cobwebs that draped from one support. The inspector snatched them from my fingers.

"Evidence," he said.

"Of what?"

"Sloppy maintenance. A broom is the best fire prevention aid in a stable there is."

"But cobwebs?"

He looked at me with scorn. "Dust and straw accumulate in the webs. They can spread a fire across a barn in minutes."

His tone said everyone should know that. Well, now I did.

I pointed to a fire extinguisher on the wall. "So why didn't they use that?"

"Probably didn't know how. Have *you* ever used one?" He didn't wait for my denial. "Anyway, it's only a five pounder. Would have lasted ten seconds at best. Only good for spot fires, not anything fully engaged."

I pointed to a light bulb on the wall that was bulging in an odd fashion. "Fire does weird things to glass."

He pounced on my comment. "And why might that be important?"

What was this, Twenty Questions?

He assumed a professorial pose. "Glass is one of the primary indicators of direction of fire. The inert gases inside cause the bulb to bulge in the direction of the hottest blaze. Which in this case would be—here." He pointed to the edge of the one remaining wall of the barn office.

I remembered the day I'd talked to Gil Streicker and Amanda Riordan. Then, the office had been an oasis of calm in the midst of a thriving concern. Now, it was just a jumble of charred wood.

We crunched over broken glass and entered the space. The greasy imprint of what might have been Gil Streicker's body streaked the bare cement floor. Switching on his flashlight, the arson inspector traced the wall in a standardized search pattern.

Finally, he pointed to a sharp triangular flare pattern following blackened wires that led to a charred electrical outlet box. That answered why the alarm didn't trigger. No power.

"There it is," he announced with satisfaction. "Not usually this apparent. Rodents, probably. Always rats in a barn, feeding on the grain."

I thought of the pregnant barn cat Amanda had worried about. Was it still around? No mice to eat here anymore.

Just for the sake of argument, I asked, "Are you *sure* it was rodents? Couldn't it be man-made?"

"That's *your* job." He touched the tip of his pencil to the sooty flare on the wall. "Got your evidence case ready? Snip that piece of wire off and send it to forensics," he ordered.

The man's superior tone grated my nerves. Surely he had brought an evidence kit of his own? Or maybe it was more fun to make the rookie do it. I trudged back to my car, retrieved the evidence box from my trunk, and returned to the barn.

After the inspector had photographed the burned wire, I snipped it at both ends and gently put it in a box for the trip to the lab. I tried not to disturb the soot on the outside of the wire, hoping for latent fingerprints underneath.

The forensics folks were like archaeologists on a dig, laboriously removing layers, a fragment at a time, to discover treasures underneath. The painstaking efforts sometimes yielded evidence that solved a crime. Maybe we'd get lucky this time around.

The inspector closed the metal cover of his clipboard and turned to leave.

"So, how are you going to call it?" I asked, waiting to see if he'd go for mice or men, rodents or potential murderers.

"Undetermined!" He chortled triumphantly.

Definitely in a better humor than when we first met earlier this morning. His wife should hire me.

I'd seen enough. Leaving him to photograph the scene, I walked up to the big house.

Marguerite, Heinrich Spine's daughter, greeted me at the door. "We're about to sit down for a light lunch. Would you like to join us?"

It seemed an unusual invitation to make to a police officer, but

I never turn down free food. Marguerite showed me to the bathroom where I washed up and then joined them at a table set for four.

There would be me, Marguerite, her daughter Amanda. That was three. Rosa would be serving and the nurse, Fancy, would probably have lunch upstairs with Heinrich. Who else was coming?

Marguerite's face brightened as a man entered the dining room. "Raven, I was so hoping you could join us."

"My dear, I wouldn't miss it."

I turned in my chair to see a man, mid-forties, dressed all in black with dark hair flowing to his shoulders. I stood and his height matched my own. His eyes were a brilliant blue and had that particular intensity gained by opening them even a little wider. A crystal amulet hung around his neck.

"You must be Peg. I've heard about you. I'm Raven LightDancer." His handshake was soft. I sensed unease about the man and my alertness went up a notch. Past history with the law? Some former convicts I'd known shared his hesitant manner.

Amanda joined us, and Marguerite rang a silver bell. "Rosa, you may serve us now." The woman brought in plate after plate of cold dishes for summer fare. Sparkling apple cider with mango. A mango lassi, that sweet Indian drink made from yogurt. Mango quinoa salad. I detected a pattern here.

"Nice lunch," I commented. The mango cider *was* tasty.

"You like it?" Raven seemed genuinely pleased.

"It's for my diet," Marguerite explained. "Raven thinks that I'll become more spiritually aware if we alter what I eat." She patted his arm. "Raven is my CAM consultant."

"CAM?" I asked.

"Complementary and Alternative Medicine," she said with a social smile as she picked at her salad. "The medical doctors don't know everything."

"Bunch of crap," Amanda muttered under her breath.

Raven put up his hand like a traffic cop. In a sotto voice, he intoned, "Negativity interferes with the vibrational field."

Like a good family liaison officer, I turned to Amanda to sooth the negative vibrations. "Are you attending college?"

She shoved black-rimmed glasses back on a snub nose. "I want to be a vet, but I'm taking a little vacation from school right now."

"Dropped out. Why don't you tell her the truth," her mother said.

The overweight girl ducked her head as though warding off a blow. She put an extra scoop of mango on her plate. "I'm helping grandfather with the ranch business."

"Feeding the horses. Mucking out the stables!" Marguerite exclaimed. "Is that proper work for a Riordan?"

Amanda gripped the arms of her chair, her knuckles white. "Heinrich promised me a salary as soon as I learn how the system works."

"Call him grandfather, dear. He *is* paying for your room and board."

"And your *alternative* medical expenses, too. Don't forget that," Amanda said under her breath.

Marguerite looked at the plate that Amanda had heaped. "Do you really need to eat that much food? Portions, dear, portions."

Raven intervened. "Please, Marguerite, Amanda. We have a guest."

Mother and daughter ignored him, intent on skewering each other.

"I don't know why you didn't inherit my genes instead of your father's." Marguerite flung words at her daughter like shards of broken glass. "Keeping your figure is important if you ever hope to..." It sounded like an argument they'd had many times before.

Amanda glared back. "If I ever hope to what? Marry some loser like dad?" Her eyes filled with tears. Abruptly she shoved her plate aside, untouched. She rose, tipping over her chair as she rushed from the room.

There was a moment of uneasy silence, and then Marguerite spoke. "Well! I am sorry you had to witness that. I don't know what got into my daughter. You understand, I'm sure, with that family therapy business you're in." She gave me one of those smiles that are all teeth.

I shifted back from her fixed stare. "Family liaison officer, Ma'am," I corrected. I doubted the mother heard me. Somehow, she didn't seem the empathic type.

Raven righted Amanda's chair and addressed Marguerite. "After lunch, don't forget, we've got crystal bowls therapy." His voice was authoritarian.

"No, I won't forget," Marguerite said, chastened.

I made my excuses and left the dining room, not staying for dessert. It probably would be something like mango mousse, anyway.

Outside, I passed the ruins of the barn and tasted bitter ashes in my mouth. I would wait for the results of the autopsy, and then I'd be back. Murders were often committed by those close to the victim. Here, that might be Heinrich Spine or some other family member.

My cell phone buzzed as I got into my Jetta. It was Charlie Doon, one of the other deputies, and his voice was somber.

"Suicide, out Lake Montezuma way," he said. "Meet you there."

Charlie Doon was everything that I wasn't as a cop—early to work, late to leave, well connected with the right crowd. Every comment he made was spit-shined for maximum effect. While I stalled in my FLO job, rumor had it he was on a fast track for promotion to detective. Maybe I needed to cultivate Doon's perfect smoothness. I contemplated it for a slow moment, then discarded the idea. Not even for a promotion, would I turn into a Charlie Doon clone.

CHAPTER FOUR

About a half hour later, I pulled into the drive of a small white house with blue shutters. Charlie Doon was getting ready to leave, and we positioned the cars nose-to-tail for the briefing.

We rolled down our windows and Charlie consulted his notebook for the interview he'd just taken. His shirt still had crisp creases from the cleaners. I glanced down at mine, wrinkled from the heat and bearing a smudge of ash. I scrubbed at it and the motion caught Charlie's eye. Rats.

Charlie's notes were precise and well ordered. "Deceased is one Johnny Miller—age 18. History of depression. Looks like an overdose. Single mother, one Mrs. Janet Miller. No husband. Another little kid in the house."

It didn't take him long to give me the basic circumstances of the boy's death. It didn't take him long to leave, either. His car tires made a gravely sound as he backed out of the drive. Dealing with grieving mothers was not on Charlie Doon's list of promotion-yielding activities.

I knew the statistics and they weren't pretty. Suicide was the third leading cause of death among teens, following accident and homicide. Males were four times more likely than females to succeed, and if there was a history of other suicides in the family, then the risks skyrocketed.

Dealing with people in crisis was part of my job as Family Liaison Officer. Caring and help at the right moment made it easier for folks to get through the tough times. At least that's what I told myself, preparing for the visit ahead.

The Millers' house was a peaceful place, or would have been before the events of this morning. Cicadas started up in the mesquite tree at the edge of the yard, and a mourning dove cooed. But as I approached, the EMTs loaded the gurney with its black plastic bundle into their van. One tech gave me a compassionate glance as I climbed the porch steps to the front door.

I straightened my shoulders, walked to the open screen door, and knocked on the door jamb. "Sheriff's department."

A little girl about eight came to the door. Her eyes were wide with shock. I knelt down to her height. "Hi, Honey. What's your name?"

"Holly." She opened the screen for me and pointed behind her. "Mama's back there." Then she took my hand and led me through the modest house. Small living room, two bedrooms off to the side, kitchen in front of us.

Although it was mid-afternoon, breakfast dishes still sat on the table. A spoon stuck out of a bowl of soggy cereal, and spilled juice from a glass next to it had dried into an orange smear. Time jerked to a stop for this family in tragedy.

We passed out the back door onto a covered porch where a woman sat rigid in a platform rocker. She stared blindly ahead, arms crossed tightly.

I touched her shoulder. "Ma'am? I'm Pegasus Quincy from the sheriff's department. I am so sorry for your loss. "

She started as if coming out of a nightmare. "Quincy? My uncle was named Quincy, back in Arkansas. Are you any relation? No, I guess not. Quincy was his first name..." Her features were rigid, and she stared at some point beyond my left ear.

She wasn't making any sense, but sometimes it's hard for the mind to grasp the finality of death.

"We might be kin." I gave her a smile. "Feel up to a cup of coffee?"

She nodded hesitantly and started to rise. I put a hand on her shoulder.

"I don't mind fixing it. Holly, why don't you come help?"

The coffee pot was full, and I poured two cups. Black for me.

I turned to the little girl. "How does your mama like her coffee?"

"Just cream."

I pulled a milk carton out of the refrigerator, sniffed it. Sour.

The little girl reddened. "That milk is bad. We use that." She pointed to a rounded container of powdered creamer.

My heart went out to her. Her brother was dead, and she had to make excuses for sour milk.

I poured some creamer into the cup, stirred it. Then I looked at the little girl and poured about half the coffee into the sink and wiped the bottom of the mug. I dumped the spoiled milk down the sink, too.

"Here, can you carry this to your mama?" I gave her the half-full cup that would be easier for her not to spill. I carried the other onto the porch and sat in a chair near the woman. Holly handed the mug to her mother and sat down on the floor near her. She leaned back against her mother's leg.

"Why don't you tell me what happened?" I asked Janet Miller, the mom.

"I went in to wake Johnny. He's always late for school if I don't remind him. I found him there. Those people," she gestured vaguely at the front door, "said it was an overdose. My Johnny doesn't do drugs. What did they mean?"

She covered her face with her hands. Her little girl started to cry, too, and I stroked her hair.

"Was your son depressed, ma'am?"

"I visited the guidance office at the high school just the other day. They arranged for some counseling to start soon. His cousin killed himself last year, just about this time…"

She lifted the mug to her lips and then set it down without tasting. "I slept in this morning. I never do that. If only I'd gone into his bedroom earlier!"

Then her mind darted in another direction. She poked at her daughter's arm. "Holly, you get ready for school now," she scolded. "Johnny will take you…" She stopped, realizing her son could not take his sister to school ever again. Mrs. Miller's shoulders tensed, and she gave a harsh hiccupy sob.

Getting the little girl out of the house for a time might be a good idea. "Is there a neighbor close? Maybe someone else could watch Holly for a while?"

I got the phone number and made the call. The woman said she was picking up her own kids from school and would swing by for Holly.

Then I called the counselor at the elementary school where Holly went and let her know what had happened. She said she'd call the guidance counselor at the high school, too.

I turned back to Mrs. Miller. "Ma'am, I'm here to answer any questions that you may have as you face these first hard days."

She roused. "Where are they taking my boy? We don't have any insurance. Do I have to pay for that ambulance?"

"No, the county pays for that."

"They won't have to autopsy him, will they? Our religion requires he be buried within twenty-four hours."

"Most likely an autopsy won't be necessary," I said. "We'll work with you on that. Have you thought about a funeral home?"

She shook her head, and I suggested one that was close. With her assent, I dialed the number. The funeral director told me they had a reserve fund set up for clients with financial needs. I handed over the phone to Mrs. Miller and listened as they set up a time for a meeting late that afternoon.

"Any family live close?" I asked her.

"My sister Eloise, over in Cottonwood. I haven't had the heart to call her."

Mrs. Miller gave me the number and I dialed it. When the ring tone began, I handed her the phone. She relayed the news to her sister in a wooden voice. Then she hung up the phone and turned to me with more awareness in her eyes.

"My sister's coming right over. I don't have to go down to the morgue and identify the body, do I?" She shuddered "I can't do that, I just can't!"

"No need." I kept my voice low and gentle as I explained how an ambulance would deliver her son's body to the funeral home. I put a packet of information on the table and told her so that she could read it when she was ready, or her sister could.

Then I sat there with Mrs. Miller for a while longer, holding her hand. I listened to her anguish as she replayed events in her mind, trying to make sense of the unthinkable. But nothing I could say would bring her son back.

Finally, she wiped her eyes and stood up. "I don't mean to keep you. I know you've got more important things to do."

About that time, the neighbor arrived to check on Holly. She shooed the little girl next door to play with her kids and said she'd stay until the sister arrived.

Another call came in for me, and I had to leave. I gave Mrs. Miller my card and asked her to call if she had any questions.

I'd only been there two hours, but when I stepped back into the sunlit yard, I felt like I'd traveled to a very dark place.

***

When I picked up Shepherd at the courthouse later that afternoon, he had a morose expression on his face.

"Well, was it one for the good guys, or one for the happy-hour crowd?" I asked. It felt good to return to the normalcy of cop talk after the bleak hours with Janet Miller.

"Judge was ready to throw the book at him. Third time the jerk's been before the court," Shepherd said.

"Well, that should make you happy. Now he won't be out on the street for a while."

"I wish. His attorney asked for a continuance. Said there were extenuating circumstances. Judge granted it."

I whistled. "Tough call. Got your defense prepared?"

"Guy's not going to get away with it. I can tell you that."

I believed him. Shepherd was like a bulldog with a crunchy bone when it came to wrong-doers.

"How'd you do with the fire investigator?" he asked, ready to leave his own topic.

"Well, at least I didn't start another fire. That's about the only thing I got credit for. You could've warned me about that guy."

He chuckled.

"He seems to think that the barn fire was caused by an electrical short," I said. "But there were cut marks on the wire—could be rodent damage, could be something else."

"Hope you collected the wire for analysis."

When I told him that I had, Shepherd grunted, "Good."

I liked that grunt of approval. I'd miss it when he retired, although he'd be the last person I'd tell that to.

"Looks suspicious, that's for sure," he said. "Watch your step out there. Heard some rumors about ol' Heinrich…" Before he could say more, our incoming business line rang. He waved at me that we'd talk later and reached for the call.

I walked back to my office holding the frustration of that half-expressed thought. *What* about Heinrich Spine had alerted Shepherd's suspicions? And why wasn't Shepherd declaring this a murder investigation?

Okay, the medical examiner hadn't said the death was anything but an accident—yet. I pushed away the unwelcome thought that maybe my partner was just featherbedding it, waiting out the days to retirement, not wanting to get involved in a messy situation unless absolutely necessary.

Not my call, but I wondered what I'd be doing if it were my case. I knew for sure a simple traffic ticket violator wouldn't sidetrack me. What was *wrong* with Shepherd?

***

Work picked up and I never got another chance to talk to him. The day ended, my own problems clamored for attention. As I cranked the Jetta's engine in the parking lot, the idiot light glowed an ominous red. I tapped on the glass and it blinked once, twice, then disappeared. Yes! It must be a loose fuse, that was it.

I probably should get it checked, though. How many more days until payday and would the car run until then? I'd just baby it along. I eased it downhill from the sheriff's station to my studio apartment.

Reckless brushed past me and bolted into the front yard, knocking the yellow notice on the table to the floor. "Eviction. Ten Days."

Actually *nine*, now. I resolved to visit my property owner, the bank, the next day and see what the problem was. Or call, anyway. It was probably a mistake. I examined the tattered piece of paper. Maybe it was some kid's prank. The paper didn't *seem* all that official. Shouldn't there should be a seal or something?

If I had to move, I wondered where I'd go. I'd lived with my grandfather, HT Tewksbury, when I first came to town. In fact, I'd bunked in the loft with Ben, my assistant, when his uncle had kicked him out. We were both homeless at that point. But I was nearing thirty. Kind of old to be a boomerang kid.

And it wasn't just HT. He'd let me in, easy, if I needed to go there again. I had a more problematic relationship with his housekeeper, Isabel. Sometimes we got along just fine, but other times she looked as if she wanted to skewer me with a serving fork. She was jealous, that's all. HT and I were making up for those lost years when we never spoke. A granddaughter should come before a housekeeper, that was for sure.

I changed out of my uniform and walked up the street to HT's house to talk to him about temporary shelter. My grandfather lived in a huge three-story monstrosity that used to be a boarding house for miners during the copper heydays. Now only HT and Isabel lived there. Plenty of room for me, although I didn't want to call in the free-room-and-board marker unless I had to.

When I arrived at HT's, he invited me in to sit for a while. My stomach growled, telling me it was dinnertime. Maybe there'd be enough for me. Then I could talk to HT about moving in. Slip the topic into conversation over dessert.

When I asked what they were having, Isabel said "salad" with this determined look on her face. I glanced at HT and his face was set. Okay HT had put on a little weight—blame Isabel's wonderful tamales and enchilada casseroles for that—but you didn't have to starve the man.

Not in the mood for another conflict-laden meal like I'd had at the Spine Ranch, I gave my regrets. I'd talk to HT later about housing. Now wasn't a good time.

Reckless and I headed to the Sonic Drive-in to share a couple of burgers. That was fine with my dog. When I got back to the apartment, I parked the Jetta and ran a few hills for good measure. That was okay with him, too.

As we pounded up my front steps after the run, out of breath and virtuous, my cell phone rang a Coldplay guitar rif which meant a stranger's text. It was from Amanda Riordan, Heinrich Spine's granddaughter.

Please come see me when you can. I've remembered something about Gil, the message read.

I called back but got her voice mail. I briefly debated driving back down the hill to the Spine Ranch. Then Reckless nosed my hand, reminded me the day was over. I left a message to say I'd stop by in the morning. That was soon enough to find out what she wanted.

CHAPTER FIVE

Shepherd wasn't in our office when I arrived the next morning, and I drove to the main sheriff's office in Camp Verde to check in.

Sheriff Jones caught up with me in the hall. "What's going on up there in Mingus?"

I temporized. "What do you mean?"

"Shepherd. Usually, he's right on top of things, but I've been leaving messages all morning and he's not responding. Don't you have a clerk up there to answer the phone?"

"Gone. Budget cuts," I reminded him.

"Oh, yeah. Well, when you talk to Shepherd, have him call me. You free this morning? Got a project for you."

Never volunteer, I kept reminding myself. Never volunteer.

Too late. The sheriff said we'd had a rash of break-ins in the small town of Beaver Creek. He wanted me to go door-to-door handing out flyers on burglar-proofing homes. Community service, he called it.

Seemed like a waste of good patrol time to be stopping at each house. Couldn't we just send out an email blast or something? But chores like this put bread on the table and dog food in the dish. I checked a map to plot out a likely route and angled my stops to finish near the Spine Ranch.

I'd visit with Amanda Riordan then and find out what new information she wanted to give me. Shepherd might be steering away from calling Gil Streicker's death a homicide, but more and more, that's what it seemed like to me.

As I neared the ranch, a mailbox to the left of the road read "Serena and Hank Battle." Pitchfork Woman and her brother. I'd passed it before, but perhaps it was time to become better acquainted with the Battles.

I turned onto a dirt drive which disintegrated into ruts patched together by big boulders. Before my Jetta could high-center, I parked and set the emergency brake. Then I hiked toward to a small house squatting at the bottom of the hill. Sharp stones embedded in the roadbed poked the soles of my shoes.

The farm was close to the Verde River, and high humidity turned the air swampy. A herd of goats and one dispirited cow grazed in a weedy meadow. They looked miserable in the summer heat. I knew how they felt.

An empty irrigation ditch fronted the meadow, and there a huge bulk of a man, with wispy dirty-blond hair, held onto a noose-pole. He shouted at me as I walked closer.

"Killed a rattler right there yesterday. Looking for his little brother."

I jumped a little in spite of myself, but little brother must have gone home. I swatted at a mosquito. Hope it didn't carry West Nile virus. From the red smear on my fingers, it was too late to ask it.

"I'm looking for Serena Battle."

He gave me an odd look as if trying to figure out a response to my statement. "I live by myself in my trailer. My name is Hank."

He pointed to his hat. It was pink felt with his name written in sparkly letters, the kind you get at a carney booth at the county fair. He was missing a few teeth in front, too. Didn't appear to bother him. I tried not to let it bother me, either.

Hank left abruptly, without saying goodbye, sweeping his snake stick through the long grass. I stuck to the short grass I could see through and made my way cautiously to a small house at the end of the road.

A motor coughed behind me and I swung around to watch as a decrepit Ford half-encased in gray primer and missing a back fender barreled down the hill. The vehicle tilted this way and that, missing the boulders—probably knew them all on a first-name basis—and pitched to a stop six inches from my foot.

I didn't flinch. I must have used up my startle response on Hank's rattlers.

Serena Battle climbed out of the vehicle, solid on her feet, with that gray-black hair tamed into a rough knot. "Deputy Quincy, isn't it? Is that miserable Gil Streicker pressing charges? God knows I've got more to complain about than he does."

"No, that's not why I'm here. I have a few questions for you."

She smoothed her hair back in an exasperated manner. "Well, then, you might as well come into the house. It's hot out here."

I wiped sweat-dampened palms on my trousers and followed her. Large tin cans lined the front porch, planted with tomato vines that struggled against the summer heat. The next cool breeze wouldn't arrive until late September, almost three months from now.

Serena flipped the switch on a swamp cooler that filled the air with a musty blast of dampness. The room was a combination kitchen/living room, with one end reserved for a small dining table. The floor was a rust-colored painted cement, cracked in places. Neat, but sparse.

"The cooler takes just a minute to cool things down. Sit there." She gestured toward a worn couch, its cushions sunken with use. "What can I get you? Water? Lemonade?"

"Water would be fine."

She pulled two glasses from the cupboard, filled them, and handed one to me. Then she dropped into the chair across from me, pushed the glass against her forehead. "Ah, that feels good. Sorry I was abrupt out there. I've been at the courthouse, filing a citizen's complaint."

"Against Dr. Spine?"

She nodded. "You saw that empty ditch in front of the field? We depend on it for irrigation, have for years. Under the laws of prior appropriation, that water is mine. I've tried to reason with those people up there, but they won't listen. Told me to get a lawyer."

She laughed bitterly. "Look around you. I've barely got enough money to keep myself and Hank fed. I live here quiet, everybody can tell you. Don't want any trouble. But those greedy bastards..." She clenched her fist.

"Did you know Gil Streicker died there Tuesday morning?"

"Oh, no!" Her posture stiffened, and her eyes held a blank look

43

for a moment. "I saw the firetrucks going by, but I didn't realize that someone lost their life. What happened?"

She listened intently as I told her the story of the barn fire and finding Gil Streicker's body.

"I'm so sorry," she said. "I know that sounds funny, given how angry I was the other day. But I was just defending my brother. I don't—didn't—really have anything against the man, in particular, just that creep he works for. And the horses?"

"The horses are fine."

"That's a blessing, anyway."

What was it with these ranching people? One life, whether animal or human, was as important as the next. It was hard to understand that.

"Can you account for your actions Monday night and Tuesday morning?"

"You don't think it was an accident then." She thought a moment and then gave me a precise accounting of her hours.

"We went to the store Monday afternoon. I remember Hank and I had an argument over squash—he doesn't like it. Said hello to the checkout clerk who always wears those western shirts, but I don't know her name. After dinner, I said good night to Hank, then went to bed. I struggle with insomnia, but for some reason, I slept through the entire night."

"And Tuesday morning, early?" I asked.

"I was here."

"Can anyone vouch for that?"

"I said hello to Mabel next door when I went out for the paper—she said she was up with her colicky baby. The propane guy came about seven to refill our tank and I talked to him for a moment. Then somebody came by to buy a carton of eggs. I keep them in that old refrigerator on the porch. Have a box where they can put their money, so I didn't talk to them. Mail came about eleven. But by the time I walked up for it, the truck was gone. Don't think he saw me."

I listened to her recounting, event by commonplace event. A quiet life by all accounts, yet I'd seen her rouse to anger with Gil Streicker. And she seemed very protective of that brother.

"I met Hank as I came in," I said.

Sorrow drifted over her face. "Two years ago he was attending

44

college, wanted to be an Aggie man. Then the accident happened. The medical bills took all of our savings and then some."

"That had to be hard. No other family?"

She shook her head. "Just Hank and me. When my father died I wanted to sell this place and move to Phoenix, but with Hank the way he is—you saw him. He'd have trouble in a big city."

"Were his injuries bad?"

"Couple of cracked ribs, broken ankle. But the worst was the blow to the head—memory loss, difficulty concentrating, gets upset easily. Hank used to be the most gentle, kind man, but now..."

"Hank knew you were upset with the people at the Spine Ranch."

She slammed her glass of water down on the coffee table, spilling a few drops. "Hank had nothing to do with that accident. He couldn't!"

"Easy. Nobody is accusing him of anything. But there's an ongoing investigation. Both of you need to stay close."

"Where would we go? We have no money." She gave a short, bitter laugh. "We're right here, twenty-four seven. You'll have no problem finding us."

I didn't leave her one of the Sheriff's burglary flyers. She had enough on her plate without that worry. Anyway, the rattlers would attack anyone foolish enough to travel the rutted road leading to the Battle farm.

It was time visit the Spine Horse Ranch and find out what Amanda Riordan wanted.

CHAPTER SIX

When I drove under the sign to the Spine Ranch, Raven LightDancer was working a skip-loader, scraping blackened timbers and ash off the barn foundation.

Yellow crime tape waved in tatters from the loaded blade. A stack of new timbers edged the boundary of the cement, and a contractor held a blueprint, marking locations for the new wall framing.

"Hey!" I shouted to Raven. "What are you doing? That's a possible crime scene."

He looked down and shrugged. "Heinrich's orders. You need to check with him."

Perhaps they'd gotten an "all clear" from the sheriff's office, that Gil's death *was* accidental. Even so, that voice in the back of my head muttered, "uh-oh," as any possible traces of homicide vanished in a huff of sooty ash.

By now it was after lunchtime, and my stomach growled at me. I told it to shut up. I'd grab something in Camp Verde before I reported to the sheriff's office, but first I wanted to hear what Amanda Riordan had to say. I walked to the house and knocked on the door. Rosa let me in the and I asked about Amanda.

"Marguerite wants to speak to you first." She led me to an office off the main living area.

Marguerite had a phone to her ear and looked up when I entered. "Good. You're here. Take this phone for me. I'm on hold."

She handed me the cell phone and I listened to three variations of the Pachelbel Canon in D before I switched it on speaker and set it down on the desk where it continued to play in a tinny fashion.

"Oh. I never thought of that," Marguerite said.

She waved a hand-held vac back and forth over the computer keyboard. A long-haired cat watched in fascination until she gently lifted him off the desk and set him on the floor. "Darling kitty," she said in dulcet tones. "Mommy's fixing the computer. You can't be here."

He jumped back up. Marguerite dropped the vacuum, snatched the cat, and tossed him outside the room, slamming the door. There was a frustrated yowl from the other side and then silence.

Marguerite sat down again, carefully straightening her designer skirt. "The computer isn't working, and Amanda says it's full of cat hair. Why would she say that? My daughter's been spending too much time around those nasty smelly animals in the barn."

The phone beeped into service and she grabbed it. An East Indian voice came through the loudspeaker and she hit speaker-off, putting the phone to her ear. "Yes, the C key sticks. I hit it and the screen turns blue...no, I've tried that. No, you can't have control of my computer monitor. How do I know where you're calling from— Ohio? Yes, the weather is fine here."

I tried not to laugh. I'd been there, too.

Finally, Marguerite slammed down the phone in frustration. "I *know* that man was lying. Did he sound like he was from Ohio to you? I was on hold for forty-five minutes for that? I think I've ruined my manicure." She turned her hand this way and that, fretfully examining her fingernails.

"What was the final verdict?"

"What?"

"About the computer," I said.

"Oh. He suggested I take it to a local repair shop."

She flashed me a runway smile. "Can't you fix it for me? Isn't that what you're supposed to do? Help people?"

I shook my head. Never volunteer.

Then I had a thought. My former assistant, Ben, was a computer whiz. Perhaps he could assist her and gain a little more information about the family in the process. Ben had helped me that way in the past. And he always could use extra money.

He'd given me some business cards, and I dug in my billfold for one to give to Marguerite. Then I headed to the auxiliary barn to find Amanda.

***

Detouring around the construction site to a second barn, I followed the sound of running water. Amanda in old clothes and tall rubber boots was giving the huge black stallion a shower. The horse seemed to enjoy the attention, standing patiently as Amanda scrubbed each leg in turn, rinsed twice, and applied—was that hair conditioner?—to the long hair on the horse's ankles.

I looked closer. Yes, I recognized the turquoise palm trees on the legend. There was a bottle just like it on my shower shelf.

Amanda turned off the water hose. Her hair was tousled as if she'd forgotten to run a comb through it that morning, and she had dark circles under her eyes. She wore a wrinkled white blouse tucked crookedly into blue stretch jeans.

A brown streak decorated one sleeve. I didn't examine that closer. My investigative talents had limits.

"Beautiful horse," I said, admiring the black stallion. Its tail was so long it touched the ground, and each fetlock created a silken ruff of black hair.

"Thanks. This big guy is my favorite. He's a Friesian. His name is Black Onyx."

I put out a tentative hand to give his wet neck a pat. "Heard of Friesians, I think. Don't they use them for matched pairs, like on Downton Abbey?"

Amanda gave me a tiny smile.

Rapport established, I moved on to the real purpose of my visit and asked her what she'd called about.

She lowered her voice. "What I'm about to tell you has to be kept in strict confidence."

It was the usual quandary. If what she told me concerned this case, I'd be obligated to report it. So I didn't promise, just gave a noncommittal, "go ahead." I hoped I wouldn't have to use what she told me against her.

"It's my fault Gil died."

"What do you mean?"

"Well," she began, "I lied when you asked me about the fire."

I motioned her to continue.

"This is hard." She stroked the stallion's rump with a nervous gesture. "You remember I said Gil was helping get the horses out? Well, he wasn't. The last time I saw him was the evening before, and he was sick as a dog then. I didn't see him at all at the barn the morning of the fire. And I was so intent on rescuing the horses, I didn't check the office."

She started to cry, and I patted her shoulder. "You did the best you could in a rough situation."

She scrubbed at the horse's mane in silence, carefully lathering the mass of hair. Silent tears dripped down her cheeks. "All I know is that Gil wasn't there to help when we rescued the horses. But he *would* have been." She buried her head in the horse's shoulder, sobbing.

On Perry Mason, the murderer always confessed. Maybe I needed to develop a better scowl. Or maybe none of this family was actually connected to Gil Streicker's death? It was too soon to tell.

"I need to take a look at Gil's living quarters," I said. At least *they* hadn't been destroyed by Raven's bulldozer. "Can you help me with that?"

"No! They're private."

"Amanda, Gil's dead. But maybe there's something there that can explain why."

I left it at that, silently urging her to cooperate. I didn't want this unhappy girl to be associated with a possible murder.

Amanda's agreement didn't come for a while, as she returned to sudsing and rinsing. The big stallion leaned into her body as she stroked one ear.

I waited.

Finally, she said in a sulky voice, "You won't touch anything of Gil's?"

"Not one thing," I promised.

She turned off the water and pulled another hose from the overhead roll. Hot air hissed from the nozzle. She handed it to me. "Dry the fetlocks, while I go get the key."

"What?"

"Everything has to be totally dry, or Onyx will develop greasy heel."

Right. She disappeared toward the big house, leaving me a very large horse with wet feet. The hose in my hand whooshed. Black Onyx turned to look at me with curious eyes.

"Not your fault you got stuck with a novice," I muttered, as I bent to dry the long hair. It was coarse and heavy in my hand, but with the conditioner, dried tangle free.

I backed up as he shifted weight, and moved to the other side to start work on the second front hoof. Amanda returned before I had to tackle the back two, the ones that could kick me into the middle of next week.

She poked a ring of keys in my hand. "Gil lives—lived—in the bunkhouse." She stumbled over the words and drew in a ragged breath. "It's across the yard. Lock up when you leave." She grabbed the hose from me.

When I left the stables, she was redoing the work I'd just done.

Sorry, horse.

CHAPTER SEVEN

I walked across the hot, sunlit courtyard to the bunkhouse. The front was a communal sleeping arrangement for the ranch hands, and to the rear, with a separate entrance, was the ranch manager's quarters. Amanda said Gil lived there.

I unlocked the door and pushed it open. It seemed strange to be going through the personal effects of a man I had met in person a few days ago, now dead.

The room was Spartan, containing a single bed made with military precision. Beyond was a rude pine student desk, and above it, a small window framed by muslin curtains.

To one side was an old steamer trunk, the hasp closed with a simple metal lock, firmly shut. I always like chests, ever since I read *Treasure Island* as a kid. Especially ones with locks. I opened the center drawer of the desk, pulled out a paper clip, and straightened it. Sometimes these simple locks could be jiggered and they'd snap open. All I needed to do was be patient and trust my fingers.

I crouched and poked the metal wire into the lock carefully. There! The latch snapped open with a satisfying click. I lifted the hasp and opened the lid. No pirate doubloons. Instead, Gil had used the trunk as a dresser, with T-shirts and boxers folded neatly to the left, socks to the right, a Dopp kit nestled on top, its old leather folds cracked and worn. I set the Dopp on the ground and slipped my hand through the stacks of underwear, searching. Nothing.

Next, I unzipped the Dopp kit. Inside were a straight razor, toothbrush, a bar of soap. I sniffed. Old Spice. There wasn't a bathroom in this small living space. Gil probably used the communal shower for the ranch hands. I put the kit back in the trunk, closed the lid, and straightened. My knees popped as I rose from the crouched position—I definitely needed to hit the gym more often.

I started on the desk contents. The file drawer to the left held a stack of receipts. No utility bills—these quarters would be part of the main ranch system—but some bank statements.

I leafed through a few. They showed regular bi-weekly deposits—Gil's salary? Withdrawals for cash and one regular monthly payment for the same amount, the same day of the month.

That could be an automatic payment—if so, to whom? There was no evidence of a big screen TV or other high-end purchase in the living quarters, but Amanda had mentioned a daughter. From the amount of the withdrawal, it might be a child support payment. Under the bank statements was the receipt for rental of a storage locker marked "paid" in a black angular script. I set that to one side along with the bank statements to examine further.

The center desk drawer held the usual jumble of scissors, paper clips, and pencils. I angled a blank pad of paper, but couldn't pick up any writing impressions. The desk drawer jammed when I tried to close it. I pulled it out further and reached with searching fingers.

A crumpled photo was wedged in the back, one of those tiny pictures grade schools send home each year. I smoothed out the wrinkles. It was a young girl, maybe eight or so, smiling with that row of crooked teeth that kids get when they've lost a few. Looked cuter on her than Hank Battle's missing teeth.

I set the crumpled photo on top of the papers I had collected thus far and moved to the closet. A long curtain, sagging on wooden rings obscured the opening. I pushed it aside. Jeans hung in a neat row to the left, long-sleeved work shirts to the right. Checked the pockets. Nothing.

On the floor, a pair of cowboy boots fashioned from bumpy ostrich leather. Gil had been wearing work boots when they'd pulled him from the fire. These fancy ones must be for Saturday night trips to town. An empty plastic laundry basket.

The shelf above the clothes held only a black fur Stetson hat. I pulled the hat down and sniffed the earthy musk of Brylcreem on the inside sweatband. Definitely for Saturday nights. I returned it to the shelf.

I tripped over a small rag rug near the bed. As I straightened it, a small irregular lump caught my eye. I pulled the rug back to examine the back of it. Stuck inside one warp end was a safe deposit key. I wiggled it free and set it on the desk. I might get lucky there.

The bed was next. A Hudson Bay blanket, white with red and green stripes, served as a coverlet. It was worn to the threads in the center. I lifted the thin, cotton-stuffed mattress. He'd used newspaper sheets for insulation to cover the metal springs, but not a single porn magazine among them. A few dust bunnies the housekeeper had missed held court under the bed.

And that was it. The room was as bare of personality as a motel room. All it lacked was the Gideon bible. If I died tomorrow, what would they find at my apartment? I set that uneasy picture of clutter out of my mind. I'd definitely clean the place—soon.

I put the photograph and key in my shirt pocket and grabbed the bank statements and storage receipt. Then I locked the door and returned to the stable. I had more questions for Amanda.

The young woman was still grooming Black Onyx. The horse's mane was parted in big hunks, loosely knotted like hanks of yarn. Amanda undid each one and combed it through, murmuring to the horse as she did so. He stood patiently under her ministrations. Maybe it felt like a massage.

"Did you discover anything in Gil's room?" she asked.

"It looked clean. Do you have a housekeeper?"

"I straightened up a little after, you know..."

"That include washing his clothes?" I asked.

She sniffed. "Well, I didn't want anybody to see the room in that condition. Things tossed all over."

"Find any interesting reading material?"

Her face reddened. "Gil wasn't like that!"

Uh-huh.

Then she paused. "Now that I think of it, it looked as though somebody had been there before me. Not Gil."

"Maybe a person was looking for something?" The words came out before I could censure them. Leading the witness. Bad idea. I knew better.

"Yes, that had to be it!"

I filed that piece of information away for further thought. Maybe it was a stranger, and maybe Amanda had been the one doing the searching.

"Did Gil smoke?"

"No! He knew how dangerous that would be around barns."

"What about extracurricular activities?"

Amanda's fingers stilled on the horse's neck. "Like what?"

"Alcohol, drugs, that sort of thing."

"Gil used to drink, but said he stopped when his little girl asked him to."

"Did he attend AA?" I asked.

"He went to meetings in town for a while. Then he quit going." Amanda's head lifted proudly, in defense of the man. "Gil said he could do better on his own without some fool poking through his business."

More likely the man had secrets he didn't want to share. "What about drugs?"

"After Gil stopped drinking, he said he treated his body like a temple."

A temple he shared freely with female acolytes? I thought back to the play he'd made for me when we first came to the ranch. "What about girlfriends?"

Amanda hesitated. "Well, you'll find out about this sooner or later. Gil and I were…"

"Lovers?"

She reddened and then lifted her chin defensively. "No."

I tried again. "What about boyfriend-girlfriend?"

The girl nodded slowly. "We couldn't tell anybody about our love, because of Heinrich."

The horse stamped a foot impatiently. Amanda untied another hank of long black hair and combed through it with gentle movements.

"Heinrich…" I prompted.

"I'm due to inherit when Heinrich dies. Gil said we'd wait a little. Well, you know."

So Amanda was due to inherit, not her mother? Something I'd need to check out.

"Other than that, did Gil and your grandfather get along?"

"Not exactly," Amanda admitted reluctantly. "Heinrich threatened to shut down the horse operation and raise cattle. Cows, instead of horses! Gil set him straight on that point, for sure."

"They argued?"

Amanda's mouth clamped shut. Interesting. I'd run that bit of information by Shepherd.

I tried another topic. "We were called out here the day before Gil died. What can you tell me about the argument?"

"That Serena Battle! Who cares about those stupid irrigation ditches, anyway? There's plenty of water to go around. That brother of hers is just plain creepy. Gil said if he ever saw him around here again, he'd…"

"He'd what?"

"Never mind. Gil just wanted to keep me safe." Her eyes welled with tears.

I was getting a broader image of the ranch manager, volatile in temper as well as passionate about the opposite sex. It would be easy to make enemies that way.

I pulled the picture out of my pocket. "Know this little girl?" I handed it to her.

"Veronica!"

"Who?"

"Veronica Streicker, Gil's daughter. See the resemblance?"

She flashed the picture at me, but I couldn't match Gil's masculine appearance to the little girl. Maybe a loving parent could. Was Gil that sort of father?

"Gil left her back East when the family split up," Amanda said. "He wanted to bring her here, to live with us after we married. That will never happen now." Her tears spilled over.

"Can I keep this as a remembrance?" She clutched the picture to her chest.

I held out my hand. "I'll make you a copy." Reluctantly she surrendered it.

"If you want a good suspect, there's always Raven," she said. "His name isn't LightDancer. Never has been. Everybody knows that except *Mother*."

Her voice held contempt, and I wasn't sure whether it was for

Raven, her mother, or both. Tension there, and it sounded like a lot of back history.

Amanda unhooked Black Onyx from the restraining lines and snapped on a lead. I jumped out of the way as she backed the large animal out of the grooming stall and went down the center aisle of the barn toward the paddock.

There, she loosed him into the pasture. Onyx hip-hopped once and then broke into a canter that lengthened to a gallop, his black mane and tail flying. Beautiful, wild, and free. And tangling all that black hair into more knots for Amanda to unsnarl.

I had a few worry knots of my own, starting with the death of Gil Streicker and then Shepherd's curious reluctance to investigate it. My partner was stalling and I wanted to know why.

CHAPTER EIGHT

The next morning, our small office was empty—no sign of Shepherd. So I drove over to the far side of the Verde Valley and finished distributing the sheriff's burglary brochures.

Then I stopped by the side of the road and pulled out the notebook I'd started on Gil Streicker's death. It wasn't a murder book yet—my partner Shepherd would have to make that call—but it was a start.

I examined the storage receipt from Gil Streicker's desk. The rental was close, and I figured I'd drop by. I plugged the address into my GPS, but when I arrived at the location, a building-free lot crowded with sunflowers greeted me.

Sighing, I pulled out the storage receipt and dialed the main number. A sad day when you couldn't trust a smart phone's Google Earth. The man who answered the phone gave me the directions— turn left, not right at the four-way stop. He said I couldn't miss it.

Ten minutes later, I drove into the yard. The rental place was a single-story orange edifice that proclaimed in big letters, "Skeet's Rental. Cheapest in the Verde Valley." The facility was surrounded by a chain-link fence to deter theft, but the front gate was wide open. The front office could monitor the gate, if anyone was there, which they didn't appear to be. A big sign on the front door said, "Back in five minutes."

I turned off the motor and dialed Shepherd. "You call the sheriff? He's looking for you."

"It'll be fine. What you got for me on the Streicker case? You been out to the ranch?"

I told him about finding the storage receipt in Gil's quarters. "I'm at the front gate of the rental place now."

"I'll check in with Sheriff Jones. Meant to do that anyway. Hey! Did you know the Peace Store had a great deal on night binoculars? I picked up a pair."

Night-vision binoculars? The tight sheriff's department budget didn't allow for such extravagances. Which meant Shepherd might be planning some off-the-record surveillance. He could persist to the point of mania when tracking the solution to a puzzle, and I wondered which one he was working on now.

Once he had me searching night and day for a missing shoe. I wore out a uniform on that one, climbing in and out of dumpsters. But the recovered footwear led to a break in a case, and a bad guy was convicted.

I remembered his disappointment about the court hearing on the Porsche driver. Was that the issue causing this sudden interest in night-view binocs? I hoped not. Surely, Shepherd had better sense than conducting an off-the-grid stakeout that could get us both in trouble.

He said we'd talk at lunch and I could bring him up to speed. We set up a rendezvous at Beto's, a Mexican restaurant in Camp Verde specializing in authentic home-cooked food.

Before I could question him further, Shepherd cut the conversation short. "Got to go, things to do. You can tell me what you find in the storage unit at lunch."

He rang off before I could respond.

I frowned. Conflict with colleagues was difficult for me. Yet I had to confront Shepherd on his faulty sense of priorities before it was too late. I needed this job, meager as the pay was.

***

I waited for another ten minutes outside the storage company office. Still no sign of the clerk and the interior of the car was heating up in the summer sun. I buzzed up the windows and got out. Time to investigate on my own. At least I could find out where Gil's unit was.

Comparing the number on the receipt with the numbers on the

storage roll-down doors, I worked my way toward the rear of the complex. Gil's unit was in a far back corner of the fenced-in area, unobservable from the front office. Although the corrugated door to his unit was closed and padlocked, the round safety lock swung free, its hasp severed with bolt cutters. No key needed.

I touched the metal lock. It was fire-hot from the sun's heat. I wedged it free and dropped it to the ground. Then, I shook my fingers a little to bring some life into the seared digits and tried to lift the rim-edge of the door. Arizona in the summer.

I debated returning to my car for a pair of gloves but spotted a half brick by the corner of another unit door. Somebody had the same problem. I grabbed the chunk of brick, wedged it under the rim of the door, and hoisted upward with my shoulder.

The roll-up lifted in a screech of metal. The bolt-cutting thieves had stripped the unit. The entire eight-by-ten-foot space was empty, except two items in a far corner: a stained corrugated box, its top flaps ripped open, and a child's sled tilted forlornly against the wall.

I crouched down and shined my flashlight level with the cement floor. At that extreme angle, a jumble of undistinguished footprints and the narrow-wheel tracks of a dolly appeared in the beam of light.

The missing contents of the unit had undoubtedly been scattered to yard sales across the valley, proof of ownership gone. This practice made items impossible to trace unless you had serial numbers and sales receipts. And the honest folks who had purchased an item in good faith would put up resistance to returning it. That's why insurance companies paid claims without question, and people reluctantly replaced lost items. A lesson, there, about having too much stuff to take care of.

I bent down and examined the contents of the cardboard box. Children's books—*Alice in Wonderland, The Little Engine That Could, The Poky Little Puppy.* I riffled through the last one. It had been one of my favorite books as a kid—drove HT crazy reading it to me, over and over. Even then, I loved the rule-breakers in life, especially in puppy form.

All of the children's books were inscribed, "From Daddy to Ronny." He had saved them all this time. Maybe they reminded him of what he had lost in the divorce. At the bottom of the box was a kindergarten report card for one Veronica Streicker. I opened it. She made all As except for a C in deportment. A summary comment read, "Does not play well with others." Way to go, Veronica. I didn't either.

And that's when things shifted in my mind. My father abandoned my mother and me when I was about the age of this little girl. He sent checks and cards for a while, and then they stopped coming. I wondered where he was or what he was doing now. Perhaps he was no longer living.

Gil Streicker's little girl didn't need to be like me. She deserved to know what had happened to her daddy. I'd do the best I could to find out, even if it meant bending a rule or two.

I shoved the contents back in the box and refolded the flaps. Then I hoisted it to one shoulder and grabbed the sled. I'd return these to Veronica, with news of her father, as soon as I could. I walked out of the unit, set them down and yanked the metal door down, ignoring my blistered fingers. I'd reexamine the contents in a cooler location.

Then I walked to the front of the complex to put the sled and box in my car trunk. The sign had disappeared from the window. When I entered the main office, the clerk wiped greasy fingers on a napkin. He held a McDonald's cup in one hand and took a hasty sip as I approached.

"I must have just missed you. Across the street. Morning break," he explained. From the look of his ample belly, he and Mickey D kept good company.

I showed him my ID and the rental receipt, told him about Gil Streicker's death, and asked about the unit.

The clerk swiveled and opened a metal file cabinet behind him.

"Streicker, Streicker…Here it is." He pulled a slim manila file from the drawer. Opened it and looked at the contract.

"Mr. Streicker always paid a year in advance. Not too many of our tenants do that."

"Did he visit the unit often?"

"Can't say."

When I told him about the break-in, the man was apologetic. "I'm not always at the front office. Have to make rounds, you understand." Then he admitted this wasn't the only unit theft.

There'd been a rash of break-ins recently.

My irritation rose. The truth was, security at the place was non-existent. Whatever Gil had stored there had vanished into the underground economy. Perhaps even with the complicity of the overweight clerk sitting in front of me.

"Still had six months to go on the lease," the clerk said. "What should I do with the refund?"

I told him to mail it in care of Amanda Riordan and gave the address. Maybe Amanda could donate it to a humane shelter in honor of Veronica. Gil might like that. I told the clerk he could re-rent the unit if he wanted. Streicker wouldn't need it anymore. When I left the office, he was rummaging in the paper sack for spud rubble hiding in the bottom.

***

It was time for lunch. Beto's Corner in Camp Verde was off the beaten path, and that's why I liked it. I turned east at the Middle Verde exit off I-17 and curved through the roundabout at the Cliff Castle Casino.

The casino parking lot was filled with tourist buses and the big sedans that some retirees favored. Casinos had been a mixed blessing for our Native American communities in Arizona. The gambling centers brought needed wealth, but also a dimension of unhealthy living that was tough to explain to the Native kids I met.

This one was run and operated by the Yavapai Indian tribe, which means the law enforcement at the casino fell to them, too. I'd had dealings with the Yavapai Nation Police before and found them to be competent and cooperative. Unlike my partner, Shepherd Malone. My stomach tightened at the conversation with him that lay ahead.

I turned left into the Beto's Corner parking lot. A big "Open" flag fluttered in the warm breeze. My stomach rumbled as I stared at the menu written mostly in Spanish that hung over the order window. I knew what I was going to have, but stared anyway. It seemed the right thing to do.

The owner took my order. He had been a miner in the southern part of the state until he was injured and had to retire. I was happy that their business had prospered. I liked their tequila lime burritos much better than fast food hot dogs. Even though it was Taco

61

Tuesday, I ordered the burrito anyway, with extra hot sauce and an iced tea to cool it down.

When my order was ready, I walked to a group of picnic tables shaded by old cottonwood trees to wait for Shepherd. It was quiet, before the lunch crowd hit, a good place to organize how I wanted to confront my partner.

Shepherd arrived, stared at the menu board just like I had, ordered a combo plate with a glass of water, and slid in across from me at the picnic table.

"How's the day going for you, Quincy?"

"The sheriff called again. Have you talked to him?"

Shepherd frowned at me. He had dark, baggy circles under his eyes, and his hands shook as he sipped the water. My determination to call him on his derelict behavior dissolved, and my family liaison officer empathy surfaced instead.

"Everything okay?" I asked. "You don't look so hot."

"I'm fine," he snapped. "Just a little tired, that's all."

The server interrupted us with Shepherd's food, and we unrolled plastic ware and napkins. I took a bite of the burrito and wiped lime salsa from one corner of my mouth. Something had put Shepherd in a foul mood.

"What's up?" I asked.

"Remember that red Porsche we caught speeding?"

I nodded.

"His fancy lawyer filed an appeal. He's claiming discrimination and profiling."

"That's ridiculous! The judge denied it, right?"

"Nope. Rescheduled the case, for further consideration."

I nodded sympathetically. "What's their claim? Was the driver Hispanic?"

Since the Arizona legislature passed tightened immigration laws, we'd had allegations of pulling people over on spurious stops to check for legal status.

Shepherd pounded his fist on the table in frustration, spilling his water glass. I handed him a bunch of napkins. Then I waited while he mopped up the mess.

"Neither," he said. "Would you believe it was because he was driving a *Porsche*? I was picking on him because he's a rich dude."

"Discrimination by auto. That's a new one. Who's the attorney?"

He mumbled something.

"What? Can't hear you." Then I hooted. "Myra. Bet it's Myra Banks, right?"

Myra was Shepherd's nemesis, ever since she represented his wife in divorce proceedings. Old defeats never die.

"Suing you, are they? Have you notified the sheriff's office?" I asked.

Shepherd squirmed. "Not yet. If I can track him, *prove* he's guilty, maybe I can still get him put away."

He took a large bite of chilies rellenos. "Driver like that's not safe on the streets. He was speeding near a school zone."

"I was with you. Nowhere near a school zone. Apologize to the man and let it go, Shepherd."

"Don't tell me what to do." He scowled.

I glared back. "Yeah, well somebody needs to. What about Gil Streicker's death? While you're out running around after this drunk, a killer may be loose. That's part of your job, too."

"My *job* is none of your damn business. This thing with the Porsche driver is personal. I can't let it go, Peg, I just can't." His eyes appealed for understanding.

"Yeah? Convince me."

He sighed. "All my life I've been a by-the-books cop. Compiled good evidence, seen case after case tossed out. *Guilty criminals* back free on the street endangering innocent people.

"Just once, before I retire," he said, "I want to nail one of those sons-a-bitches, put him behind bars for so long even his mother forgets him." His fists clenched until the knuckles whitened.

"But the situation out at the Spine Ranch..."

"You're doing just fine on the Streicker thing. It hasn't been declared a homicide and maybe it won't ever be. He could have tripped over something, hit his head."

"What about that stripped wire?"

"Points to arson, serious, but not homicide."

My jaw set. Shepherd was wrong.

"You want to be a detective?" he asked. "Now's your chance. Detect, if you are so determined. Leave me alone to handle this problem and then I'll be back. Another couple of days, tops. Trust me on this one."

Maybe this *was* the best way to handle it. The fact was, Heinrich Spine's construction crew had destroyed any possible evidence at the barn, and his granddaughter Amanda had finished the job at the sleeping quarters.

If it was a homicide, we were so far behind that we might never catch up. I could lose my job over this one. Small consolation that Shepherd wouldn't be far behind me.

"I've got a plan," he said. "Fill me in on what you discover and I'll report back to the sheriff's office. They'll never know that I'm…"

"…That you're tailing this drunk driver on company time."

"Never mind. I'll figure something else out."

"Not so fast. I'll cover for you. But you've got to help me, too." I recapped my visit to the Spine Ranch ending with Amanda's assertion that Gil had been her Intended.

He nodded. "So where would you go next, if this *were* a homicide?"

"I'd keep plugging away," I said. "Go to the bank to check the accounts there, try out that safe deposit key that I found.

"And I'd investigate the secondary witnesses," I continued. "For instance, talk to the nurse, Fancy. She might know something. Maybe I'd question the absent husband, Dr. Theo Riordan. If both his wife and daughter were involved with Streicker, there might be a jealousy angle."

"Good," Shepherd said. "I agree. Go see these folks. Follow any leads you find there."

There was an echo of the old Shepherd in his structured, precise statements. If I held on long enough, perhaps my partner would give up this crazy Porsche driver vendetta and rejoin me in the real world.

"Something else," I said. "Amanda mentioned their cook might have a back history. Does the name Raven LightDancer mean anything to you?"

"Tall skinny guy?" Shepherd asked. "Long black hair, dresses like Johnny Cash?"

"That's the one."

"Think he has another name. Talk to Rory Stevens. He had some dealings with LightDancer a time back. I'll meet up with you tonight. You can bring me up to speed on the case then." With that, Shepherd departed.

His last suggestion raised a small problem.

Rory Stevens had been a SEAL and was now on the underwater recovery team for the sheriff's office. Even though he was shorter than me, he was intelligent and incredibly buff. That's why he'd been my on-again-off-again boyfriend.

Right now we were most definitely off, but I dialed his number before I got cold feet. I needed the background on Raven LightDancer, and I needed it now.

CHAPTER NINE

Rory answered on the first ring. "Well as I live and breathe. Peg-the-rat-Quincy."

The warmth I once knew had turned suspicious and cautious.

"No, you can't borrow my Hummer again."

I back-pedaled. "It wasn't like that. I swear I didn't know that fire hydrant was so close."

"You got any idea how much one of those fenders cost to repair? Not to mention that hydrant spewing dirty water all over my baby. Which hydrant I also got to pay for, I might add."

How much did it cost to fix a Hummer? A lot probably. Couldn't blame Rory for being a little peeved. I pushed ahead and apologized. I even tried to sound sincere. He had information I wanted.

There was silence, then, "All right, you wouldn't be calling me unless you needed something important. Spill it."

I let out the breath I'd been holding. "Shepherd says you know something about one Raven LightDancer."

"He still around? Thought we ran him out of town."

"Yup, still here," I said. "He's working as a cook at the Spine Ranch. What can you tell me about him?"

"Better clue the family in. He can get expensive."

"What do you mean?"

"What's it worth to know?" Rory's voice turned calculating.

A chance to redeem myself with Rory and get some information at the same time. It was worth substantial to me, but my wallet was flat. How much would it take?

"What about a bottle of Arizona Stronghold's Mangas wine?" I bargained. It was a local Arizona vintner, one that Rory was particularly fond of.

"A start. What else?"

What did he mean, *what else?* Wine was expensive. I thought hard. "How about a massage?"

That was my hole card in this poker game. Would it be enough?

"All right. Next Saturday. Wet Beaver Creek, the far side of the water. But I'll meet you there. I'm not letting you near my Hummer again. And this is not a date," he cautioned.

"Right," I agreed, "Not a date. Thanks, Rory, I owe you."

"Not nearly enough, Quincy. We have scores to settle." He hung up.

I felt like I'd scaled a very slippery castle wall. But he'd said he'd help.

Still, I considered his last words. *Did* I owe Rory something? Of course not. He was being unreasonable. I brushed away the guilt niggling at the back of my mind. He should have known better than to loan a friend a car too big to negotiate the winding streets of Mingus.

On the other hand, a bribe never hurt.

I drove down to a vacant lot on the outskirts of Cottonwood and parked in the middle of it to finish the paperwork on the FLO call for the teen who had killed himself. The Verde Valley wasn't the center of criminal activity, but old training dies hard.

Many of the law officers here had come from larger cities, where it wasn't safe to park in an unattended area without clear views to the rear. This lot had nice visibility all four directions and was a favorite for both the sheriff's department and the town police.

Next, I debated filling out a burglary report on the storage unit. Nah, a waste of time. Instead, I pulled out the bank statements I'd retrieved from Gil Streicker's room. I'd struck out at the storage unit, but perhaps the bank would be more productive.

There was a chance that safe deposit key I'd found in Gil

Streicker's quarters fit a box there, too. Worth a try. I checked my watch. It was almost closing time, which meant Loretta Stone should be working the front counter. Maybe I'd get a break and pick up some small town gossip on Gil Streicker along with information about his accounts.

I fingered the deposit key in my pocket. I didn't have official sanction to look at the contents of the box but figured I could finagle my way in, if I talked to Loretta.

Time to pull in a few favors. I had driven her under-age daughter home from a party that had gotten too wild down in Clarkdale. The daughter was furious, but the mother had been grateful. I hoped she'd remember that now.

Three clerks stood behind the counter waiting on customers, with Lorena in the middle slot. The bank had one of those arrangements where customers stood in a single line. The process lowered the frustration of choosing the wrong queue, behind the guy who wanted to chat up the cute teller. It also meant you couldn't predict which bank clerk you'd get.

I was at the front of the line, with three customers doing business with three tellers. If they all finished at the same time, I'd have my pick of clerks. Or could be I'd be shunted toward someone that I didn't want at all if the business transaction times were uneven. I stood rocking on my heels, tuning in to the conversations at the front counter.

One guy wore a dirty, ripped T-shirt and was cashing his construction wage check. The clerk on the end position gave him the once-over and made him thumb-print the back of the check. Not fair to an honest working stiff, but part of the unconscious bias at some financial institutions. You are what you wear. Hmmm. I wet a finger and scrubbed at a spot of lime salsa on my shirt sleeve.

At the other end of the long counter, a man in a business suit and the male teller exchanged football stories about favored teams. No discrimination there.

At the center window where Loretta stood, a frail woman with white hair leaned on a cane while she conducted her business. I willed the lady to talk faster, to *finish* whatever matters she had and leave, so I could talk to Loretta. Sweat spouted at my hairline. I breathed deeper to calm my impatience.

Football guy finished his story and left.

"Next." The male clerk beckoned to me. I looked behind me. No one else in line. I pointed with my finger toward Loretta and made gestures that I wanted to talk to her. He shrugged and turned to straighten up his piles of deposit slips. I made eye contact with Loretta who gave me a non-verbal signal about the slowness of some customers. I smiled back.

Finally, the older woman completed her deposit slip, received her cash, counted it twice, unclicked her purse, and pulled out her wallet. She put the bills inside, changed her mind and pulled them back out and sorted them by denomination.

My toes started to itch.

She returned the money to the wallet and the wallet to her purse. She clicked it shut, gathered her cane, and walked slowly toward the exit.

At last, my turn.

Loretta smiled apologetically. "Sometimes they're like that. She lost her husband last year. She just likes to come in to talk. We all help each other. Like you did for me. My daughter wasn't too happy when you brought her home, but I'll be forever grateful."

She remembered my good deed! "I'm here to check on the bank accounts of Gil Streicker." I put the bank statement on the counter and turned it so she could see the name.

"I always enjoy Gil's visits. He's so easy to talk to." She blushed.

Another Gil Streicker conquest.

"He has such a sweet little girl. I remember when he brought her in one day. This little towhead, holding on to her daddy's hand, skipping all the way. She did like her free lollipop. I gave her a choice and she picked a red one. They always do that." She looked at me with concern. "I hope there's no problem."

"Gil Streicker is dead." No way to tell that news easy. "His only living relative is that little girl, living back east with her mother."

I stopped here and crossed my fingers. I *assumed* that I was saying was true. But whatever, Gil wasn't around to correct me.

"Oh, no!" Her face paled. "He was just in a week or two ago. What happened?"

I lowered my voice and leaned closer before I spoke, assuming that tone of just-us-girls sharing a secret. "His death is under investigation. Best that you don't ask more right now."

Loretta nodded. She took off her glasses and swiped at them. Settled them back on her nose, then turned businesslike "Whatever I can do to help." She clicked the keys on her computer. "Gil had the one bank account and also a savings account."

"Current balances?"

"A little under a thousand in the checking account. The savings account was zeroed out. I know, because I sent out the warning notice myself last week. People always forget about the final service fee."

I got caught in that once myself. Never could figure out why you have to pay a bank to use *your* money. But Gil's zero balance jibed with what I'd seen in the statement. Now came the hard part.

"I have Gil's safe deposit key," I said. "I need to take a look at the content of his box."

I held up my hand, staving off her objections. "I won't take a thing. You can be there the whole time. I just want to be sure little Veronica is taken care of in a timely manner."

"Oh, that poor little girl." It was clear that Loretta wanted to help, but she hesitated. "Our manager is down at the main office this afternoon, but I imagine she'd be okay with you just *looking* since there's a good reason…"

She put a "closed" sign at her spot.

I ignored the dirty look from the guy next in line.

We went to the entrance to the safe deposit vault and I showed Loretta the key. She checked the number and pulled a signature card from the drawer. I signed as an officer of the law, checking the signatures above mine. Unlike the storage unit, Gil Streicker had been here often.

"Gil a regular customer?" I asked.

"There's a story behind that, let me tell you. That man didn't know much about banking. He came in with this fistful of money, wanted to open a savings account. I got all the paperwork done—there's a ton, let me tell you!—and then he asked if he could draw the money out anytime he wanted."

Loretta looked around us to be sure no one was listening and then continued. "Well, of *course,* I had to tell him about the cash withdrawal limit of $10,000, and he got this funny expression on his face, said never mind, how much to open a safe deposit box? I had to start the paperwork all over. I remember because I was supposed to pick up my daughter from band practice, and he just kept talking, nervous like."

"Then he started coming in on a regular basis?"

Loretta nodded. "First of the month, like clockwork. Would ask to visit his safe deposit box, always asked for that little room for privacy. Of *course*, I never asked him what he was putting in. Several months later, he asked for a *bigger* box. What do you think he had in there? None of my business I'm sure, but..."

Loretta unlocked the vault door and we entered the dim little hall of the bank. The place looked like a dungeon. Can't banks afford light bulbs?

I followed her down a short hall lined with safe deposit boxes. Some were old, some brand new, and Loretta explained. "With the bank mergers and all, we just collect the boxes and bring them here to a central location and continue to use them. Some of these are over a hundred years old."

She stopped in front of a newer section. "Here it is. Number 543." I handed her the key and she put in hers and turned both. She opened the door and pulled out the box.

"I'll have to stay with you to be sure nothing is taken." Then she gave me an apologetic smile.

We went into a small room with two chairs, and I pulled back the lid on the large box. It was almost entirely empty, except for a few papers scattered on the bottom. Some odd tax receipts. A birth certificate showing Gil Streicker had been born in Montana. He had the same birthday as mine, November eighth. Did that make us related in some sort of cosmic way?

A folded piece of paper—that lined paper with the holes on the side that kids used to write school reports. I unwrapped it to discover a brief, hand-written will leaving everything to his daughter, Veronica Streicker. He declared he was of sound mind and body when he wrote it. I wondered if that were the case.

There was a disturbance at the main entrance to the vault.

"Loretta, you in there? Closing time. I need the outside door key."

Loretta hesitated, torn between closing routines and the need to stay to supervise me.

I patted her hand. "You go right ahead. I'll be fine here."

"Well, just a minute and I'll be *right* back."

We'd almost gotten to the bottom of the box. I lifted the last stack of papers and peered at two remaining objects. The first was a wedding band, heavy gold. I tried it on. Even as big as my hands are, it slid around on my finger.

Funny how we hold onto things like that. I'd wanted to dump mine in the deepest ocean after the split from my one-time husband, but a friend convinced me to keep the ring. It was still back in Tennessee in her jewelry box. Gold was worth a fortune. I wondered if I should sell it. Maybe, someday.

I replaced the ring in the box and picked up the second item, a Yale padlock key, tarnished with age. The lock at the rental unit had been brand new. Which meant this belonged to a different padlock.

Take it or leave it? Loretta's footsteps approached, and the moment of decision wavered, shimmering in the air. I snatched the key and stuck it in my pocket. Bad Peg.

I scooped everything else back into the container and closed the lid just as Loretta re-entered the room. I handed the box to her. We walked to the right row and she shoved the box in the slot, closed the outer door, secured both locks and handed the key back to me. I stuck it in my other pocket.

We moved toward the entrance. Not soon enough for me. I felt my heart race and took some deep breaths. Closed spaces like bank vaults give me claustrophobia.

Loretta clucked her tongue as we entered the bank open area. "My goodness, that huge box for those few scraps of paper. Doesn't make sense to me." Then she stopped so abruptly that I bumped into her. "So *that's* what he was up to."

"What do you mean?"

"Several weeks ago, just as I was leaving, Gil came into the bank. He held the door open for me, always *so* polite. He was carrying this Whole Foods bag, you know, that reusable kind? I made a joke about his making a run on the bank. He just gave me this funny look."

She clutched my arm. "What if he was *emptying* his safe

deposit box, not putting something in? I wonder what he kept in there? Now we'll never know, I guess."

"I suppose not." I touched her hand. "Thanks! You've been very helpful. I'll make sure little Veronica's guardian knows about the documents in the safe deposit box."

As I walked out of the bank, I reflected on the end of a life. Not much to show for all those years of living on this earth—a child's sled, a box of books, some papers and a ring in a bank vault. So much for immortality. I hoped at least Veronica had some happy memories to remember her daddy.

Or perhaps there was more. I touched the padlock key in my pocket. Did Gil Streicker transfer his deposit box contents to a closer location? I wondered if he had a premonition, something was about to happen to him. Something *did* happen, and I needed to find out why.

My mind deep in thought, I drove with a heavy foot on the road back to Mingus. Blue-and-red lights flashed in the rearview mirror as Charlie Doon's patrol car slid into the slot right behind me.

Damn, it would have to be him! I put on the Jetta's turn signal and pulled to the side of the road.

CHAPTER TEN

Normally cops don't stop other cops for traffic violations. It could be Charlie Doon didn't recognize my Jetta. Or perhaps he relished the opportunity to show me up. He hitched his equipment belt and strutted to my car in an irritating duck walk, heels in, toes out.

I tucked in my wrinkled shirt and rolled down my window as he approached.

"License and registration please."

I flashed my cop's ID.

He leaned down further and gave me a look over the top of his mirrored sunglasses. "Peg Quincy. What, you speeding? You *know* I'm always behind the Gecko Insurance billboard this time of the afternoon. If I didn't know better, I'd say you were propositioning me."

"Don't I wish. Too bad you're a happily married man." I gritted my teeth and flashed what I hoped would pass for a charming smile. "I was thinking about a case. I'll slow it down."

"You know, Peg, that we set an example for the people we serve and protect. If *we* aren't law-abiding citizens…"

Charlie let his pompous voice trail off. I kept my face neutral. Blah de blah blah. When Charlie had a few too many at P.J.s, a favorite sports bar in the Village of Oak Creek, he'd drive his own car home afterward, good law-abiding citizen that he was. Pot and kettle.

He waited to see if I would grovel a bit more and when I was silent, finally let me off the hook. "You watch that speed now. Little kids around."

I gave him a two-fingered salute and he did the same. He sauntered to his patrol car and I signaled to pull back out into traffic.

One of the curses of living in a rural area. That humiliating traffic stop would be all over the sheriff's department lunchroom by the shift's end. Maybe I could report in tomorrow with a bag over my head.

I set the cruise control for two miles under the speed limit. Reaching into my pocket, I pulled out some gum, popped it into my mouth, and chewed hard. It was hard to stop thinking about cases when the workday was done, but not fun to be on the receiving end of a traffic stop, either. It was unsettling to live in a world with no room for error 24/7.

With the shorter days, dark shadows crisscrossed the road as my Jetta whined up the last steep grade into Mingus. Shepherd paced back and forth in my driveway as I pulled in.

"Figured I'd stop by and check on the Streicker case," he said.

About time he was coming to his senses. I was tired of doing this by myself. I needed my partner back.

I popped the car trunk and retrieved the sled and box of children's things from Gil Streicker's storage unit.

"Need some help?"

"Take the box, I'll handle the sled." Shepherd followed me up the interior stairs, lugging the carton. Reckless pushed past both of us in his eagerness to be first. He stood at the top of the steps, baying, urging us forward.

"That dog does have a mouth on him. How're your neighbors handling it?"

I set the sled down near the closet and motioned Shepherd to put the box next to it. "Not so good," I admitted. "I need to think about moving."

"Somewhere here in Mingus or down the hill?" Shepard asked. "Some nice places around where I live."

"That would accept a dog like Reckless?"

"Good point. That bay of his carries."

"And the bank's been after me, too," I admitted.

"Saw the eviction notice on the table downstairs. I heard they

75

were planning to tear down this old building, put up some condos."

Why was I the last person on earth to find out these things?

I shoved a pair of underwear under the bed with one foot and tucked my sleeping T-shirt further under my pillow. Awkward, entertaining men in a studio apartment.

I grabbed a pair of jeans from the closet and a dark T-shirt, my get-free-popcorn from the local theater. Last year's model, so I was trying to get some wear out of it. Waving Shepherd toward the coffee pot in my micro-kitchen, I went into the bathroom to change.

Shepherd hollered through the door, "What's with the sled? Second childhood?"

"Just a minute." I hung my holster on the bathroom hook, yanked off my uniform and pulled on my casuals. I opened the door to an enthusiastic greeting from Reckless. You'd think I'd been gone for days.

Shepherd was sitting on the couch drinking from my favorite coffee mug. I poured coffee into my second-best mug, the one with the crack in the lip, and told Shepherd about the break-in at Gil Streicker's storage shed.

"Nothing left after the thieves pulled out," I said, "just this sled and a box of kid stuff. Do you think they found anything of value to steal?"

"Streicker was divorced. Sometimes, what the guy gets at the end of a marriage isn't worth spitting at." His tone was bitter and I remembered he'd had been through an unpleasant divorce, similar to mine. Shepherd was pretty much of a loner. So was I, come to think of it.

Reckless laid a satisfied head on my bare foot, his soft breath tickling my toes while I brought Shepherd up to speed on my visit to the Spine ranch, including the bulldozing of the fire-damaged barn.

"What's worse," I continued, "Amanda cleaned Gil's place, right down to washing his undies. If his death was more than an accident, those folks sure have taken the steps to destroy the evidence."

I waited for Shepherd to acknowledge we should have been more proactive, but he ignored my hint.

So I continued my report. "I found a key hidden in Gil's room and visited the bank this afternoon." I told Shepherd about the bank teller's story of the missing contents of the safe deposit box.

"You thinking Streicker was hiding money there?"

Shepherd gave me a shrewd look. "What else would it be— diamonds? Not likely, here in Arizona. But where would a ranch hand find that much cash? Drugs, you suppose?"

"If you want to believe Amanda, she said Gil was substance free. Regular AA attendance for a while. Could be blackmail, though."

"Folks get upset when they are paying to have secrets kept. Murder would silence him permanently." Shepherd leaned down and scratched Reckless's ear.

"Shepherd, you ever think about getting another pet?" He'd had a black-and-white kitty for a while, at total odds with his tough-guy persona. I wondered if he was lonely since his daughter took it with her.

He snorted. "Watching you with Reckless is entertainment enough, thanks." He got up from the couch. "I got to be going. Things to do tonight."

A shiver ran up my back. "Shepherd, I can't keep covering for you forever."

"Didn't ask you to. This is *my* business, not yours." His lips tightened at my rebuke. "You keep following up on the blackmail angle on Streicker. Do some more talking to those folks out at the ranch. When we get the medical examiner's statement, I'll make a decision whether to label it a homicide, not before. Did you check in with the ME's office like I asked you to?"

That was Shepherd. Always a comeback that put me on the defensive. "No, but I will."

"Good. See that you do. I'll expect you to call me with regular updates," he ordered. His preemptive tone indicated he had returned to a supervisor role, with me being the underling.

Fine. I could live with that. But if Shepherd got into trouble, it was on *his* shoulders, not mine.

The loose board by the landing creaked once as Shepherd turned the doorknob to let himself out, then the house was quiet. Too quiet. The episode with Charlie Doon and this continuing feud with Shepherd left me too frazzled to sleep.

I snapped a leash on Reckless and we went for a late night stroll. The streets were silent in the darkness, palpable warmth still emanating from the old brick buildings. The ailanthus trees waved ghostly branches against the summer moonlight as I stretched tight leg muscles on the steep hills. Reckless pulled at the leash, his nose discovering nighttime creatures.

My mind returned to the mystery of Gil Streicker's death as my feet adjusted to the cracked and broken sidewalks of the old mining town. If we declared his death a murder, the sheriff's office would assign more manpower. That would mean folks nosing around our part of the woods, which would shine a spotlight on Shepherd's extra-curricular activities—which could be a bad or a good thing, depending. My partner-loyalty warred against my instinct for self-preservation.

Reckless stopped to investigate the smells of trash left out for early morning pickup, and I gave the leash a yank. The theft at the storage unit was probably a crime of opportunity, or was it?

And there was the possible illicit money stored at the bank. Who at the Spine Ranch had secrets worth paying for? Perhaps that Raven LightDancer, or whatever his name was, for one. Heinrich Spine? He was an unpleasant sort of a guy, but old enough to have been active in World War II. Perhaps chemical warfare then—or after. His daughter Marguerite? Or even her absent husband?

Too much to consider. As my mind started spiraling in worn circles, I headed for home. When we arrived at the apartment ten minutes later, the front door was ajar. My mind flashed to my service weapon, hanging on on the hook in the bathroom where I'd left it. No help for it now.

I loosed Reckless's leash as we entered the building. "Search," I commanded.

With an excited bay, the dog leaped up the steps.

CHAPTER ELEVEN

Reckless barked incessantly from the floor above, but not the wuff-wuff-wuff of a coonhound's announcement chop at discovering live game. Maybe whoever had been there was gone. At least I hoped so.

I scrambled up the remaining stairs and dived into the bathroom. I locked the door behind me and grabbed my weapon belt from beneath my bathrobe. I paused a moment catching my breath, cursing my carelessness at being unarmed.

Reckless paced back and forth outside the room, his nails clicking on the hardwood floor. Drawing my Glock out of the holster I slowly opened the door. Silence. I walked into the one-room apartment and checked the closet, with Reckless crowding my shins. No evidence that anyone had disturbed the box of Streicker's belongings.

That left the outside. When I opened the back door, my dog pushed past me and dashed into the small yard. The moon had risen, casting long tree shadows over my back shed and the small patch of grass beyond.

"Anything, Reckless?"

He tested the breeze, tail waving. Other than a woof of acknowledgment to the neighborhood stray cat perched on the back fence, Reckless didn't move. I relied on his keen nose more than my own night-dim senses and breathed easier when he didn't sense human danger.

I jiggled the hinged padlock on the storage shed. It seemed

secure. We walked to the rear of the yard, and I opened the gate to the street beyond. At this time of night, no traffic. A barn owl hooted in the big Aleppo pine and late-night crickets chirped in the bushes. No scrape of boot heels on the asphalt of the street, no brush of leaves by something passing by.

I closed the gate again, walked to one side of the house, and shined the flashlight down the side yard. Then I paced to the other end of the house and did the same. Still nothing.

We returned to the house, and Reckless dashed into the apartment, ran around once for good measure, and leaped up on the bed. For once, I didn't even argue. I propped a chair under the door handle. Tomorrow I'd get the locksmith out and redo the master lock.

Had it been a casual thief looking for valuable items to fence for drugs? He'd have slim pickings here. I didn't even own a television. Or could it be they were looking for something more specific?

I crossed to the open closet door and picked up the sled. I turned it over, carefully examining the bottom. Unless there was gold under the rust, nothing there. The tattered Kraft box held kids' books— nothing that would be worth a burglary. But maybe they didn't know that....

Stop it! I chided myself. Quit inventing things that don't exist.

But, too charged up to sleep, I reheated a cup of coffee in the microwave and walked out onto the front balcony, Reckless padding behind me. I sat in the old rocker, listening as an underpowered car labored up the hill toward town.

The full moon illuminated the foothills below and reached to the red rocks near Sedona on the far side of the valley. Finally, I tossed the dregs of the coffee over the railing and walked back inside. Three hours of sleep, if I was lucky.

***

Reckless woke me at dawn, and I did a slow jog in the hills above the mining town, while he ran three times as far, hunting for varmints. I stood for a moment on the ridge catching my breath and looked down on the empty space where the grand Montana Hotel had once stood before fire destroyed it, and farther, into the mining pit where the man had died the first week I came to this town.

Mingus had a history of violence from the mining days, and I carried my own ghosts with me as well. People I'd been too late to help, and one person I'd sent to the hereafter, who would be waiting when I arrived. The memory of that shooting never faded. It haunted my midnight dreams and even returned on sunny mornings like this.

I returned to the house to prepare for work. An incoming phone call vibrated my cell as I walked dripping out of the shower. I grabbed a towel, and draped it around the strategic places. It was Shepherd's ID.

"Yeah?"

There was traffic noise behind his voice, so he wasn't at the office.

"Sorry I barked at you last night. This is my affair, not yours. I shouldn't have pulled you into it."

"What partners do," I grunted.

Niceties finished, he went on to the real purpose of the call. "The medical examiner's office called this morning. Said you'd ordered a heavy metal test?"

I braced, waiting for criticism of the budget expense. His reaction surprised me.

"Good call. There were traces of arsenic."

"Does that mean we're investigating a murder?"

"Not sure. Don't know if there was enough in Streicker's body to kill him. With these drought conditions, many of the shallower wells in the valley have elevated arsenic counts. There was enough to make him awfully sick, though."

"So he could have been impaired when he went into the barn?"

"Could be. But another way of looking at it, he might not have been the intended victim," Shepherd said.

"Meaning?"

"You know how sometimes a person wanting to commit suicide will make hesitation marks first?"

I made the connection. "You mean somebody was looking for the optimum killing dosage but hadn't reached it yet?"

"Poison is premeditated, not a crime of passion. But it's still filled with risks. Sometimes the wrong person gets hurt."

So was Gil Streicker the intended victim or just a stand-in? I shivered.

"Shepherd, there was an attempted break-in at my apartment last night."

"They take anything valuable?"

"You know I operate on a shoe-string."

"Getting the lock repaired?"

"Yeah, they're coming this morning."

"Good, although it seems like a waste of money, seeing that you're leaving that place anyway. Talk to Bettina Schwartz," he ordered. "She's good for Mingus real estate, knows what will be coming available."

For somebody that was AWOL himself, Shepherd was doing a lot of none-of-his-business supervising my personal affairs.

"Anything else?" My tone was sharper than I intended.

"No, that's it."

"And you're going to be back on the job when?"

"I've got your back. Talked to the sheriff this morning. Everything's fine."

It was strange to hear a defensive tone in Shepherd's voice. Then he quashed it.

"Anyway, don't forget the case hasn't been declared a homicide yet. I'll tell you when."

Saying he had my back didn't help much when he was miles away doing unauthorized surveillance. I closed the connection with a little more force than necessary.

How much longer would Shepherd be conducting this vendetta? More importantly, how long would I choose to be his unwilling accomplice?

CHAPTER TWELVE

When the locksmith finished and the studio apartment was again secure, I dropped my dog at my grandfather's house and continued up to the sheriff's station. The office was empty, Shepherd nowhere in sight.

I tried his cell and listened to the phone ring eleven times. Finally, I received the message, "Party out of range; please leave your message after the beep." I hung up without leaving a return voice mail. What was the point?

The fax machine's idiot light blinked that it was out of paper. I stuffed some in, the machine geared into action, and sheets spilled onto the floor. No way to tell if any of it was important. And no telling how long the machine had sat there, unattended.

The hair on the back of my neck tightened. Shepherd knew I'd be late with the lock problem. His job was to be here, providing coverage, manning the office.

I stacked the spilled paper into an untidy bundle and started to read. The first batch was from Solemn Sidney at the medical examiner's office. Sidney's report spelled out in exacting detail what Shepherd had mentioned this morning. At least my partner had to sit through Sidney's lame jokes this time, not me.

I skimmed through the report. Inconclusive signs of carbon monoxide poisoning, so the man may still have been alive when the fire swept through the barn. Traces of arsenic: Possibly chronic, from the physical signs—Mee's lines on the fingernails, redness of

83

the cheeks. Bruising to the back of the head, perhaps sustained in a fall. Again, inconclusive.

The report ended with a hand-written note from Sidney suggesting we search the premises for arsenic. Sidney liked to get in on the action whenever he could—Worse than Shepherd at poking his nose in.

The message-box-full indicator on the station phone blinked accusingly. I punched the play-back button and worked through the stack. The first two messages were from the sheriff, asking Shepherd to call him. My partner's problem, not mine, since he said he'd made contact already.

Another message invited us to the annual town barbeque. Nice. I wrote the date on our lunchroom calendar. I deleted the next three calls that offered an assortment of roofing deals, screaming mortgage rates, and upcoming sales at the local discount store— didn't those folks even know what number they were dialing?

The last message was from the forensics lab. I called back, and the agent on duty picked up.

When I gave him the case number, he checked it for me. "Just gave this to Shepherd Malone," he grumbled. "Don't you guys talk to each other?"

Apparently not.

"Okay, here it is. Cuts on the wire are definitely man-made."

"Any clue as to the instrument?"

"Not an ordinary pocket knife. Something with a small, crescent-shaped blade."

"Like a surgical scalpel?" I asked.

"Could be. Look, you guys need to get your act together over there. It's a waste of my time to report this information twice."

Tell me about it. I thanked him and rang off.

The fire was deliberately set, then. Sometimes that meant an insurance scam, especially if the ranch were in financial difficulties. Was it a coincidence that few of the horses were in their stalls the night of the fire or just the happenstance of a summer night's outside pasturing?

On the other hand, Gil Streicker had lost his life in that fire. The blaze may have been set to destroy evidence of a murder.

I decided to head out to the Spine Ranch to follow up on the arsenic angle once Shepherd returned with the department SUV. Dr. Spine had been a chemist, so possibly he'd have some in his supplies. Or there was always the barn and gardening shed, where old rat poison might be stored. That stuff used to contain arsenic.

I tried Shepherd's phone again. This time he answered.

"Where you at?" I asked, hearing the ding of a cash register.

"Safeway. Dude came in here for groceries." He was whispering like the announcer at the 18th hole of the Master's Golf Tournament.

"That's not an arrestable offense."

"It is if he samples that wine he's buying, on the way home. Wait! He just picked up some peanuts to go with the liquor."

"Shepherd! If he spots you..."

"Nah, I'm fine. I'm hidden over here behind the donuts." The phone clicked as he hung up.

I was on my own, in a suspicious death case that was rapidly spinning out of control, while my partner played his little game of hide and seek.

My cell phone rang and I grabbed it. At first, I thought it might be Shepherd calling me back, but the number on the caller ID was unfamiliar. I pressed the connect button.

It was Marguerite Spine-Riordan. "Officer Quincy. Thank goodness I reached you. Please, you've got to come at once."

"What seems to be the—"

"There's a strange man out in the yard. With a gun."

"Didn't you call the sheriff's office?"

"They put me on hold," she said.

"Did you tell them it was important?"

"Well, I didn't want to be *rude* about it. I gave them my name and my address and told them that I was Heinrich Spine's daughter. That should have been enough."

"So then you called me."

"Well, you *left* your card on the table." Her voice was querulous and whiny.

I felt a sudden kinship with the sheriff's office dispatcher. Maybe it would be simpler to deal with her problem myself. I'd meant to visit the ranch later today anyway.

"The man. Where is he right now?"

"Out by the barn. He's arguing with our gardeners."

"And you are sure there's a gun?"

"Well, I saw something shiny. It *looked* like a gun. I locked the door right away and came up here into the study. Amanda is in town and Heinrich is asleep and I certainly couldn't call Rosa or *Fancy*." Her voice crackled with disgust at the last name.

"Stay where you are. I'll be there soon."

"Well, where else would I be?"

She slammed the phone in my ear ending the connection. I did likewise, taking out my rudeness on the device. I called dispatch and informed them of my destination. They said they'd stand by.

***

When I drove through the Spine Ranch gate, I counted three men near the new barn construction. Two were ranch hands I'd seen there before. The third man brandished an iron crowbar.

It could fit Marguerite's description of something shiny. And a crowbar could be a deadly weapon, too. I'd attended an exhibition once where a man tossed one twenty feet and put an outsized gash in a wooden post. Wouldn't want one used on my skull.

The squad car with light bar flashing would have made a better entrance, but the Jetta would have to do. At least I was in uniform. I jerked on the parking brake, got out and strode toward the group.

"What's the problem?"

The men looked up at my approach, and one of the unarmed men started speaking to me in rapid Spanish.

My high school Spanish class was a decade behind me. Now I wished I'd paid more attention.

"English, *por favor*."

"This man, he rips open the turnout gate on the drainage ditch."

"Our water!" Crowbar Man shouted.

As I drew closer, I recognized blond scraggly hair and that pink beanie. It was Serena Battle's brother, Hank.

"Not yours." His fist clenched the bar tightly, his stance aggressive. "You stole it from us."

"*Idiota*!" Another torrent of Spanish, curse words spat out like machine gun bullets.

I kept my eye on the crowbar. I was facing an angry man who was also brain-damaged. Even so, the outcome would be the same

86

if he threw the bar. I touched the Glock at my hip, not wanting to escalate the situation, but ready if I had to.

"Hank, remember me?" I asked. "You were hunting snakes when I came to visit your sister, Serena."

Some clarity returned to his eyes. "Serena..."

The hand with the crowbar dropped to his side and Hank shook his head. He looked at the two angry men and me in uniform.

Then he dropped the bar. He ran in an awkward, uneven gait for the side of the big house and disappeared behind it.

"Stay here," I ordered the men and gave chase. I'd had the record for the hundred-yard dash in the police academy, but the ten pounds of duty belt and my Glock slowed me some. That, and too many lunches at Beto's Mexican Restaurant.

Hank had a twenty-five-yard advantage on me. As I rounded the corner, he increased that lead, darting across the backyard. In a one-handed vault, he cleared the barbed-wire fence into a paddock beyond. I jumped the fence, too, and doubled my speed.

Hank swerved around two grazing cows that jerked up their heads, and then bounded over a far fence. Picking up speed, he vanished into the woods beyond.

I jerked to a halt.

A Brahma bull appeared from behind the cows and trotted aggressively in my direction. Criminals I faced without fear. But bull vs. cop? I knew who'd win that contest.

I paused, hands on knees, assessing its reaction. With no picador's lance, my only option would be flight. I took a quick glance behind me at the fence, some twenty paces distant. Then I edged sideways, trying to put the cows between the bull and me. That confused him for a moment, and I pivoted, racing for the fence.

If the ground shook, I didn't feel it. But hot breath dusted my neck as I vaulted the fence one-handed. I landed on the other side in a splatter of dust. One palm was bleeding, and my uniform pant leg was ripped at the knee.

But I was on one side of that barbed-wire fence and the bull was on the other. I had made it!

The bull chuffed, uprooting plugs of grass with its hooves. We made eye-contact for a moment, then it whirled and trotted heavily back to the cows, honor satisfied.

I rose shakily to my feet and threw the finger. More than one kind of honor. Anyway, I knew where Hank lived. Maybe Serena could calm him down a little before I got there.

The two men looked up as I returned from behind the house. One held out his hand. "I'm Ray Morales, head gardener here at the ranch."

Unlike the first man, his English was unaccented, prep-school perfect. Bilingual? I'd always admired the ability of people who can speak two languages fluently. I often had trouble making even one language work for me.

I winced a little as we shook hands. He turned my hand over and examined my palm.

"Ol' One-Eye stopped you, did he? Come back to the barn and let's clean that out."

At the faucet, he washed the scrape gently, then applied some disinfectant ointment from the office first aid kit.

"You want a bandage?" He quirked an eyebrow at me. "Didn't think so. Interferes with the shooting hand, right?" He mimicked a six-shooter draw.

"Thanks. That feels much better." I smiled and then queried him about the incident. "Hank Battle. He bother you before this?"

Ray nodded. "Some. It's not his fault, though. He and I used to go motorcycling, over to Prescott and down Yarnell Hill before, you know..." He tapped his head.

"Still, he threatened you. Want to press charges?"

"Not for me to say. Up to the Boss Man." He pointed to the big house. "But Hank and his sister are entitled to some of that water, too."

He gestured to the luxurious lawn and magnificent weeping willow trees framing the house entrance "This place feels like a goddam golf course." His voice deepened with intensity.

I couldn't argue with that observation.

"But don't repeat that to Dr. Spine? I need this job. Got a wife and three kids at home."

I promised him what he said would remain with me. "Got a quick question for you, though. Any arsenic around the ranch?"

"You mean rat poison, that sort of thing?" he asked.

I nodded.

Ray shook his head. "No, I'd rather foster the barn cats and let *them* destroy the rats. Dangerous to keep poison like that around, with the horses and ranch animals."

I gave him my card. He promised to call if Hank trespassed again.

Then I walked up to the big house to talk to Ms. Marguerite and the Boss Man.

CHAPTER THIRTEEN

The nurse, Fancy Morgan, opened the front door. She was dressed in jeans and a man's gray shirt rolled at the sleeves. Without makeup, her face looked vulnerable and tired, as though she'd kept too many late nights.

"Is Marguerite or her father around?"

"Heinrich is napping. Marguerite is in her room with a migraine."

Her words were matter-of-fact, without emotion, and she made no effort to open the door wider.

"Marguerite called me," I said.

"About the fight. Yes. She might be down later."

"Might I wait inside?"

Fancy sighed and her lips tightened.

Something had irritated her, and it couldn't be me since I'd just arrived. If Heinrich was asleep that only left Marguerite. Having dealt with Marguerite myself, I wasn't surprised.

"Suit yourself. I was about to make some tea anyway," Fancy said. "I'll set an extra place."

She turned and headed back to the kitchen.

I entered, closed the door, and followed her. I'd rather have coffee than tea, but the invitation gave me a chance to learn more about the nurse and her interactions with the family.

In the kitchen, I sat on a bar stool while Fancy spooned tea leaves from a metal container into a fine china teapot and added steaming water from the built-in dispenser in the wall.

Reaching into a cupboard behind her, she carefully lifted down two teacups and saucers so thin they were translucent, together with linen napkins edged in lace. She set them down on the table and poured hot water into the beautiful old teapot.

I turned over a teacup to examine the maker: Spode.

"Careful!" Fancy reached over, took the teacup and set it carefully back on the saucer. "These was Mrs. Spine's wedding china. She said I could use them whenever I wanted." Her voice was defensive like a little girl caught doing something bad. "And now that she's dead, Marguerite could care less."

I wave my hand in agreement. Not my territory.

Fancy lifted the teapot lid, judged the color of the tea and poured two cups. Next, she offered me cream and sugar which I declined. She took her cup delicately in one hand, a pinky crooked, and took a sip.

I followed her action. Not as good as the Jamaica Blue Mountain coffee that Ben used to prepare at the office, but not bad, for tea.

Fancy looked around the kitchen. "Raven LightDancer's in town getting supplies. This is his place, that is when he's not helping himself to the family's money."

I raised an eyebrow. "What's his background?"

"Everybody's got a back story," Fancy said evasively.

"Even you?"

"Let me check upstairs again."

She dialed an internal number, there was a short pause, and Marguerite's slurred voice mumbled something. Fancy put the phone down with unnecessary force.

"Your tea about finished? I wouldn't bother waiting for Marguerite. In her current condition, she may never show."

"I'm in no hurry." I stirred a little sugar into my cup and settled back. "Your name is unusual."

"My mother had pretensions. I always hated the name. It sounded like some dance hall girl's."

Fancy didn't look much like an entertainer these days.

"How did you meet Heinrich?"

"It's a long story."

She paused and I had the feeling it was a tale she didn't want to share. I waited in the silence, hoping she would.

"I took care of my parents, back where I grew up," she said. "A little town in the Midwest—just a slow place in the road."

Her eyes had a far-away look. "When my mother died, I took care of my father. When *he* died, I headed west. I met Heinrich Spine at a truckstop coffee shop. We hit it off, and I came here, first as a nurse to his wife, then as a housekeeper. That changed back to nurse when he got more infirm. End of story."

Her brief statement summed up years of hard living.

"How did your parents..."

"Let me get you some more tea." Fancy snatched my cup so fast that some of the dregs slopped onto the floor. She placed the cup on the counter and grabbed a paper towel. She scrubbed at the floor nervously.

"Clumsy of me." Then she poured us more hot tea.

"How is the family here doing since Gil Streicker's death?" I asked.

"As good as can be expected, I suppose. You know." She shrugged.

I pushed a little. "Amanda said that she and Gil were a couple. How did Heinrich react to that?"

Fancy's mouth twisted, and she got a peculiar expression, like anticipating guilty pleasure from hurtful gossip.

"He didn't know," she said. "Gil and Amanda kept quiet about the whole thing after what happened with Marguerite."

I took a sip of the bitter liquid. "Marguerite?"

Fancy gave me a direct look, made a decision, and went further. "Gil first went after Marguerite. When Heinrich found out about the relationship, the old man changed his will, leaving everything to Amanda. Gil broke it off with Marguerite the next day and started courting the daughter. Some women have all the luck."

She gave a polite smile, showing her disdain for some women.

"Marguerite must have been livid. Did she and her daughter have words?"

"Amanda pretended the prior relationship had never happened. They never talked about it, far as I know."

Poor Amanda! Not particularly attractive, but being wooed by the handsome Gil Streicker. I could see her need to minimize the affair he'd had with her mother, or pretend it didn't exist.

"Heinrich's in ill health," Fancy said, "and he wasn't going to last forever. Gil aimed to get this ranch, whatever it took."

Interesting. A jealous Marguerite—that could be a motive for murder. Or if Amanda finally owned up to the earlier relationship that Gil had with her mother? More complications.

I set my teacup and saucer carefully in the sink. "Where around this place might I find a medical scalpel or arsenic?"

"How should I know? This a scavenger hunt or something?"

"It could concern Gil Streicker's death."

"His death was an accident," Fancy said flatly.

"Still under investigation," I countered.

She thought a moment. "Well, a scalpel...Nothing around here. You might check with Dr. Theodore Riordan, Marguerite's soon-to-be-ex-husband. He's supposed to help out when Heinrich gets fussy, but somehow he's always unavailable when that happens."

Fancy's voice turned self-righteous, as she described another person who had failed her when times got rough.

"Where's Dr. Riordan live?"

"Not here. Heinrich would never allow it. A camping trailer down by Beaver Creek is good enough for him." She scribbled hasty directions to the campground on a slip of paper and handed it to me.

"And what about arsenic? Where might I find that around the ranch?" I asked.

"You mean, other than the stuff in our water? Surprised that hasn't killed me before now. Might be some in the gardening shed— use it for rat poison. You'd have to check with Ray."

"He says there's nothing there. Does Dr. Spine have a chemistry lab for his experiments?"

"He doesn't allow visitors." Her mouth pursed in proper gatekeeper refusal.

The hair on the back of my neck bristled. "Police business. Call up and ask if I can take a look."

With an exaggerated sigh, Fancy picked up the house phone once more. "Marguerite, the policewoman wants to see your father's chemistry lab." There was a muffled response and a click as the other receiver disconnected.

"Marguerite says she is totally indisposed and can't meet with you. Her way of dealing with troubles."

Fancy grabbed a ring of keys hanging by the side of the kitchen door. "If you *must,* follow me."

We walked through the dark cool of the house, our footsteps echoing from the Saltillo tile. This Spanish-style hacienda seemed an unlikely setting for a full-blown chemistry lab but perhaps it fit Heinrich.

I'd always had a fondness for chemistry. In high school, I had this wild-eyed science teacher. On the last day of class before summer, he spewed a thousand ping-pong balls out of a bucket filled with liquid nitrogen. We looked on in awe as the balls erupted in all directions. I don't think they renewed his teaching contract after that. Pity.

I tried to picture this big house filled with ping-pong balls scattering in all directions. No, from the sound of it, Heinrich practiced a darker kind of chemistry.

Fancy stopped in front of a closed door toward the back of the house. She fit one key into a padlock hanging from a metal latch. We passed into a small, enclosed entryway, perhaps four feet square. Lights flashed on automatically at our entrance. A circulating fan whirred to speed as the door shut behind us, forming a negative pressure. The small entry room created a buffer for noxious fumes that might otherwise enter the main house.

Fancy fit another key into the lock of a second door at the far side of the vestibule. A blast of musty air rushed to meet us as we entered the lab proper. The room was long and narrow, with high clerestory windows and a huge ventilation hood hovering from the ceiling. The double-door barrier blanketed the room with stillness. With the new air circulation, an acrid smell permeated the air.

Maple cabinets with black rubber counters lined the walls. I touched one surface and recoiled at the greasy smear on my finger. I wiped it hastily on my pant leg. Dim sunlight glinted off retorts and glass test tubes, some still holding a dark residue in the rounded bottoms.

A row of Bunsen burners was tethered to a strip of gas outlets on the wall above the counter. I sniffed but caught no scent of gas. Papers were scattered across the counter as though a complicated test were in progress, but a thick layer of dust covered everything. This lab had not been used for some time.

I walked over to the counter and casually reached for the papers.

Fancy intervened. "Please don't touch anything. Heinrich absolutely forbids it."

I walked along, hands behind my back as requested. It seriously hampered my snooping style.

I sneezed, disturbing the dust layer. Row after row of glass bottles lined the shelves—some clear, some amber colored, with tight stoppers. Nothing was labeled "Arsenic." Didn't mean it wasn't there, though. As I walked farther into the lab, the air turned foul. My vision blurred and an instant headache throbbed at my temples.

"I detest coming in here," Fancy said. "Air giving you problems?"

I coughed in assent. She walked to the end of the room and unlocked a final door that led to the outside. We walked into a semi-shaded garden. Even in the heat of the day, it was cool, with high velvet mesquite trees arching overhead. Filtered sunlight drifted across a small pond, and a covey of quail dashed to cover beneath lavender, bee-filled Russian sage.

"Nice garden," I said.

"Thanks. Hardly anyone comes back here now except me." Fancy visibly relaxed as she dropped to a red sandstone bench. She patted the seat next to her and I sat.

"See there?" She pointed to a bed of spiky-leafed plants. "I've planted some hybrid iris— there are a ruffled peach and gold bicolor and a deep red that's a re-bloomer. The corms won't bloom until next spring, but they're worth the wait. I love flowers. Never had any when I was growing up."

It was a side of Fancy that she hadn't shared before.

"Mind if I smoke?" she asked.

Without waiting for my answer, she reached into her pocket and withdrew a pack. She lit one, breathed a puff of smoke into the air, and sighed. A bucket of sand next to the bench was piled high with butts, evidence that she came here often.

"No! Get out of here. Shoo!"

Fancy's birthmark splashed deep purple against her pale cheek as she reached down and lobbed a good-sized rock at a gray-and-white cat prowling about the garden. The stone hit its hind leg, hard.

The cat yelped once and limped into the brush.

"Ouch. That had to hurt," I said.

Fancy seemed to notice my judgmental tone. "That cat buries turds in my garden. I catch it here again, I'll kill it." She pulled a bit of tobacco off her lip with a precise gesture. "Sorry. I didn't mean that, of course."

Of course. "Who has keys to the chemistry lab?" I asked.

"Heinrich installed the locks when Marguerite began giving her soirees. Said he didn't want the whole world with access to his work. So he's got keys. Marguerite, too, probably. She's got her nose into everything. Then the ring of keys that hangs in the kitchen."

"Heinrich's not worked in the lab for a while?"

Fancy shook her head. "He had a series of small strokes. All of a sudden the Riordans showed up—mother and daughter. Then about a month ago, the doctor. Convenient, that. I always wondered about that. Dr. Theo Riordan, a doctor, just when Heinrich needed medical help…"

Fancy took another draw on her cigarette and I looked at her sideways. Up close, she had a hardness about her face, lines where there shouldn't be any. My grandfather used to call that "rode hard, put up wet." It couldn't be easy for her, taking care of the rigid German chemist.

Fancy stubbed out the cigarette and rose abruptly. "Time to be getting back. Heinrich will be waking soon. You can reach the front parking lot that way." She pointed to a gate at the far end of the garden. Before I could respond, she had turned and re-entered the chemistry lab. She locked the door carefully behind her.

The lab had yielded no sign of arsenic, but we could return with a court order if necessary and have a closer look. My meeting with Marguerite could wait, too, since the "man with a gun" was no longer at the ranch.

It was time for me to check on Hank Battle before the confrontation at the irrigation ditch slipped from his memory.

CHAPTER FOURTEEN

During my stay at the Spine Ranch, the hot sun had turned the inside of my parked Jetta into a sauna. Black upholstery—good in winter, bad in summer. I held my breath, opened all windows, and turned the AC up to max. Then I steered the wheel with my palms until it was cool enough inside to breathe again.

At the Battle farm, Hank's old truck was parked by his trailer, but I turned right instead and parked the Jetta in front of Serena's house. The irrigation ditch was running full, the gush of water cooling the summer air. Maybe Ray Morales had opened the floodgates at the Spine Ranch, letting the waters flow again. Smart man.

Serena answered my knock. "I heard you drive up. Come in."

I followed her into the house, small in comparison to the Spine mansion. I sat on the same dusty couch I had the first time I was here. I didn't like conflict—no cop did—but Serena's blind spot when it came to her brother was going to cause trouble.

She perched on the edge of a small chair opposite me, a stubborn expression on her face. "Hank told me what happened at the ranch. He didn't mean anything by it. He gets carried away sometimes."

"Well, this time he was waving a crowbar around. That's dangerous."

"Hank was just protecting what is rightfully ours. Anyway, no charges are being filed, are they?"

She seemed unconcerned. Someone must have called her from the ranch. Unlikely as it seemed, the Battle family might have allies there. Ray, perhaps. Or even Fancy or Amanda? It was possible.

I tried again. "Serena, Hank was threatening people. He's out of control."

"No, you don't know my brother. Folks around here have learned to live with his moods. We didn't have any trouble—that is, until the Riordans moved in."

"Now you're blaming Hank's problems on the water shortage?"

"Why not? Heinrich's got plenty of water. And yet he insists on using ours, too. I think Marguerite puts him up to it." Her fists clenched, white-knuckled.

She noticed me looking at them and hid her hands under a fold of her skirt.

"My brother was different before."

She gestured toward a bookshelf where a picture of a smiling Hank stood beside Serena and an older man—their father?

"Hank took AP classes all through high school—knew that he wanted a career in agriculture since he was four. He had this uncanny ability to connect with anything on four legs—horses, our pigs and goats, even wild creatures." Tears glinted in her eyes.

I contrasted the smiling boy in the picture to the unkempt, confused man I confronted earlier in the day. I hesitated. Perhaps Serena was right.

"We'll leave it at a warning for now," I said slowly. "But if Heinrich Spine files a formal complaint against Hank, I'll have no option but to arrest him."

"I'll watch him closer, I promise."

I left the farm with a troubled mind. Serena could say what she wanted, but the situation was dangerously unstable. Like those bottles in Heinrich's chemistry lab: Inert chemicals collecting dust in a vacant room, but enter a catalyst and the roof could blow off. Maybe the Battles, brother and sister, were that catalyst to violence. I hoped not.

It was early afternoon, and my stomach reminded me that I hadn't eaten lunch. I thought about Beto's and then remembered my lagging feet and winded breath on the dash across the bull's paddock. Maybe it was time to eat healthier.

I pulled into a grocery store parking lot. Inside, I filled a plastic container with healthy greens at the salad bar and picked up a diet Coke. Then I drove out to the picnic area near Montezuma's Well.

The Well had nothing to do with the Aztec chieftain who had never visited Arizona, but rather, was a natural limestone sinkhole filled from springs that created a cool blue-green pool in the crater. The little lake held unique species of leeches and water scorpions, but fish couldn't survive there, because the calcium carbonate levels were too high. A local entrepreneur discovered this much to his consternation when he tried to stock it as a trout farm. Nevertheless, it was a great place for a midday stop.

The tall cottonwoods formed a green ring around a grassy picnic area, their summer leaves rustling overhead. I stepped over an old irrigation ditch carrying water from Montezuma's Well to farmlands before it reentered Wet Beaver Creek. The walls of the ditch were hardened limestone, leached from the mineral-rich water of the Well. The sound of the water soothed me as I sat in the shade, munching on my greens, rabbit-like.

I rang Shepherd to fill him in on happenings at the Spine Ranch, but there was no answer on his cell. I'd catch him tonight at the Mingus sheriff's station and we'd have this out. One way or the other, he needed to focus on the job, not this crazy obsession of his.

And the *job* was figuring out who might have killed Gil Streicker. The Riordan women, Marguerite and Amanda, were possible candidates. So were Serena Battle and her brother, Hank.

I couldn't rule out Ray Morales. He seemed calm, but there could have been a disagreement. And Raven LightDancer? I knew next to nothing about the man, except for the innuendos that Amanda had hurled. Still too many unanswered questions. I dumped the remains of the uneaten salad in the trash and returned to my car.

I'm usually good with directions, but the ones that Fancy had given me to Dr. Theo Riordan's trailer made no sense at all. I turned off I-17 at the Sedona exit, then turned west down a narrow paved road. At about the two-mile mark, I crossed over Red Tank Draw, a dry slash in the red earth. And a half-mile beyond that, I drove over another bridge at the Wet Beaver Creek.

The road switched to dirt just after the creek and then forked in a T-intersection. To the left was a sign to a private boy's school and to the right was the entrance to the V Bar V Ranch. No longer a working ranch, it was designated a Heritage Site because of the petroglyph cliff located there. Nothing either direction looked promising for the trailer that Fancy had described.

I U-turned and rattled back across the bridge and into a day-use picnic area. Maybe someone here knew where Dr. Riordan lived. The parking lot was full, with only the "Service Vehicles" spot vacant. I pulled into it and got out to stretch my legs.

A lanky man wearing khaki Bermuda shorts, a pocketed vest, and an orange T-shirt emerged from the Camp Host trailer. He waved his arms wildly. "Hey! You can't park there. It's reserved."

"Sorry, I just need some directions."

I knelt down to pet the camp cat, a well-fed orange tabby missing half of one ear. He sniffed me once, put his tail in the air, and stalked off, his ample belly swaying from side to side. I bet he had a good diet of camp scraps and didn't have to settle for spinach and kale salad.

As the man drew closer, I pulled out my badge. "Pegasus Quincy, sheriff's department."

"Oh! I thought you folks drove official vehicles." He looked scornfully at my dusty car. "How can I help you?"

A good start would be not dissing my Jetta. "I'm looking for a Dr. Theo Riordan. He's supposed to be camping somewhere around here."

The camp host pulled off a baseball cap and wiped the sweat from his brow. "He better not be camping in these grounds. It's a Day Park only. No overnights. Kids sneak in here at night, and I have to run them off." He pointed to the sign at the entrance: "See? Says right there, 'day use only'. Makes my job a lot tougher when people don't pay attention."

"Must be hard," I said, trying to sound sympathetic. "Say, I could use some water. You don't have a vending machine or anything here, do you?"

"Sorry. No electricity, no machines. This is a *picnic* area. Most people prefer it that way."

His tone implied I should know that. My parched throat didn't care. It needed water. I debated asking whether he might have some in that fancy camper of his but decided not to. Accommodating thirsty law officers probably wasn't in the camp rulebook.

The wind shifted and shadows darkened the park as clouds deepened overhead. I looked up. "Thought June was too early for the monsoon rains."

The camp host shook his head. "These are from a subtropical depression in the Baja Peninsula. Bad news."

"Why? I thought rain was good for the desert."

He looked at me as though I was a tourist, asking too many dumb questions. I felt like one. The sun beat down on my bare head, and a nascent sunburn tightened the bridge of my nose.

"This year we've already had bad fires on the Mogollon Rim to the north of us," he said. "When the forests burn, pine needles drop to the ground and form this waxy coating. Water runs right off it. A flash flood can hit in the mountains and within minutes, that little stream you see there can rise bank to bank."

The clear limpid flow of the small creek in front of us seemed an unlikely place for a flood, with little kids playing in the shallows, hopping from rock to rock, and diving off into the deeper pools.

I pointed at a glint of silver under a sycamore beyond the far side of the park. "What's that?"

The host whipped out pocket binoculars and peered at the shape. He didn't bother to share the view with me.

"Looks like a trailer. Might be your guy. If it is, he's parked illegally. You should arrest him."

"Why don't you?"

"Out of the park boundaries. Not my responsibility."

I wished my job was that easily defined.

I thanked him and left. I backtracked to a turnoff I'd missed. Maybe this was it. The rutted, dirt road angled back toward the creek. About five hundred yards in, the humped silver shape of an old Airstream trailer emerged from the shadows. The area near the creek was damp and cool, and cicadas buzzed in a nearby grove of cottonwoods.

Dr. Theo Riordan greeted me at the front steps of his trailer, holding a plate and glass. The doctor was in his mid-fifties, on the plump side, with a florid round face and a buzz cut balanced by a stubby white beard. He wore Teva river-runner sandals, a white T-shirt and Bermuda shorts. A birder's olive-green, broad-brimmed hat completed the outfit. The good doctor had gone native.

"Good morning, Officer," he said. "Fancy called and said you might be along." He put his dishes down on a picnic table and held out a big hand. "Theodore Riordan at your service. Call me Dr. Theo."

It was a cool, slightly damp handshake from the glass he'd been holding.

"Pull up a chair," Dr. Theo said. "I was just starting lunch. Want to join me?"

"Just some water," I said, being virtuous.

He entered the trailer for a moment and came out with another big glass of ice water. He sat in a camp chair across from me and dived into his sandwich with gusto. Remembering the discarded salad, I looked at the homemade bread, ham, and cheese with envy.

The creek bubbled over a red sandstone ledge beyond the trailer, and a Crissal thrasher warbled a rich phrase of song in the alder branch across the water. Easy to see why he liked it here.

I brought my mind back to law enforcement with difficulty. "The camp host across the way says you're parked illegally."

"What does he know?" Dr. Theo said, gesturing about him. "This land is free for everyone. Free air. Free water."

"But..."

He shook a finger at me in mock disapproval. "Don't believe everything you hear. Dr. Spine owns this land. He gives me permission to park here as long as I want."

I considered returning to the campground to let the site host know. Nah, let him stew about rule-breakers. He seemed to be good at that.

"You know about the fire at the ranch," I said. "Gil Streicker, the ranch manager died."

"My daughter Amanda told me. Sorry to hear it."

I took another sip of water. "You mind if I take a few notes?"

Dr. Theo waved at me with half a sandwich. "Fire away. I've got no secrets."

"Amanda tells me that you and your wife are separated."

"In a way. I still keep an eye on her, balance her bank account, that sort of thing. Marguerite is somewhat of a spendthrift. Oh, that reminds me. She was going shopping in Phoenix today and hasn't checked in. Just a moment."

He pulled his cell phone from his pocket and manipulated the touchscreen. A map flashed up. He enlarged it with thumb and forefinger and studied it for a moment. Then he smiled, closed the connection, and tucked the phone back in his pocket.

"Her phone is registering at the ranch. She must have changed her mind about the trip."

"You keep *track* of where she is?"

"Well, somebody has to. What if she had car trouble?"

"She knows you do this?"

"Easy enough to put a locator app on her cell." The tops of his ears turned red. "I pay the phone bill," he said defensively. "I just want to be sure she's safe."

Uh-huh. Another word for control in my book.

"Think the two of you might get back together?" I asked.

"That's what I want. Heinrich is on my side—he doesn't believe in divorce. I don't either."

"Marguerite agree with you?"

His lips firmed. "She will."

"What was your relationship with Gil Streicker?"

"Gil was a good ranch manager. Period." Dr. Theo picked up his sandwich again and took another bite.

"I heard Gil once had a relationship with Marguerite."

Dr. Theo choked. "Heinrich put an end to that foolishness. It was done. Finito." A look of satisfaction spread over his pink face.

That seemed definite. Maybe too definite. I made a note. "What's your assessment of Dr. Spine?"

Theo shifted and the camp chair creaked under his weight. He wiped a dribble of mayo off his chin.

"He's made a lot of enemies here in the valley."

"Enemies?"

"The good doctor seems to think he can do whatever he wants. The neighbors take offense at that sometimes. Gil Streicker was good at running interference. Don't know who will get that job now."

"Perhaps Amanda? She said something about bookkeeping at lunch the other day."

"I hope not. Tried to talk her into medicine, take over my practice someday. But she loves animals, wants to go into veterinary instead. I'd hate to see her get sidetracked here."

Interesting. I wondered if Dr. Theo micro-managed his daughter's life like he did his wife's. Gil Streicker would have been an impediment to that sort of activity.

Dr. Theo shrugged. "I shouldn't be talking ill of Heinrich. He's been supporting my family for several years now."

"What happened?"

"To be honest, I'm not sure. One day my practice back in Michigan was doing great, and the next, my partner had absconded with the proceeds of our bank accounts. Stuck me with a mountain of bills. I had to declare bankruptcy. Part of the troubles between Marguerite and me. I've made adjustments, but she still lives in this fantasy world, like nothing has changed." His tone was bitter.

"What kind of practice do you have?" A neutral lead-in. Interesting things sometimes emerged if a person was patient.

Dr. Theo took the bait. "Back home? Pediatrics, all the way. Love kids. Out here, whatever comes in the door. It's hard to start a new practice at my age."

"Did you ever do surgery?"

"I assisted a few times. Then the malpractice insurance fees went through the roof, and I had to stop. They're doing a lot with robotics, these days, especially with the little kiddos. Those tiny veins were hard for big hands like these to find." He held up two paws of stubby fingers.

"Still have any of your old equipment?"

"No, left all that behind when I closed the practice. I'm making a new start here."

He sounded casual talking about it, but a small scalpel wouldn't take up much room, even in a travel trailer. I made a note. "Got another question for you."

"Name it. I'd like to put this affair behind us. It's been upsetting for the whole family."

"What do you know about arsenic?"

He glanced at the peaceful surroundings. "Seems strange to talk about poisons in a beautiful spot like this." He popped one last chip in his mouth and wiped his lips. Then he leaned back and proceeded to lecture the uninformed.

"Arsenic: Odorless, colorless. Used to be the preferred poison in the Middle Ages. Production of arsenic stopped in the eighties here in the States."

Right. Get to the point, doc. "Ever prescribe any in your medical practice?"

"I didn't. My old office partner did, though. Used it as a leukemia treatment for a patient of his." He gave me a sharp-eyed look. "You're talking about Gil Streicker, aren't you? Think that's how he died?"

"It might have contributed," I said. "He showed traces in his system. But Fancy said arsenic was in the water at the ranch."

"She's being paranoid. First thing I did when we moved here was check the water condition. The arsenic deposits seem to be localized to specific areas of the Verde Valley, not near the ranch property, thank goodness."

I took one last drink of water, wondering if the liquid flowing down my throat contained arsenic. Odorless, colorless. I'd never know until it was too late. Perhaps that's what happened to Gil Streicker.

I tucked the notebook in my pocket and stood. "Thanks for talking to me. I'll keep you posted." After all, that was my job, good family liaison officer that I was.

I walked back to my car. By the time I had turned around in the drive to leave, Dr. Theo had stretched out on the grass in front of the trailer for an afternoon nap, hat tilted over his eyes. He presented the picture of a man with nothing to hide.

But, pleasant as Dr. Theo appeared, the good doctor had an edge that disturbed me. He'd had access to both a scalpel and arsenic in his practice. And he seemed highly protective of both wife and daughter. The relationships that Gil Streicker had with Marguerite and later with Amanda would be problematic to Dr. Theo. Might the strain be enough to drive him over the edge to eliminate a rival?

I punched Shepherd's phone number into my cell and listened to the empty rings. My partner was still off the grid. When we started work as partners, he had promised to always be there for me when I needed backup. What had happened to that promise and the man who had made it?

Tomorrow began the weekend. Saturday morning was the scheduled massage for Rory Stevens. Part fun, part business. By the end of the day, at least I'd know more about Raven LightDancer.

Amanda felt Raven was the key to what happened to Gil Streicker. I wasn't sure about that, but I planned to keep turning over stones to disturb whatever shadowy creatures lived there.

Gil Streicker's little daughter, Veronica, deserved no less.

CHAPTER FIFTEEN

By the time I rose Saturday morning, I convinced myself that my meeting with Rory Stevens was strictly business. I was only going because I needed to know more about Raven LightDancer, or whatever his name turned out to be.

At least somebody cared about law enforcement, I told myself as I shopped for the needed supplies, unlike my supervisor. The grocery store had a special section for Arizona wines, and the black bottles with the red-and-black labels of the Arizona Stronghold Vineyard called to me.

I picked up a bottle of their *Dala* cabernet, a corkscrew, and a couple of heavy-duty wine glasses. Rory was more of a screw-top person, but I was going all out for this occasion. I picked out a pot of miniature yellow roses in the flower section to add some class.

I could have pried the information out of Rory without this massage trip, but maybe I'd been a *little* at fault with his Hummer. He was a good friend, and I needed to make it up to him. This wine and a massage would serve as my apology.

Although I've been on the receiving end of massages, I hadn't actually *given* one, but it shouldn't be too hard. Just fake what I didn't know and make up the rest.

I'd gone to Isabel, my grandfather's housekeeper, for advice. She'd been a masseuse when she was younger.

"Always start with the face," she said. "Then the fingers and toes. And don't forget about atmosphere. Scented candles, soft music. People like that."

I mentally repeated her directions. Face first, then fingers and toes. I could handle this. No problem.

From the grocery store, I dropped by the Patchouli Palace and picked up a bottle of almond-scented massage oil and a thick gold-colored candle. I grabbed a New Age CD from their stock and stood impatiently as they checked me out. I was ready.

It took me about forty-five minutes to drive Highway-260 through Cottonwood, a short zag north on I-17 and a right at the Sedona exit. Two miles later, I passed over Red Tank Wash, as I had the day before.

The wash was dry with only small puddles of moisture reflecting back the small canyon's steep red rock walls. The narrow one-lane bridge that crossed the wash was in disrepair, its guardrail whacked by a too-wide truck, it looked like. One end dangled precariously over the water. I made a note to call the highway patrol to report the damage.

The Verde Valley had a love/hate relationship with water. This time of year, drought and low water levels pitted people like Serena Battle and Heinrich Spine against each other. But in the winter, snowmelts on the Mogollon Rim near Flagstaff flooded the Valley streams, causing damage to houses and house trailers like Dr. Theo's that parked too close to the creek.

I could use some of that snowmelt today. The summer heat beat on the outside of the Jetta. I switched on the AC to combat it. Sneaking a glance into the picnic area, I checked to see if the camp host was about. He was, so I parked on the other side of the road, in a no-fee area at the edge of Wet Beaver Creek. I didn't want him ruining my fun this morning.

Rory's atomic-orange Hummer was already there, taking more than his fair share of two parking spaces. I squeezed my Jetta in next to him and struggled to get out, turning sideways and scraping past the Hummer. I smoothed out the butt mark I made on the dusty vehicle with my palm, in a peacekeeping gesture. No sense getting on Rory's wrong side. Again.

I opened the trunk and got ready to load. A low table went on my back with a headband to steady it. I grabbed a blanket, sheets, and towels in one hand, slipped a bag over my shoulder with the massage oil and wine supplies. Then I tucked my boom box under my arm. That left my left hand to heft the rose plant. I slammed the trunk door down with my elbow. I shifted the load to get comfortable, feeling a little like a Himalayan Sherpa.

I hiked across the bridge at Wet Beaver Creek and up the hill to Rory's designated spot across the creek. It was a quiet place. He said it used to be a nudist beach, but I didn't see any bare bodies this morning. Good thing. Let privates be private was my motto.

As I struggled up the hill, Rory sat on a rock, dressed in swim shorts and sandals, a baseball hat shading his eyes.

"You need some help with that?"

He didn't expect a response. Didn't get one. Rory treated me as an independent woman, which suited me just fine.

I dropped the bag and linens and carefully set down the yellow rose plant. Then I raised both hands, lifted the carry strap from my forehead and lowered the small table. The binding had made a bruise-hard welt on my forehead and I rubbed it. I positioned the candle on the table and lit it. Next, I arranged the flowers and the boom box next to it. Finally, I spread the blanket on a ledge of red rock and put a sheet on top.

"Here, do the honors." I handed the bottle of wine to Rory.

He uncorked the wine and poured two glasses, set them down carefully on the sandstone ledge.

"Pretty cool," he commented, taking a gulp of the wine. Then he set down the glass and sprawled on the sheet on his stomach.

I slipped in the new CD. Soon romantic Enya waltzes serenaded the creek side, blending with the soft ripple of the water from the creek below us. Perfect!

"What's that caterwauling?" Rory jerked upright. He grabbed the radio and switched off the CD. Then he twisted the dial until he found our local country radio station, KAFF. Brad Paisley was wailing something about crushing beer cans on weekends.

"Ah, that's better." Rory cranked the volume up loud. Real loud. He settled back down on the blanket.

"Start with my back," he ordered.

A red tail hawk flapped out of the tall sycamore above us and left for quieter parts. I lowered the radio volume to a whisper.

"Turn over. I'm starting with your face."

"My face? My face isn't sore. My *back* is sore. What sort of a massage is this, anyway?" Rory remained stolid, unmoving, on his stomach.

"Whatever. I'll rub, you talk."

He was *ruining* the mood Isabel had suggested I create. I scowled and poured half the bottle of oil in the middle of his back and smeared it around. Some dribbled on the sheet, puddling. Too bad.

"Tell me about Raven LightDancer," I said.

"A little bit harder on that left shoulder."

Rory settled deeper into the sheet-covered blanket. "Raven... Well, first of all, his name's not Raven LightDancer. It's Marty Zielinski."

"What?"

"Scratch right there, just under the shoulder blade."

"Zielinski, you said?"

I nudged the oil around a little with one finger.

"Yeah, the guy is Romany, from Poland."

"You mean, like a gypsy?"

I scraped up some of the excess oil and started to rub his left arm, all the way down to his fingers. Then I started on his foot, rubbing the heel, stroking the instep.

Rory twitched, then shifted the foot out of reach. "Not there. Do my other arm. Keep things even."

I abandoned the foot and worked on the arm as directed. Okay, maybe I leaned a little too hard into it, but hey, Rory was a former SEAL—he could handle it.

"Ouch! Softer."

Hmmm. Guess not.

"What else about this Marty Zielinski?" I asked.

"Well, he might have been a gypsy at one time, but now he's a career opportunist—card shark, spiritualist, all-around con man. Gets caught, he skips and reinvents himself."

I dropped that arm, palmed some oil onto the nape of Rory's neck. Then I circled his ears with my fingers.

"That figures," I said. "Right now he's posing as a New Age guru using sound therapies and weird diets over at the Spine Horse Ranch." I thought of the mango feast and burped.

My own back was cramping as I squatted in the awkward position. Now I realized why masseuses always used massage tables. And chairs! Didn't they have those little stools that they sat on?

I stopped and pried a pebble out of my kneecap.

"Hey, don't stop now, this feels *good.*"

The radio DJ had come on, hawking the gun show at the fairgrounds. I turned the volume down more.

"I want to hear that." Rory reached over and punched in more volume. "Don't forget my legs. You've been working on my head long enough. Feels fine. Start on my legs."

"Who's giving this massage anyway," I muttered.

"What?"

"Never mind."

I switched from shoulders to legs, working on the hard, tanned muscular thighs. The thighs led to the calves, roped with tension. Rory was a swimmer, on the volunteer underwater recovery team for the sheriff's office. It showed.

"*Now* turn over."

I slapped his thigh like you would the side of a horse you wanted to shift.

"Already? I was enjoying this. One more turn on my back? I think you missed a spot there."

"Over!"

He reluctantly complied, lying on his back, front upwards.

I leaned back and started on his feet, first rubbing the top of the foot, then circling each toe with my fingers. I didn't know how he felt about it, but the gestures were oddly stimulating to me. Was I getting a foot fetish?

Isabel said you should keep quiet during a massage, let the customer enjoy the experience. Unfortunately, the raucous descriptions of Berettas and S&W specials killed the ambiance. My budding foot fetish faded.

"I'm being forced to move from my studio apartment," I said to drown out the gun show. I explained about the eviction notice and my aborted attempts to find lodging that would accept Reckless.

"I don't mind dogs. You could always move in with me."

"What?"

"You know, bunk on my couch. As a friend, like." He shifted on the blanket.

I wasn't sure I wanted to room with Rory. I heard my instructor's voice from the police academy: Never sleep with a workmate, especially on his couch. Asking for trouble.

I contemplated being Rory's roommate for another nanosecond.

"Sun's in my eyes," he complained.

Nope. Would never work.

I plopped his cap on his face. "Better?" The man had just forfeited a face rub.

I started on the chest and arms. Then I worked on the fingers, pulling and stretching each in turn.

"My legs. Don't forget the front of my legs. They're stiff with all the work you did on the other side."

My back cramped again, and my own fingers were getting sore. This massage stuff was hard work. I scratched at a mosquito bite on my arm—the breeze had brought the critters up from the creek, eager for fresh meat. I brushed at another bug that buzzed my head.

"Keep going, you're doing fine," Rory purred. "You can do this every weekend for me."

In your dreams, frogman!

"When I'm finished, what about giving *me* a turn?" I asked. I thought about the bliss of having someone rub my feet.

There was silence, then a snore erupted beneath the hat brim. Rory had tuned me out completely and was sound asleep.

Sitting on my haunches a moment, I wiped the sweat from my eyes. Then I took another swig of the now hot wine and looked up at the sun, climbing in the sky.

A person could get a bad sunburn, lying in the sun like this. I contemplated that fact for a moment. Then I switched off the boom box and picked up the roses. I loaded up the rest of the gear and strolled back to the Jetta. Rory had had his wine and massage. I had the information I came for. Fair trade.

An Abert's towhee chuckled from under a red barberry bush near the car as I loaded up. I thought briefly about disconnecting Rory's distributor, like my cousins in Tennessee had done as a prank to my old car.

Instead, I scrawled a big "Wash Me" with one fingertip in the dust on the Hummer's hood, right where Rory couldn't miss it. That would be a good job for a capable man like him when he woke up. It might cool down that sunburn he had gotten, maybe.

***

The Jetta's transmission made grinding noises as I drove up the final hill into Mingus. Come on, old girl, you can do it. I shifted the car into low and the noise smoothed out.

But another unpleasant surprise awaited me at the apartment. A new eviction notice replaced the one I had torn down. This one, taped to the front door, announced in big red letters, "Final Notice." They weren't kidding.

I didn't have many possessions, but I didn't want them sitting out on the street waiting for me one night when I got home from work. Time to get serious about finding another place to stay.

I kicked off my shoes at the top of the interior stairs to the apartment and dropped onto my red sofa. Then I pulled out my cell and dashed off a text to Bettina Schwartz.

"I'm getting desperate," I typed. "Something, anything?"

Her response beeped back like she'd been waiting for my text. I guess that real estate people keep the same weird hours we law folks do. Bettina said we'd not stop looking until we found just the right place for me. I liked her can-do attitude—it resonated with my own. And I needed a place to land, fast.

We set a time to meet the next morning.

CHAPTER SIXTEEN

Just as she had promised, Bettina honked outside my building early the next morning. I rubbed the sleep out of my eyes, threw on some clothes, and dashed downstairs to greet her. What was I thinking, to give up a weekend day for this?

Bettina Schwartz was a petite woman, with a huge head of platinum blond hair and a cowboy vest whose Conchos jingled in hard-to-miss places. She shook my hand firmly. "Isn't it a lovely morning? Call me Bett."

Real estate agents are the first in town to have the new cars. It was just my luck that Bettina Schwartz picked a SmartCar, not a Tesla. I squeezed my six-foot frame into the front seat and we started up the hill.

Bettina asked questions like a police interviewer. I tried to be cooperative, but what did my sock size or my last three boyfriends have to do with renting a house? Finally, she took a hint at my noncommittal responses and we lapsed into silence for the rest of the drive.

She shifted the little car into low and it wound up the curves to the top of Walker Street, where many of the lovely wood-frame Queen Annes built for mine executives had fallen into disrepair. The roofs went first, then the house would implode, everything falling into the cellar with a splintering of rotten wood. We passed several in this sorry state and stopped in front of the final house on the street. This residence seemed to be intact, at least at this point.

"The owners are so excited that you're looking to lease their lovely home," Bettina said. "They'll make you a great deal. And the neighbors would love to have a lawman—oops, make that a law *person*—in the neighborhood. It will raise the value of their property if they decide to sell."

She pulled into the driveway of the unoccupied house. A tattered "For Sale" sign drooped in a yard covered with litter and debris from last winter's storms. A broken tree branch leaned against the sagging roof.

"They'll fix that," Bettina assured me with a dismissing wave.

She struggled to open a front door warped by the house settling, and we walked in to discover another tree limb had crashed through a front window.

"Look at that view," Bettina gushed, pointing to a strip of the valley barely visible through a high bathroom window.

The boards creaked under our feet. Termites?

Bettina gestured uncertainly upward. "Bedrooms are up there. They'll fix the stairs, I'm sure."

Fixing up the old house was a challenge I might have tackled until she mentioned the rent.

"They want that much?" I gasped.

"Well, it's an authentic turn-of-the-century home. Make a great Bed and Breakfast."

Changing sheets wasn't my idea of fun.

"What's next on your list?"

"I was so sure you'd like this one. There *is* something *lower* on the hill." She sniffed just a teensy bit.

I jack-knifed my legs back into her fashionista car and we headed down on the status scale. The next house, tiny, backed up to the town's rowdiest saloon. When we opened the car door, we were greeted by the sound of an out-of-patience mother screaming at her kids next door. A jackhammer from some Main Street construction entered the cacophony.

"Maybe we can come back another time when it's quieter," she said.

Right. Like never.

She studied the computer print-out. "You don't want Clarkdale?"

"No," I said definitively. The man I had killed lived there. I didn't want that constant reminder every day driving to work.

"And Cottonwood is too far…"

I nodded. I'd been there to pick up Shepherd during his recovery from an injury, and it was a longish drive from where my grandfather lived in Mingus. Anyway, I liked it here in this little town. I wanted to settle here permanently, if this budget crisis at the sheriff's department ever lifted.

"Those are the only two I've got so far, but I'll keep looking." Bettina sighed.

I stretched out my legs with relief when I exited her car at my apartment's front door. We said polite goodbyes and she left. I was disappointed, but no sense rushing into anything. Didn't property owners need to give 30 days' notice? I had plenty of time.

***

It was near noon, and I pulled cheddar cheese, a loaf of sourdough deli bread, and my favorite horseradish from my microfridge. Setting my cast iron skillet on the small stove, I poured in a bit of olive oil. Then I buttered both pieces of bread, put slices of cheese in between the bread, slathered the horseradish on top of the cheese and pressed the two slices together.

When the oil was hot, I tipped the sandwich into the pan to toast. I flipped the sandwich once and when it was done, slid it onto a plate along with some pickles.

I grabbed a beer and walked out on the balcony to eat. Traffic backed up on the road below me as tourists from Phoenix looked for parking places so that they could visit the Copper Museum and the fudge company. Pedestrians gathered in knots and family groups, snapping pictures of the million-dollar view, and window-shopping for the stained-glass and watercolor treasures in the art galleries. Their dollars paid our salaries, so I didn't complain.

After lunch, an afternoon with no set plans loomed. My grandfather, HT, and Isabel had headed over the mountain into Prescott for their quarterly Costco and Trader Joe's run. I didn't think I'd be talking to Rory Stevens anytime soon.

I paced in the small apartment for a while and then grabbed my car keys and headed down the stairs for a drive. The Gil Streicker case was weighing on me, and I always thought better behind the wheel.

The Jetta started smoothly, its sulks from the day before forgotten. I drove aimlessly across the valley, enjoying the pre-monsoon clouds on the horizon, and the fresh quiet of the weekend.

When the Jetta stopped in front of a white house with blue shutters—Janet Miller's home—I looked up in surprise. Maybe subconsciously my car, like an old country doctor's horse, had delivered me where I needed to be. I'd been wondering how she was doing after her son's suicide.

Janet sat in an old platform rocker on the porch when I pulled up. She reminded me of someone I knew. I didn't have Shepherd's facility with names and faces yet, but he had thirty years on me. If it was important, my brain would sort through all the possibilities and fish out the person I was struggling to remember.

"Just stopping by to see how things are going," I said, walking up to the porch.

A stupid remark. How good could things be, with your child dead by his own hand? I was still learning this family liaison, FLO, thing. Occasionally I had some awkward moments as I fumbled with the right thing to say. Sometimes there *was* no right thing.

But Janet didn't seem to take offense.

"I wanted to thank you for stopping by the other day, Officer Quincy. Johnny would have liked that." Her eyes filled with tears.

"Did you reach the funeral director?"

"Yes. We've made arrangements to scatter his ashes over the red rocks. He loved them so. He was studying to be a journalist, you know. Now that never will happen."

She started to cry silently, making no motion to brush away her tears. They dripped on her cotton blouse, making a trail of dark splotches.

"I'm organizing a mother's group," she said after a moment, "to hold an assembly at the high school. Sometimes there are copy-cat sui...suicides." She stumbled over the word. "Would you be a speaker?"

I didn't know much about teen suicides, other than they left heartbreak and destruction behind them. But I promised I'd put something together.

I left soon after that. It was just a drop-in call to let her know she wasn't alone.

Between the aborted real estate hunting trip and the visit with Janet Miller, my Sunday so far was a downer. When I got back to my studio apartment, Reckless greeted me with the unabashed enthusiasm of a redbone coonhound. I let him out in the backyard to check out the ground squirrels and pocket gophers.

The structure was built into the hillside, and beyond the backyard, the road climbed steeply into the main part of town. One little kid spotted me in the yard and waved. I waved back and my mood lifted. Maybe life wasn't so bad.

It turned even better a moment later when my phone rang. It was Flint Tanner. Flint was a geologist that had come to town about the same time I had. A tall drink of water, keenly intelligent, and sexy as all get out.

He was no longer part of my life, but late on sleepless nights the timbre of his voice, the easy way he had of moving, his strong presence, haunted my bedroom still. I'd never understood the phrase, "carrying a torch," before I met Flint. Now I did.

"Peg, I know this is short notice, but would you like to have dinner with me tonight?"

I considered playing hard to get, but inside I was panting like my dog Reckless.

"Where?" There was an unbecoming squeak in my voice.

"How about Grapes? That's close to you."

I hesitated. Grapes was the favorite hangout for Rory Stevens and me when we were "on" rather than "off." After the massage-on-the-rocks episode, I wasn't sure which category fit, but it would be awkward to run into him at Grapes with an old flame on my arm.

So I countered Flint's offer with a suggestion that we meet at Nic's, in the Old Town section of Cottonwood. They had thick, *expensive* steaks. A girl had to eat.

Flint was agreeable and rang off.

I scritched Reckless's ear for good luck and headed for my closet. Time was a-wasting. I pushed hangers around on the closet rod pondering the age-old problem of what to wear for the evening. It had been so long since I'd been on an official date, everything looked unsuitable.

Finally, I grabbed a pink silk blouse that didn't look girly on me with my height and red hair. Brown pants that I'd tuck into my new chestnut suede boots with the fringe around the top. I took a leisurely shower and washed my hair. I even painted my toenails all-I-want-for-Christmas pink and shaved my legs for good luck. I was ready to rumble.

At a quarter to six, I let Reckless out one last time, climbed into the Jetta, and headed down the hill to Old Town.

I arrived just as Flint drove up. He unfolded long legs and got out of his pickup truck. Flint was six-two, two inches taller than I was. I'd always appreciated that fact. He gave me a smile that began at one corner of his mouth and crinkled his gray eyes.

"Peg, it's been too long."

We both hesitated over a handshake and then he enveloped me in a hug instead. It felt good, warm. Better than warm. A little embarrassed, I pulled back. Flint held the door open for me and we entered the restaurant.

He touched my back as he held the chair out for me at the table. I felt a responsive jolt of electricity. Maybe there was *still* something there between us...

We'd had a brief affair I'd hoped might develop into something more. Then the new bank manager, Jocelyn Hunter, caught his eye, and Flint moved on. I cried for weeks. Could those banked coals burst into flame once more?

Stop it, Peg!

I snatched up the menu. It trembled in my fingers as I deliberately hunted for the most extravagant item on the menu. Anything to distract me from the handsome man sitting across the table.

Flint was attentive over dinner: brushing my hand as he refreshed our wine from the carafe, offering me a bite of his lobster soaked in butter. I licked the butter from my lips and looked into his eyes, deeply. A movie moment. All it needed was the slow motion and violins.

A small tingle grew below my belt line as I anticipated what the evening might bring. We lingered over coffee, making small talk. When the check came, Flint didn't even glance at it, just put his American Express card in the slot and let the waitress take it.

He gave me a soft look, holding the glance a moment longer

than necessary. Then he sighed and straightened in his chair.

"Some bad news, Peg, at least for me."

"Oh, no. What?"

"I've been laid off as a geologist. Budget cuts." He shrugged, trying to be matter of fact about it.

Flint had been instrumental in the mining survey for the town, but there'd been a dearth of activity in that area since the town voted down new mining development. Could be that's why I hadn't seen him around.

"What are you going to do?" I thought guiltily of the expensive dinner I'd just consumed. Maybe I should have offered to go Dutch.

"This is awkward." He hesitated. "I need to ask a favor. I can't go to my girlfriend Jocelyn for this—you understand."

My heart took a nosedive at the mention of the bank manager's name and the accompanying adjective. Girlfriend as in, we go bowling together, or *girlfriend*, as in we're sharing the same bed? I backpedaled like crazy, trying to retreat from the cliff I'd almost leaped over.

"Uh, sure, anything."

"I need a job recommendation. They want a professional reference." He shoved a piece of paper across the table, suddenly all business, turning that romance off like a light switch.

I glanced blankly at the sheet of paper, desperately trying to change directions. Business, Peg. This is all about business. Flint's name appeared in rough letters on the first line. Then my eyes jumped to the legend topping the page.

"You're applying for a job at the Spine Ranch?"

"Sure. There's an opening there. Something happened to the manager."

He died, in fact.

Flint didn't notice my hesitancy and plowed on. "And I grew up on a ranch. I had a range management specialty with my geology degree."

I could see him gearing up with the elevator pitch that we all practice for that awful moment we might actually need it. But how could Flint *consider* working for Heinrich Spine?

"Uh. I'm sort of working the case out there," I said. "Could be a conflict of interest, to recommend you."

"I heard that was Shepherd's case." Flint's voice became strident. His urgency to reach his goal brushed my own concerns out of the way.

I hated Shepherd Malone for putting me in this bind! And Flint wasn't listening either. Did I mean nothing to these men? Obviously, I still *felt* and Flint didn't. My cheeks glowed poker-hot.

I yanked a pen out of my purse and scribbled the usual platitudes across the sheet—excellent worker, well-organized, good team player—and slid it back across the table to him.

"Thanks before I could change my mind.

Flint grabbed the paper and tucked it into his shirt pocket.

"Compliments of the house," said the waitress at his shoulder. "Special chocolate lava cake." She set a huge dish of cake swimming in chocolate sauce in the middle of the table.

"Stay here and enjoy your dessert," I told Flint. "Catch up with you later."

I tripped on the carpet in my haste to rise and grabbed the corner of the table. The lava cake tilted ominously. But it didn't feel as awful as I did. Before Flint could protest, I strode out of the restaurant into the dark night.

I'd been dreaming of romance and all he wanted was a job reference—was *paying* for it, in fact, with an over-the-top dinner. I should have known better. Jocelyn-the-bank-person could keep the bum.

I stormed down the street to my Jetta. Ramming my foot on the accelerator, I roared up the hill to Mingus. The tires squealed when I slammed into the parking spot next to my building. I yanked the key out of the ignition and stomped to the apartment.

Then I jerked the offending Eviction Notice off the ground floor window. No reason to advertise to the world that I was headed for the same black hole that Flint Tanner found himself in.

Reckless greeted me with a pounce, and I stomped up my interior stairs tripping over him the whole way. He jumped up in my lap with a heavy thud when I slumped onto the sofa. I rubbed him behind the ears just where he liked and hugged him close.

Maybe I should become a nun. I vowed celibacy for 60 days—well 30 days, anyway.

The world seemed a quiet and dark place as I walked out on the balcony for a late night survey of the town. It would be nice, just once, to have a person to share this life of mine.

Would I settle for even a slug like Flint Tanner? Nah, I wouldn't stoop that low. I'd carried a torch for that man long enough.

I locked the balcony door behind me and retired for the night. Tomorrow was Monday, time for my regular work life.

No more Ms. Nice Person. I meant it.

CHAPTER SEVENTEEN

The next morning at the office I had just settled with my first cup of coffee and croissant from the bakery down the street when I got a call from the horse ranch.

"Someone is poisoning me," Heinrich Spine said.

"Do you need to call 911? Are you in danger?"

"No, of course not. If I were, I wouldn't call you."

Right. "How do you know you're being poisoned?"

"How soon can you be here?" His voice was sharp with irritation. "I need to talk to you in person."

He didn't sound too sick to me, but at his age, you couldn't be sure. I told him I'd be there in a half hour. I tossed the remains of the croissant in the trash and dumped the coffee in the sink. I told Shepherd where I was going and he grunted at me. "Stay safe."

***

The housekeeper, Rosa, met me at the door and gestured to the second floor. "Please hurry. Dr. Spine is fighting with his daughter."

I took the steps two at a time and opened the door to Heinrich's study. Marguerite was on her hands and knees picking up pieces of a broken bowl. It looked as though the old man had tipped over a tray of food on the carpet.

He looked up when I entered. "Took your time." He pointed with a shaking finger at his daughter, his watery eyes glared fiercely. "She's trying to poison me."

"Now father," Marguerite began.

"That's *Doctor* Spine to you. Leave. I don't need you here." His voice held fierce contempt.

"I'll be right outside." Marguerite threw her father a look of frustrated bitterness and retreated out the door.

"I could use a drink of whiskey. Liquor cabinet's over there."

"Fix your own," I snapped. I wasn't his daughter and he didn't pay my salary.

Leaning heavily on his cane, Heinrich walked to the sidebar. With a shaky hand, he poured a whiskey from a crystal decanter. He lifted it toward me.

"Want one?"

"No," I said, pointedly looking at my watch. What was the man doing drinking at this time of the morning, anyway? And wasting my time while he did it?

"Water, then," he suggested.

"No, thanks. You really being poisoned?"

"Could be, the food's bad enough here." He settled back in his chair. Took a sip of his whiskey. "It's one way to get rid of that woman. She hovers."

"And you play games," I said.

"What else has an old man to keep life interesting?"

I wasn't buying his "poor me" attitude.

"You could be nicer to Marguerite—she's your daughter. What'd you call me for?"

He shrugged. "Gil Streicker's death. Was it accidental?"

"Possibly not. We're still waiting for the final report."

"But I understand arsenic was involved?" He took another sip of his drink.

"Who told you that?"

"Never mind. I wanted to inform you that someone's been in my chemistry lab," he announced. "The bottle of arsenic I kept there for experiments is missing. I've been robbed."

"And this happened when?"

For once, he seemed nonplussed. "I'm not sure. I don't remember when I was last in there. Several years ago. But when Fancy said you'd paid a visit, I went to look. The arsenic was gone."

That was convenient. Covering his bases, now that we were taking a closer look.

He gave me a gimlet-eyed stare. "*You* didn't take it, did you?"

Heat started at my throat and moved upwards. Only I wasn't embarrassed, but rather, angry.

"Gotcha," he said. "Anyway, forget that for now. I wanted to discuss this job application I got from one..." He opened a folded piece of paper with his arthritic fingers and smoothed it out on his knee. Pulled a pair of reading glasses out of his pocket and settled them firmly on his nose. "...Flint Tanner. He says you know him. Do you?"

I considered my answer. I was angry at Flint, but the man needed a job. "He's reliable. You could do worse."

"Or I could do better. What about you?"

I choked back indignation. "Dr. Spine, I—"

He waved a hand at me. "Never mind. I was just checking. You'd need to know about horses before I'd consider you, and you don't look like a horse person."

He got that one right.

"What are you doing this Saturday?" he asked.

"Why?"

No way did I want a closer connection with Dr. Heinrich Spine and his entourage. The man was a dredge anchor on my good intentions.

"Marguerite's giving one of her summer soirees. You're invited."

"I'll think about it," I muttered as I left the room. Heinrich's chuckle followed me down the stairs.

This visit had been a waste of my time. The old man's statements were just a smoke screen to deflect attention that missing arsenic from his lab could have killed his ranch manager.

When Fancy showed me around the chemistry lab, she claimed the room was kept locked. But that big ring hung by the kitchen door held a copy of the entry key. Everybody passed through the kitchen at one time or another: Amanda, Marguerite, even Raven LightDancer. Maybe it was time to visit the man in black.

***

As I neared the kitchen, I heard the syncopated rhythm of flamenco. The melody conjured up images of smoky campfires and wagon caravans, very unlike the New Age tones I associated with

Raven LightDancer.

Raven was alone in the kitchen. Steam rose from a large stockpot on the six-burner gas stove, pastry was resting on a marble slab, and a clear glass bowl held a golden-brown filling.

"Peg Quincy, I didn't expect to see you again so soon. Are you looking for Marguerite? I think she went to the store."

He switched off the CD player on the counter, but the music still echoed in my mind.

"Actually, I didn't want to see her, I wanted to visit with you."

His manner turned formal, almost old-world courteous. "Coffee?"

At my nod, he walked over to the built-in coffee maker in a side wall and steamed an espresso. He looked at me and asked, "A double?"

I nodded. He hit the brew button again. Liquid black gold steamed into the cup.

He made one for himself as well. "Have a seat." He handed me the espresso and pulled up a chair beside me.

His actions were hospitable, but the look in his eyes was cautious, measured. "You know."

"I do. Rory Stevens told me."

"Ah, Rory. We both are swimmers, in our own way." He took a small sip of espresso.

"Marty Zielinski is a long way from Raven LightDancer," I said. "Why'd you change your name?"

"*Officially*, I haven't. LightDancer is my nom de plume. And I'm good at what I do."

"Which is what?"

"Let me show you." He rose and lifted the lid from the bubbling pot on the stove. Steam belched forth.

"Here you see the makings of an organic vegetable broth. Don't tell Heinrich, but I get the vegetables from Serena Battle's truck garden."

He poured the boiling mixture of vegetables and liquid into a second colander-lined pot waiting in the sink. Then he tipped the vegetables into the trash and held out the remaining broth to me. "What do you smell?"

I leaned closer and my nose caught an earthy fragrance.

"Curry?"

"Close. Garam marsala, actually. A five-spice mixture of cumin, coriander, cardamom pods, black peppercorns, dried red pepper—seeds discarded, of course—"

Of course.

He reached into a drawer for a spoon and dipped out a sample. "Try some."

It *was* good, a rich buttery essence on my tongue.

"You plan to tell Marguerite and her father my real background?"

When I remembered his fake guru act at the mango lunch, I was tempted.

"Look, I tell Marguerite what she wants to hear, and I help the family eat better, even Heinrich." He held out open-palmed hands. "I'm a reformed man."

I wasn't so sure. The honest demeanor he presented now could be an act, too. Likely it was. But I needed information.

"I just came from Heinrich's room. He says someone is poisoning him."

"Heinrich has a good imagination. Marguerite takes after him. Sometimes, she'd rather not see the world the way it really is."

"What's your relationship with the family?"

"Chief cook and father confessor, most days." His face held a wry expression.

In spite of what I knew, I warmed to his surface cheerfulness, as I suspected many people did. But I also detected an edgy intelligence. I wondered if such intelligence had seen a potential rival in Gil Streicker and acted upon it.

"Where were you the night Gil died?"

"You think I had something to do with it?"

His expression was all innocence.

"Did you?" I asked.

"Not a chance. I was over in Rimrock taking care of my ailing mother."

"All night?"

"All night. She'll testify to that."

I just bet she would. "And might your mother's last name be Zielinski, like yours is, *Marty*?" My voice hardened as I remembered his falsehood to the Spine family.

"So I use two names. Arrest me." He held out his arms for imaginary handcuffs.

"It's not something to joke about. You're no more a spiritual healer than I am."

"Don't be so sure, Miss Pegasus Quincy."

His voice deepened, the vowels lengthening. "I sense an aura about you." He cocked his head and squinted. "Pink—No, more turquoise, I think. Definitely spiritual in nature."

He gave me another disarming smile. "People believe what they choose to believe. I am just the channel."

I shook my head. What a load of malarkey. This man was paid exceedingly well for the gibberish he spouted to Marguerite. If his past history as a con man was revealed, that income would vanish.

Was Gil a blackmailer that had threatened to unveil him? My eyes went involuntarily to the big ring of keys hanging near the door. Easy enough to set out a drink for the ranch manager laced with arsenic. Odorless, colorless. Gil would never have known. And the man in front of me would never admit to it without further proof.

"I'll catch up with you later, Marty." I rose from my seat.

"Do that. And the name is *Raven*, please. I've got a reputation to maintain."

As I walked out the front door, the strains of an East Indian sitar floated out from the kitchen. The brief glimpse of Romany gypsy vanished as the New Age Raven LightDancer returned. The man presented an unsettling element here at the Spine Ranch.

I'd do well to remember that.

CHAPTER EIGHTEEN

Later that afternoon, I received a telephone call from Bettina Schwartz inviting me on another house hunt.

"We'll find something exactly right for you," she promised.

Her voice held that fake bravado that Shepherd used about his Porsche obsession. But the lady was tenacious, had to give her that.

I agreed to meet her after work. It would be cooler then, and the longer summer hours would give us daylight to look at houses. I'd settle for anything at this point. I just needed four walls and a roof that didn't leak.

I knew the odds were slim when Bettina didn't meet my gaze, but rather pulled out a stapled sheaf of papers from the side pocket of the car door. She ran her finger down the computer-generated list.

"We've seen most everything here in Mingus. Maybe something will open up soon. That nice couple from Canada says they are thinking of putting their place on the market soon..."

We were in trouble if that was the best she had. HT had told me about that house—a five-bedroom monstrosity rumored to be in the low seven figures. That was about four zeros beyond what I could pay in rent.

"Surely there's something else?"

"Well, there's one place, but you won't like it, I can guarantee that."

My ears perked up. "Why not?"

"All sorts of complications. The owner, Mrs. Dorothy Harper, lives in a nursing home now. Possible tax foreclosure. Plus it's been vacant for months—probably infested with scorpions and packrats. And you can't even get to the house in mud season."

"How long is mud season?" First I'd heard of this climate event. This wasn't the East Coast after all, but rather the high desert of Arizona.

"I want to look."

"You won't like it."

"I don't care." My chin set.

She sighed, undoubtedly relegating me to that purgatory of time-wasters that all real-estate agents face.

"All right, we'll take a short peek. It's on the way down the hill to Clarkdale, and I have some lovely properties there." She drove her car down the switchbacks and then yanked a hard right at the turn to Desolation Gulch.

The Gulch had a checkered history during the mining days at Mingus: fistfights that turned into long-running feuds, cockfights, ladies of ill repute. As the crow flies, or the cop runs, the location wasn't far from Mingus at all. But the primitive road was an impossible challenge for the little SmartCar, even on a dry summer day.

Bettina high centered the car twice and finally gave up. She pulled on the emergency brake and we hoofed it down the hill, deeper into the Gulch. The real estate agent teetered in her high heels for a few steps, then yanked them off to walk barefoot. The last of her chirpy manner vanished as a run appeared in her stocking. I liked this house already.

We hiked for another five hundred yards and stopped at the end of a weedy drive.

"That's it," she declared, pointing at a dilapidated structure ahead of us.

"Seen enough? My feet are killing me." She started back up the rutted trail.

"Wait a minute, I want a closer look." I kept walking.

The house was small but solid. The walls were constructed of round river rock, the front door half-ajar. I slowly walked around it, judging the construction. The roof looked sound. Two rusted hulks of cars populated the backyard. There was a small shed of corrugated tin, and was that an outhouse?

"It doesn't have indoor plumbing?"

"Well water, septic system."

"But no indoor plumbing."

Bettina rubbed one foot. "The owner was going to put it in, got the pipes up to the foundation of the house, but never got around to connecting it."

"What about electricity?"

"It has an emergency generator and propane," Bettina said. Her voice was I-told-you-so triumphant.

Not so fast, real estate lady. "Heat?"

"A fireplace." She was getting a might sulky at my persistence.

I walked up onto a small wooden porch, my footsteps echoing on the boards. There was a hand-made rocker, where the owner must have sat. The unlocked front door opened with the screech of rusty hinges.

The inside was compact. A small living room with a fireplace held an old but serviceable sofa. An archway led to an eat-in kitchen with a small wooden table and chairs. I wandered through another doorway into a bedroom just large enough for bed and dresser.

There was no closet, but built-in shelves would do for folded clothes. I bounced on the double bed. Mattress seemed intact. No sign of water leakage from the roof above. And it was way bigger than my small studio apartment.

I turned around and walked back out on the porch, considering the possibilities. An unobstructed vista spread all the way down the gulch to Clarkdale. Facing east, so I'd see both moonrise and the early morning sun.

The little house even had a tin roof. I'd always liked tin roofs in the rainy—correction, make that mud—season. And it was quiet, away from neighbors that might be bothered by a baying hound like Restless. If I moved here I could build a fenced yard so he'd have a place to stay when I was at work. A doghouse, even. The house had a solid, set-down feeling to it.

"I'm interested," I said, pulling the front door shut with a scrape across the floor.

Bettina was quiet all the way back to my apartment. As we pulled into the parking lot she said, "I'm sure something else will turn up if you'll just be patient."

My patience meter had swung all the way over to the red zone. "See when I can occupy."

"I can't promise anything, but I'll approach the owner. She has good days and bad days." She sniffed.

"Pick a good day. I want the place."

When I got back to the studio apartment, I felt like a new woman. I had a place to live! It would mean a lot of work, but I wanted to set down permanent roots here on the mountain. Besides, my dog Restless and I needed room to play. In my mind I was already rocking on my own front porch and...then the phone rang.

It was my partner, Shepherd. "I want to do a stakeout tonight. I need your car. Need you, too, in case we run into something interesting," he announced. "Bring your gun."

***

When Shepherd knocked late that evening, Black Mountain shrouded my apartment with deep shadows. To the north, a faint glow marked the town of Sedona. Beyond that, the Mogollon Rim and the San Francisco Peaks formed jagged outlines on the horizon. With no moon rising, the skies would be dark and optimal for surveillance.

I let him in and made one last attempt. "Shepherd, give it up. Let somebody else handle this guy."

He ignored my words and pushed ahead with his plans. "We need to use your car. The Porsche guy would recognize mine. And if anything happens, you're the officer-in-charge. I'm just along for the ride."

Were we on two different planets?

"Your job is at stake," I protested.

"Some things are way more important." His jaw set. "Now, you ready? Let's go."

Although Shepherd was dressed in a dark T-shirt and black slacks, I outfitted myself in full uniform with my Glock at my side, as he had requested. It seemed strange to be the token law enforcement officer, here.

Shepherd had been told to stay away from this guy. What did he think his defense would be, that he was a civilian ride-along? I couldn't see the judge buying that one.

But it was a waste of time arguing with Shepherd when he was in this frame of mind. Maybe we'd get lucky and the guy would commit some outrageous crime. Then we could lock him up for good and get Shepherd off this impossible mission.

I made one last pit stop. Then I filled a bottle of water that I'd ration, sip by sip. Stakeouts were tough on the female anatomy, but I was developing strong kidneys. I glanced at the back door to be sure the lock was set, and we pounded down the stairs, Reckless leading the way. I pushed the pup back into the apartment, closed and locked the door.

Shepherd and I piled into my Jetta, and I started the engine.

"Shepherd is this trip really..."

"What's that?" he asked, pointing at the dash.

"What?"

"That red light—means something's wrong." He leaned forward, listening. "Engine noise. Sounds like your timing belt is loose. Supposed to be replaced at a hundred thou. How many miles you got on this car?"

Damn it! The blasted timing belt was *my* problem, not his. On the other hand, was he telling me in his own curmudgeon way to mind my own business? I gave up and shut up.

We wound down the switchbacks from Mingus to the valley floor and then turned right at the first roundabout entering Cottonwood. The small town was a solid middle-class farming community, but a more affluent mix was starting to move in, especially in the foothills of the Black Mountains. Houses with views meant money, and I figured that's where we'd find the Porsche. I wasn't wrong.

The red sports car gleamed like a sword of fire under a streetlight in a cul-de-sac. I coasted to a stop in front of a house for sale half a block distant and switched off the Jetta's headlights. The air fan whirred for a minute and then was silent.

I pushed my seat back to its limit, trying to get comfortable for the long night ahead. Shepherd did the same.

To pass the time we talked about the weather, and sports, and the latest political shenanigans by the good folks in Washington. Shepherd was an arch-conservative, while I was a social liberal, so we sparred for a while on that.

Then Shepherd cleared his throat. "Now, on to this suspicious death out at the Spine Ranch."

"Gil Streicker."

He nodded. "Medical examiner's final report said enough arsenic in his system to make the man sick, woozy. He could have lost his balance, fallen. Plus, the arson examiner called me. He's determined the cause of the fire is man-made. That's enough to consider this a murder investigation."

He'd finally called it. We could move ahead with an official inquiry. Or could we? At Heinrich Spine's insistence, the old barn had been bulldozed to make way for the new one. At least Heinrich's wish that the dead man be cremated hadn't been honored—yet. But Amanda's tidying up of Gil's quarters meant any evidence there was long gone. Even if we dusted for fingerprints, we'd find only signs of her compulsive mopping and swiping clean all surfaces.

Why had we waited so long to collect evidence? What hadn't been destroyed by the fire was now obliterated. I expressed these regrets to Shepherd.

"Too late to do anything about that now," he said. "We'll have to play catch up. Always a good idea to start with the people. We'll need to re-interview everyone again. Begin with that nurse, Fancy Morgan. Have her come to the Mingus station for an official statement, away from the ranch influence."

"I'll call her in the morning," I said. "And Ben may have found out something when he helped Marguerite with the computer system. I'll check back with him."

Shepherd nodded. "I'll contact Dr. Spine. If need be, we can visit with him again. Maybe we can whipsaw his testimony between us."

It was good to have Shepherd on board. For the first time in many days, we were operating as a team on this murder case. But that left Shepherd's Moby Dick, the red Porsche guy down the street.

"You take the first watch," Shepherd ordered, leaning back against the headrest. He tipped his baseball hat over his forehead and closed his eyes. Soon I could hear soft snoring. The guy was beat. No wonder, with this round-the-clock obsession.

The Porsche gleamed in front of me like a siren of promise. I ate a power-bar and took a sip of water. Then I squirmed a bit in my seat and lowered the window, thinking some fresh air would help keep me alert. A mosquito flew in and bit me before I could swat it. Rolled the window back up again, rubbing at my elbow.

I felt my head nodding and jerked awake. The dog had gotten me up at dawn this morning, and it had been a long day. I needed some toothpicks to keep my eyelids up! I shifted again and glanced over at Shepherd.

Would music help? I considered switching on the radio but didn't want to wake him. Anyway, my ears needed the quiet to hear any noise from the house. I twiddled my thumbs one way. Then twiddled them the other.

When that didn't work, I tried the multiplication tables. I made it all the way up to the elevens before I got stumped. Twelve times twelve was a gross. What was a gross anyway? Something big, like an elephant.

I started counting elephants in the jungle. Nice quiet jungle. A nice *silent* jungle full of green vines waving in the gentle breeze. My eyelids closed again and stayed shut.

I jerked awake with a start. The red beacon was gone! How had the Porsche driver left without my hearing him? I cranked down the window, but the night was silent except for a wind chime on the house next door.

I poked Shepherd. "Wake up! He's gone."

"What do you mean, gone? You were supposed to be watching the car."

"Well, you were supposed to be keeping me awake, not snoring like a rusty lawnmower. What do we do now?"

"Nothing. You blew it. Can't you even do a simple stakeout?" He snorted in disgust.

"I blew it? What about you?"

"Maybe I can go investigate a little since he's gone..." He looked at the house in the cul-de-sac.

"Shepherd!" I exploded. "You don't have a warrant. And the man has committed no crime. You want to get hauled before Internal Affairs?"

I started the engine and made a backup turn using the drive of the house-for-sale. Shepherd didn't talk to me the rest of the way back to my apartment.

He got out of the car as soon as I pulled in, slammed the door and stalked to his own vehicle. Before I turned off my motor, he gunned out of the drive. Probably going to lose more sleep sitting in front of that Porsche owner's house.

I didn't care. This wasn't my problem and it shouldn't be his. Shepherd had one more day, and then this covert operation was *over,* one way or the other.

I stomped into the house, adding Shepherd's problem to the growing list I was wrestling with—Porsches, timing belts, evictions. I needed a break!

But I didn't get one.

CHAPTER NINETEEN

The following day, Fancy Morgan arranged to meet me at the office, mid-morning. Shepherd was conspicuously absent from the station, and for once, it didn't bother me. We both needed some space after my screw-up the night before. I still winced at his tongue-lashing.

Fancy walked into the office about ten. I set her up in the conference room and asked if she wanted some coffee. The room was small, with Army-surplus furniture. Ben and I had cleared out accumulated junk to convert the room into usable space, and the musty odor of old files and papers still lingered.

"I could use something stronger than coffee."

"How so?"

"Damn javelinas got in my iris beds. Tore them up, destroyed the plants."

"Oh, no!" I remembered how proud she had been of the iris when we'd sat together in the garden.

Javelina—called wild pigs by some—were incredibly damaging to vegetation in Arizona. They traveled in family herds and used their snouts and sharp hooves to tear up ground when they searched for food. It sounded as though Fancy's poor iris bed had made good pickings.

"Next time I catch them out there, I'll blow them to kingdom come."

"You don't really mean that," I said.

"Watch me." Her eyes glittered. "My uncle taught me how to

shoot when I was little. Those nasty things don't stand a chance."

Fancy sat there, tapping long fingernails on the table.

"You mind?" She pulled out a pack of cigarettes.

I did, but I also wanted a cooperative witness, so I shoved an ashtray her direction.

It would be easy for a smoker to start a barn fire—they always carried matches or a lighter. But then Heinrich was a smoker, too.

I tried to picture the old man killing Gil Streicker, but it was hard. Heinrich couldn't do it alone, I decided. Could Fancy be paid enough to assist her employer? Possibly. Everyone had their price.

I set a small recorder on the old oak table and tested to be sure it was working. Then I opened a small notebook to take notes as well. The physical act of pen to paper helped me focus on details, and sometimes, when technology failed, I was thankful for a backup system.

"Thanks for coming in this morning," I said.

She shrugged. "Don't have much choice, do I?"

I couldn't argue with that. I switched on the recorder, then, and gave the opening statement—the date, location, who was present.

"We are investigating the suspicious death of Gil Streicker," I said.

Fancy sat up straight and stubbed out her cigarette. "Wait a minute. I thought Gil's death was an accident. Do I need a lawyer here?" Her eyes narrowed.

"Up to you. But anything you can tell us would be helpful in clearing up the matter for the family." I made my tone friendly, nonchalant. This was always the tricky point in an interview. She'd not officially requested a lawyer. That meant we could continue without one if I could settle her down a little.

I started with the safe topic she brought into the office. "It must be hard, having your garden destroyed that way."

"I spent good money to buy those iris. Now they're gone." Her lips tightened. "Doesn't make any difference."

I raised an eyebrow in question.

"Outstayed my welcome. Time I was moving on."

"Would you go back home? Where is that exactly?" She'd mentioned it briefly at our last meeting, but I wanted to pin her down if I could.

"Just a stop on the road back east. You've never heard of it."

"Try me."

"Batesville," she said, "like the coffin makers." She spit out the words as though they were painful.

An unusual association. "And the state?" I asked.

"Doesn't matter. I left there years ago. Been stuck in this little piss-ant valley for too long. Thought I'd try Vegas this time. Or maybe the California coast..."

Her voice sounded empty, discouraged. Hard to look ahead to a future with no hope.

I leaned forward. "Fancy, where were you the night of the barn fire?"

"In my room. In bed. I had nothing to do with Gil's 'unfortunate accident'." Her tone held an active dislike for the involuntary self-disclosure she'd just made. I had sympathy, but gathering information was necessary if we were to find Gil Streicker's killer.

"Can anyone verify your whereabouts?"

"Sure. The two guys I was having a threesome with." She gave a laugh that choked off in the middle. "Of *course* no one can verify that. I'm a non-person around there."

"There was one thing, though..." Her mouth pursed, as though she were a six-year-old tattling to the teacher about another classmate's misbehavior.

"What? You hear anything suspicious?"

"You mean like the midnight screaming match that Gil and Marguerite had in the hall? Woke me out of a sound sleep."

"Could you hear what they were saying?"

She leaned back in the chair and lit another cigarette, drew deeply and watched the smoke curl toward the ceiling, considering her next words. "I don't know how much you know about Gil Streicker..."

I gave her a hand wave that said continue.

"He got to the ranch, not long after I did."

"When was that?"

"Five, six years back. We'd talk, sometimes, after the family went to bed. He told me he'd been poor all of his life. That's what we had in common, him and me."

"But he was going to do something about it," I prompted.

"Like I told you, he used that good old cowboy charm to entice Marguerite. Never saw anyone fall so hard as she did. They became lovers."

"Then what happened?"

"Heinrich discovered it." She smiled then, leaving little doubt who the informant was.

"He swore no cowhand would get his land when he died," she said, "and that was the end of it. Marguerite was devastated when Gil broke it off. She'd gambled that Gil loved her for herself, not for the ranch she'd inherit. Guess what—he didn't."

Her tone was world-weary. Although Fancy's employment made her invisible to the family, the woman had feelings. I wondered if Gil Streicker had made a move on her, too.

"And the late night fight? What was that about?"

"Marguerite had discovered Gil was romancing Amanda." Another short smile. "Marguerite swore to get him fired if he didn't leave her daughter alone. Then I heard her door slam and he clumped down the stairs in those big cowboy boots of his. Took me hours to get back to sleep."

"Anything else?"

"What more do you need? If anybody had reason to kill Gil Streicker, it was Marguerite. Oh, and check out her husband, too."

"Dr. Theo? Why him?"

She smiled that Cassandra smile. "The good doctor has an OxyContin problem. Ask him to explain that one."

She stood. "If you don't need me anymore, I'm leaving. I've got some things to pick up at the store before I head back to the ranch."

After she left, I reviewed my notes. The ME had found traces of poison in Gil Streicker's system, and poison was traditionally a woman's method. Two women were involved with Gil Streicker. It was time to set up formal interviews with Marguerite and her daughter Amanda.

But there were three women involved with Gil, if you counted Fancy Morgan. It couldn't hurt to check Fancy's back story. I Googled the name of the town she'd given me. Towns by the name of Batesville showed up in Missouri, Mississippi, and Ohio. No shortage of Batesvilles back east.

Fancy mentioned something about a casket company in

connection with the name. I tried that and came up with a little town called Manchester in Tennessee. That might also be a possibility.

I put in a call to Ned Jamison, one of my fellow police academy classmates back in Tennessee. He answered on the first ring, his cheerful voice booming over the distance.

"Peg! Haven't heard from you for too long. How's the West treating you?"

Ned didn't fit the police stereotype. He was a pudgy, overweight guy who wanted to be an officer so bad it hurt to watch him. His dad had been a police officer, and his uncle, too. That should have helped, but Ned tripped over his own feet. He was a computer whiz, but he'd barely made it through the obstacle course training.

"Can't complain," I responded. "You got a job yet?"

Competition for positions was fierce in Shelby County in Tennessee where Ned lived. I'd been trying to talk him into looking farther afield, but he had a wife who refused to leave her family there. Ned wanted to be a detective, and he'd be a good one. But there was the little matter of getting the time in grade. To do that, you needed a job.

Ned sighed. "I just gotta have patience. I've been teaching a class or two at the community college, waiting for an opening. What's up with you?"

"I need some background investigative work. But I'd got no money to pay you…"

"Glad to keep the old skills polished. What you need to know?"

"I got a lady here, name is Fancy Morgan. Nothing official, yet. Just poking around." I told him about the name Batesville, the towns with that name, and the reference to caskets.

"I'm looking for anything unusual," I said, "that possibly happened, some five, six years ago."

"What kind of unusual?"

"I'm not sure. I just have a sense something's off." I told him about Gil Streicker's death and the machinations the folks at the Spine Ranch were going through to keep an investigation from happening.

The sound of his scribbling pencil filled the space between us.

"Pretty vague," he said, "but let me see what I can do. Nothing but time on my hands right now, anyway."

"Something will turn up for you."

"Yeah, right." But Ned didn't sound hopeful, just resigned.

I wondered if I should give his wife a call, put a bug in her ear about how great a place Arizona was. The state didn't have much water, but the people were friendly. I doubted even that would help, though, with her kin all being in Tennessee. Family was a powerful tie.

As I hung up, Shepherd burst in the front door.

"I just saw Fancy Morgan driving out of town. Good work, Peg, getting her to come in."

It was as though the events of the previous night had never happened. Perhaps in his mind, they weren't that important. I set my own hurt feelings aside and told him about Fancy's lost irises.

"Tough," Shepherd commented.

Obviously, he wasn't much of a gardener. He perked up, though, when I related the fight Fancy said Gil and Marguerite had had the night before the barn fire.

"We need to follow up on that," he said. "The Spine Ranch is holding a garden party this weekend. Might be a good time to check out the family."

I followed him into the lunch room. There Shepherd filled a cup with water and set it in the microwave to boil. He pulled a canister of loose green tea from the cabinet and spooned some into a mug with the water.

"You going?" I asked.

"Have to. Policemen's Benevolent Fund needs replenishing. You're on the hook, too. Got a party dress?"

The PBF was the sheriff's favorite fund. He dictated no overtime this summer because of the tight budget, but he suggested we donate our time to replenish the fund used to help officers' families after a death in the line of duty. It appeared the Spine party would be one such "donation" opportunity.

"Not in uniform?"

"Nah, the Spine establishment says that would be too inhibiting to their guests. They just want us there in case of trouble."

Although I wasn't wild about obligatory events, this one meant I'd get to see Shepherd in formal party wear. *That* should be interesting. I knew how much he hated dressing up and playing nice.

"Your old beau, Flint Tanner, is invited to Marguerite's party, too. Heinrich's considering him as Gil's replacement. You know anything about that?"

"Yeah, he told me." I kept my tone neutral, but my mind was doing cart-wheelies at his news.

Flint would probably be there with his banker girlfriend, Jocelyn, in tow. That changed the game. No way was I attending alone!

Rory Stevens could escort me. I had a bribe to entice him—an atomic orange Hummer that needed washing. It even bore a sign that said so.

CHAPTER TWENTY

The day of Marguerite's garden party I stood blankly staring at my closet door wondering why I was attending this farce. I hated command performances, especially those including someone I didn't want to see, such as one Flint Tanner. At least I wasn't going alone. I had convinced Rory Stevens into taking me.

The day was June hot, and the green silk chiffon dress I'd picked would be cooler than slacks. I didn't have a garden-party hat, but I piled my red hair in an elaborate do on the top of my head and affixed a rhinestone clip on the side. Then I slipped into a pair of high-heeled sandals. That would have to do.

I packed a change of clothing in a tote bag to take along. Rory had promised me an excursion to an ancient pueblo when we finished with the cop chaperone duty. It was called Spirit Mountain, an undiscovered archaeologic treasure just across the meadow from V Bar V Ranch. The old Indian ruin had over sixty rooms—you'll love it, Rory promised me.

The look of interest in his eyes as I opened the front door made dressing up worth the effort. The party officially started at one p.m., but from the cloud of dust we ate before we reached the front gate, everyone else was arriving fashionably late, too.

Ray Morales directed traffic and he waved us to a pasture they'd chalk-striped for parking. Rory's Hummer jounced and swayed over the ruts and settled in between a Mercedes and a Stingray. It looked like an unkempt ugly uncle looming over the expensive cars.

Rory offered me an arm, and I picked my way across the hillocks in my sandals. They were totally impractical for police chases, which is what I'd been doing the last time I was in this pasture. I glanced around, but the Brahma bull hadn't been invited to the party.

The spreading lawn in front of the Spine mansion had been transformed into a gala reception area with a huge party tent and small conversation gazebos scattered on the lawn. A central pathway led to the paddock where the Friesian horses would be performing later in the afternoon.

Maybe fifty people or so had already arrived, and waiters were circulating with champagne and—was that caviar? I snagged a glass and a small plate with a cracker spread with the fancy stuff. I took a bite. Hmmm. Tasted like fish eggs. I sniffed. Smelly fish eggs.

Men arrived in polo-shirt casual, but women took the opportunity to play dress up. They wore billowing hats decorated with feathers and tulle, and long dresses punctuated with strands of pearls.

Members of the sheriff's department, betrayed by their sharp-eyed alertness, tried to blend with the party goers. Heinrich Spine was taking no chances. With the water issues in the valley, summer heat could make conflict inevitable. Shepherd stood at one side of the yard, looking uncomfortable as he tugged at the too-tight collar of a long-sleeved white shirt.

I walked to the front of the house where Marguerite stood, dressed in immaculate white linen with a wide-brimmed hat sporting an explosion of purple-dyed ostrich plumes. As I drew close, she smoothed the shoulder ruffle of a too-tight pea-green sheath that Amanda had been poured into. The girl was obviously uncomfortable and shrugged away her mother's hand with a sulky expression. Trouble there.

I deposited the empty caviar plate and glass and grabbed another glass from a passing waiter. Just another guest having a great time.

"Well, I didn't know you'd be here."

I whirled to discover Flint Tanner.

"And Rory Stevens," he said to my date who'd been trailing me around. "This is ranch land. Aren't you out of your swampy element?"

Rory scowled at Flint, not his usual cocky self. I couldn't blame him. Flint cut a tall figure in contrast to Rory's short stature.

My ex-boyfriend wore a cowboy hat, pressed blue jeans and a big smile. Next to him was a ravishing young woman, blonde and petite.

"Let me introduce my friend, Jocelyn Hunter," he said.

"We've talked on the phone," Jocelyn said, "about that studio apartment you're renting." She reached out a slim hand to me and then adjusted it upward a few inches to reach mine. "My, you must have played basketball in school."

Now my scowl matched Rory's.

Her little face set in a determined expression. "I normally don't mix business with pleasure. But you *did* get the eviction notice?"

I murmured something about stopping by the bank the next week. I congratulated Flint on his new job and exchanged hot-weather comments. That exhausted my repertoire of social niceties. When Amanda Riordan approached me, I turned away from the group with relief.

"I'm so glad you could make it," she said. "Did you see this awful dress mother chose for me? I look like an ocean wave."

"You look beautiful." I gave her shoulder a pat. "That green brings out the color of your eyes."

Which is what I always used to say to my mother when she dressed up to go out after my father left us, her eyes uncertain and a certain bravado in her voice. I felt a twinge in my heart and then let it go. Those shadowed childhood memories were best left buried. Tennessee was eons away from this sun-filled summer day in Arizona.

Amanda deserted me to greet yet another late arrival. Rory had moved to the edge of the yard talking to a group of friends. An extrovert, he shone at parties like these. That left me, standing alone in the midst of a crowd of strangers.

My cure for anxiety was food. I found it at the party tent where Raven LightDancer was presiding over an impressive array of hors-d'oeuvres.

"An interesting show," he said. "Count on these people to entertain."

"What have you got to eat?" I asked him.

"Try this." He popped a morsel into my mouth. I chewed thoughtfully on a cheese puffery with salmon and chives. "Not bad. What else you got?"

"Persimmon bruschetta, cucumber with whipped feta, or this steak tostada with chimichurri sauce."

I reached for the tostada.

"Careful, a little hot," he warned.

My eyes watered as I swallowed too fast. Then the flavor came rushing through. I could get used to this.

On the other hand, I was getting paid—or the Benevolent Fund was—to anticipate problems. Maybe I should just keep my mind on business.

"Raven, who are all of these servers?"

His cordiality disappeared like water seeping out of a leaky barrel.

"Family members."

"Did you hire them?"

"You think they're here to cause trouble and steal? Well, they're not. These are my friends. They'll be fine." His voice was defensive.

I wasn't so sure.

I retreated to the main house restroom, sanctuary of all women escaping an awkward moment. As I passed through the hall on my way to the front bathroom, I checked the door to the chemistry lab. Locked, as Fancy told me it would be.

I joined the end of the line that had formed outside the bathroom door. Attorney Myra Banks stood to the side with Janet Miller, the woman whose son had killed himself. I moved over to say hello while we waited our turn.

Janet Miller wore no makeup and appeared to have lost ten pounds in the time since her son's death. Her eyes were haunted, staring. Myra stood with a concerned arm around the woman's shoulder.

"Peg! Glad to see you." The attorney looked up with a relieved expression as I approached.

The restroom door opened, and Janet pushed past the other waiting women. She rushed in and locked the door, sobbing.

"What was that all about?" I asked.

Myra had a troubled look. "I thought the party would cheer her up. A big mistake. Ever since we arrived, she keeps going on and on about how Gil Streicker gave Johnny drugs and that's why he died."

"You think she was right?"

"We've got a big meth problem in the high school." Myra shrugged. "I didn't think my nephew Johnny was into that sort of thing, but you never can tell."

Nephew. It took me a minute to make the connection.

"You're related to Janet? She said her sister's name was *Eloise.*"

Myra looked embarrassed. "That's my first name, thanks to our mother. Eloise Myra Banks. You understand why I use my middle one for business."

I wasn't sure her choice was much better. What do parents think when they name their children? Another reason to be glad I didn't have any kids.

"I'm worried about Janet," Myra said. "She's not sleeping. The doctor prescribed sleeping pills, but she's not taking them."

"Keep an eye on her, Myra. Grief does terrible things to people."

I was glad Janet had family close. She seemed to be a woman standing on the edge of a very high cliff as she dealt with the death of her child.

Our conversation was interrupted by a commotion in the front yard. Heinrich Spine banged on his chair with his cane to gain the crowd's attention.

"Please make your way down to the paddock. We have a treat in store with an exhibit of the prized Spine Friesians." Then he took Marguerite's arm to lead the procession.

I made a hasty visit to the restroom, and then joined the crowd. A breeze had kicked up, and its breath cooled my cheek. I leaned against the rough wood of the paddock fence, watching the building thunderheads as I waited for the show to begin.

The crowd applauded spontaneously as the first black Friesians appeared, a matched pair with a Phaeton. Ray Morales sat high on the step with a top hat and a black leather whip. The animals shone with their grooming, manes elaborately braided and hooves gleaming with polish.

The carriage rounded the turn by the fence, passing within inches of the guests. The silver decorations on the harness gleamed and the single-tree jingled as they pranced by.

Next out, Flint Tanner stood tall in the English stirrups of a gelding, the horse prancing and side-stepping away from his hand.

There was a touch at my elbow and Rory Stevens joined me. He chuckled unkindly under his breath. "Be too bad if that horse gets the better of him."

"Hush," I whispered, as Flint passed close by the fence, the horse settling to his touch.

Then there was a roar of approval from the crowd as the next rider appeared from behind the barn. It was Amanda on Black Onyx. She had changed into riding jodhpurs, and competition hard hat. The young woman was superb on the black stallion. She bent over and whispered in the horse's ear. They cantered easily past us, the Friesian's luxurious mane and tail flowing in the wind.

Seated on the horse, Amanda left her own awkward body behind, transformed into a centaur of horse and rider. No wonder the girl loved Onyx! The watching group clapped as she swung by.

As a finale of the show, some of the guests were invited for a carriage ride with a spirited team of four black horses. The exhibition was impressive; I had to give Heinrich Spine credit for that.

The old man stood with difficulty and looked with rheumy eyes at the friends and business associates gathered in front of him. "First, thank you all for coming to our little party. Second, I'm officially announcing that I have signed the ownership of the Spine Ranch over to the Nature Conservancy upon my death. When I am no longer here, this beautiful ranch will live on in perpetuity."

There was a scattering of polite applause. I looked to the Riordan family for their reaction. Heinrich's announcement had apparently come as a surprise. Marguerite's face was as white as her linen shift.

"No." She shook her head, "No, you promised..."

Promised what, I wondered? I strode in her direction, but her husband, Dr. Theo, reached her first.

"Marguerite, dear. Your father has the right to do what he wants with this ranch. It was never yours."

Marguerite slapped his face. The sharp crack echoed in the sudden silence, the white imprint shocking against his ruddy cheek.

"How dare you say that! This ranch *is* mine. I've earned every miserable inch of it." Then Marguerite fled into the house.

Dr. Theo stood there, his arms hanging at his side, head bowed. Then he slowly followed after his wife. People parted on either side of his wedge of desolation.

After he left, the guests stood in knots, awkward with uncertainty. A few went up to Heinrich to murmur their appreciation for the party, but the mood of celebration had been crushed by Marguerite's exit.

The wind added to the tenseness of the moment, scattering dirt and debris as a thunderstorm moved in. Women clung to unmanageable hats, and servers scurried to bring table service and remaining food into the house. The party was over. It was time to leave.

Rory and I headed to the parking lot. It started to rain, first tentative splatters, then sheets of drenching water. He seemed to tap into the energy of the storm.

"Forget those ridiculous shoes," he shouted. "Let's run for it!"

He grabbed my hand as the thunder and lightning crashed overhead and the rain came down in a blinding rush. My impractical heels were ruined in seconds as we dashed through the puddles and mud. When we reached the Hummer, I stood hopping from one foot to the other as Rory unlocked the doors.

Safe in the vehicle, my breath steamed the windows as the rain drummed against the metal roof. I swiped the moisture off my face and took down what was left of my elegant hairdo. I shook my head like a dog to loosen the knots, liberally spraying Rory with water.

"Hey!" he exclaimed.

The sudden drop in temperature from the storm chilled the air. "Turn off the AC?"

"No can do. Need the air to demist the window. Deal."

He yanked the wheel left and right to negotiate the puddles in the yard. Mud squished between the tire treads, sending a spray to either side as he bumped onto the main road. Several miles later he turned toward Spirit Mountain.

I crossed my arms, shivering. Then I remembered the tote and twisted on the seat to get it. I zipped the bag open and pulled out a small hand towel. Once I wiped the worst of the water off my arms and legs, I dug out my Bermuda shorts and T-shirt. They were still warm from the earlier heat of the summer day.

Rory was seemingly intent on the road ahead, and I wondered whether I could change out of my wet clothes, casual-like. If surfers could skinny into wetsuits in a public Malibu parking lot, this shouldn't be too hard.

"Don't look."

"Wouldn't think of it," Rory assured me.

Kicking off the now ruined sandals, I lifted the dripping skirt. Then I pulled the Bermuda shorts up to my thighs and then slipped the dress over my head. But before I could yank the T-shirt down, Rory turned and gave me a big grin.

"Road!" I punched his shoulder and pointed ahead.

"Ow, that hurt."

"Deal," I said.

I reached in the tote one last time and pulled out a pair of Tevas, those sturdy river shoes. For general hiking, especially in muddy conditions, they often worked better than boots.

"How much farther to Spirit Mountain?" I asked.

"Probably another twenty minutes or so."

The cloudburst had stopped, and although the thunderheads were blue-black on the horizon, only spits of rain hit the windshield. Rory lowered his window, and the tangy odor of wet creosote drifted in.

"Ah," he said. "Love that stuff."

I pulled my cell out of my sopping purse and checked for messages. The blue light was blinking which meant I had one. It was from Ned Jamison, my buddy back east.

"Peg! I've found out something about the Batesville connection. When I couldn't reach you, I called your grandfather. He told me you were at the Spine's party. I left a message there, too. Call me."

I dialed his number, but just then we descended a hill dropping into a dead zone. I'd try him later.

Lightning flickered across the sky as we drove the route toward

Wet Beaver Creek. I hoped that the calm water of the creek would ease my party-strained nerves, but something much different awaited us.

"Holy cow, look at that!" Rory braked sharply and pulled to the side of the road.

CHAPTER TWENTY-ONE

In front of us, the normally dry gash of Red Tank Draw had vanished under a roaring torrent of water pouring over the road. The crossing was barely visible as the angry flood covered the roadbed with a foot of water.

An impatient horn blared behind us, and a red pickup roared past, spraying mud on the Hummer.

"Idiot," Rory said, as the truck driver plowed across the flood-covered bridge. His tires threw a ridge of water that bulged to the top of the hubcaps. Reaching the other side of the bridge, he climbed to the top of the arroyo, his big tires throwing out gouts of mud.

Another car whizzed past us, a battered blue Toyota. A woman drove, her mouth set and hands clenched to the wheel. Staring straight ahead, she followed in the wake of the pickup like a baby duckling following a parent.

"No, lady, don't try it. Don't do it," I muttered.

The Toyota reached the center of the submerged bridge and I held my breath. Would she make it over? Then a sudden tongue of water immersed the tailpipe and the car stalled. The woman cranked away at the starter, but the car was stone dead. The water lapped at the side panel of the vehicle.

Rory turned on his emergency flashers and dashed out on the roadbed. I dialed the sheriff's office and requested assistance. Then I yanked open my door and ran after him.

We'd drilled on water rescue at the police academy back in

Tennessee. But there, we were dealing with slow-rising rivers, predicted and anticipated sometimes days in advance. I'd never thought I'd use that training here. Who expects floods in an Arizona desert?

Rory waded out to the flooded Toyota, holding onto the guardrail and fighting against the current. He pounded on the driver's side window.

"Unlock your seat belt. Roll down your window and climb out. Now!"

The woman pulled out her cell phone and took a selfie.

The water continued to rise, and I waded out to assist. As I reached the Toyota's bumper, the car jerked under my hand and started to float. It shifted sideways with the force of the current and drifted closer to the jagged edge of the guardrail marking the drop-off to the torrents below.

"Too late," Rory yelled in my ear. "Car's going over." He grabbed my arm and pulled me back to the safety of the creek bank.

The Toyota caught for an instant on the broken railing. Then with a gentle sigh, the car slid into the wash. It floated upright, buoyant in the current, and slowly pin wheeled once, the heavier engine weight reversing the car.

Then the passenger-side rear tire caught on the edge of the muddy sandbank in the middle of the stream. The car hesitated for a moment, then held.

A tangle of mesquite branches bumped into the car, wedging it farther into the red mud. However, the car was turned crossways to the current. That stable position wouldn't last long. I had to rescue the driver!

I skidded down the roadway embankment parallel to the roiling creek, lost my balance, and fell seat-first in the mud. I stumbled to my feet and pushed through the remains of an old barbed-wire fence. The flooded creek lay ahead of me.

Rory dashed back to the Hummer. He ground into low gear, barreled through the fence, and paralleled my actions on the creek bank.

Downstream from the bridge, the red-brown water roiled with a mass of debris and broken branches. The stream grew in width creating waterfalls and whirlpools as it ripped down the channel.

I plunged into the creek near the car, mud sucking at my ankles. The storm had dropped the temperatures dramatically, and the water chilled me through in seconds.

The white-faced woman in the car pointed frantically to the back seat.

"There's a child in a car seat back there!" I shouted to Rory as the Hummer lurched to a stop.

"I've got to reach them before the car shifts again."

"I'm breaking out the rescue gear," Rory yelled, climbing out of his seat and running to the rear of the Hummer.

He yanked out a PFD, a Personal Flotation Device, and threw it to me. I pulled it over my shoulders and cinched it tight around my waist.

I reviewed what I knew about water rescue. Most people try to get out by opening the door of their car. Then they panic when they find out the door won't budge, that the water is stronger than they are.

If the water was above the floorboards, the next best bet was escape through a window. But there was a three-minute limit before the automatic window-opening gear jammed in rising water. This lady had already passed that threshold.

That left breaking a window manually. The car's back end was still anchored in the mud bank, but the hood swung like a pendulum, back and forth in the rushing water. The car could break loose at any moment.

Rory tossed me a ball-peen hammer from his Hummer's tool chest. It fell just short, but I grabbed it before the current did, and shoved it in my waistband.

The water nudged at my calves, and then sucked at my knees as I waded closer. The current seemed like a living animal, grabbing at me. A branch blocked my foot. I kicked it away.

I waded away from the upstream side of the car. The worst possible situation was to be swept under the car by the current, trapped under muddy water until you could no longer breathe. Drowning came next.

The woman had frozen in the front seat. She stared at me, her face a rigid mask of fear.

"Peg, here."

I looked over my shoulder as Rory yanked a rope-toss bag out of the trunk. He held one end of the rope and underhanded the canvas bag containing the rest of the cord across the water to me. Gravity pulled the rope out of the heavy bag as it zipped my direction.

I followed the arc of the canvas bag and snagged it like a shortstop with a game-winning play. Maybe it was.

Our lives could depend on it.

I tied the rope around my waist and pulled the hammer out of my waistband. No use trying to break out the windshield—that glass was fabricated to stop a good-sized deer before buckling. Best get the little kid first. I reached over and gave the back window a shortened whack.

The glass crumbled instantly, and I brushed away the shards with the handle of the hammer. The little girl in the car seat looked to be about two years old. She appeared more excited than frightened by this turn of events.

"Hi, Honey, you ready for a ride?"

I unhooked her car seat harness. She lifted her arms and let me pull her through the window. She clung tightly to my neck, tucking her head under my chin.

The woman in the front seat unfastened her seat belt and scrambled to the back. She grabbed my arm through the window opening with panic-stiffened fingers.

"Get my little girl out of this!"

The car tilted against the current. Then the vehicle shifted again, aligning with the flood waters. I needed distance from the car.

"Hold tight," I said to the little girl.

I pushed through the rolling water, testing each footstep before I moved forward toward dry ground.

Rory applied steady pressure on the rope, pulling us toward shore. By now, other people had gathered on the bank. They formed a tug-of-war line on the rope behind him, helping pull.

I heard a collective gasp and chanced a quick look behind me. The car released from the sandbar with a sucking sound. The woman trapped in the car screamed once, a shriek that echoed above the flood. Then she was silent, as the car bobbed and twisted in the downstream currents.

My attention turned toward maintaining my balance on the rocky wash bed. I slipped once and then I righted myself and continued onward, making slow agonizing progress. Rory's eyes locked on mine, urging me forward.

One step, another. Finally, I felt the current release its hold as I neared shore. I lifted the child up to Rory. He passed her to a woman behind him who swaddled the little girl in a blanket.

Rory stretched out an arm to pull me up, too. At that moment, I stumbled and the knot I had tied in the rope unraveled. The creek bank dissolved under my feet, plunging me into a deep hole of swirling darkness.

I gulped a mouthful of muddy water. By the time I surfaced, the current had pushed me to the center of the flood once more. The flotation device was still secure around my waist but the rope was a useless snake floating out of my reach.

"Stay afloat, Peg!" Rory's words were almost lost in the roar.

I pointed my feet downhill, and floated on my back, using my feet to steer off rocks and tree branches snagged in the morass. The current stiffened as the water volume increased and I felt its hard slap. It was bitter cold, and my body numbed.

A log snagged by the stream created its own waterfall ahead of me. I'd have to use my arms to push off the top of the half-submerged limb. If I slipped underneath the fallen tree, I'd drown in the snarling water. I flipped over on my stomach in anticipation.

The log pulled at me, but I eluded its grasp. From the corner of my eye, I saw the bright orange Hummer keeping pace on the edge of the bank, tearing through a blur of sagebrush and creosote.

A huge bulk loomed in front of me in the creek. The blue Toyota! It was still upright, but rapidly filling with water. The woman clung to the back seat, trying to keep her head clear in the shrinking air space.

I bumped into the side of the car and rebounded. I clutched for the bumper, felt it slip from my mud-slick hands. Then I stretched out my fingers, caught an edge, and pulled myself closer to the back fender.

The car seemed firm at this point, wedged against the far bank of the draw, but I knew that condition could change at any moment, as it had before. Hand over hand, I pulled myself to the back window.

I made eye contact with the woman. She was shrieking, terrified. I had to calm her down, or we'd both go under in our attempt to reach the far shore.

"What's your name?" I asked.

"M-M-Mary." Her lips were blue from the exposure to the water as hypothermia and shock set in.

"Well, Mary, your little girl is fine. She's up on the bank. Ready to go see her?"

She nodded stiffly.

"First, you need to climb out this window—"

"No, I can't!"

"Sure you can. How else you going to your little girl?"

"You'll be safe." I shrugged out of my flotation device and dangled it in front of me, luring her.

"As soon as you're out of the car I'll put it on you."

She was tugging at something in the front seat.

"No, leave your purse. Just you!"

She sucked in her breath and then scrambled through the back window. Panic-stricken, she grabbed the vest out of my hand and pulled it over her shoulders.

I dodged her frantic embrace and steadied both of us against the current. We only had one life vest, so we'd have to double up. But we could do this.

"Ready, Peg?" Rory shouted.

He tossed me the second rope-throw bag. I tightened that rope around me. Knotted it twice. The creek narrowed here, intensifying the coil of swiftly swirling water, but making the journey to safety much shorter. There'd be a danger if either of us lost our balance, but a risk we'd have to take.

I clung to the back of the woman's waist and together we started wading to shore, while Rory and his volunteers pulled the rope overhand, helping us along. The woman stumbled once and I gasped.

Something bumped against my leg, then wrapped tightly around my ankle. I lost precious moments untangling the sodden vine.

The woman sagged in the water, but the vest held her upright.

I pushed her hard into Rory's grasping fingers. She was safe!

Now me. One more step and I'd be there.

Yet the flood waters held me captive. My chest pounded. I couldn't breathe. The air around me blackened as I fought to control the panic I'd held at bay for these last frantic minutes.

"No," I moaned. "Not now!"

Rory led a human chain from the bank. He held out his hand and I reached for it, our fingertips almost touching. Then I plunged into a deep hole. My mouth filled with filthy water.

I stumbled to my feet, sputtering.

He tried again, and the welcome strength in his out-stretched fingers met mine. Pulled by the rescuers, we staggered to shore.

I dropped to the ground gasping, trying to catch my breath. I vomited out the muddy water and lay there, exhausted.

I leaned against the Hummer, shivering as a breeze flattened my wet clothes against my body. Rory tucked a warm blanket around my shoulders.

"Thank god you're safe, Peg. If something had happened to you..." He let his voice drift off and shoved a metal Thermos cup into my hand.

I took one gulp and started coughing. Coffee, liberally laced with Scotch. The next swallow went down slower and melted the cold right down to my hipbones.

"The EMTs need to check you out," Rory said.

"I'm fine, really."

"And these guys will make double sure."

His tone brooked no argument and for once, I surrendered my independence. He put one strong arm around my shoulders and led me to the emergency van.

The blood pressure cuff around my arm showed a sky-high, adrenaline-charged blood pressure reading. Skilled hands investigated a cut on my forehead that I'd acquired. In the midst of the rescue, I felt nothing at all, but now the wound started to throb, especially when they dabbed on antiseptic.

"Ouch." I jerked away.

"Better than the alternative," one said.

"When's your last tetanus shot?"

Without waiting for my response, he jabbed me with a needle.

Then efficient hands rinsed mud off my arms and legs, and disinfected numerous small cuts.

"Be sure to disinfect everything again once you get home," one EMT cautioned. "No telling what's in these flood waters."

Overhead a news chopper buzzed the creek scene. The Toyota woman's stupidity would be all over the evening news with the usual warnings about driving into flood waters. We were lucky. This time everyone survived. Sometimes they didn't.

The EMT gave Rory the high sign. He helped me to the Hummer, and I climbed in with unsteady legs. I tried to buckle my seat belt, failed. Rory hauled himself into the driver's seat and with gentle fingers completed the task.

He maneuvered skillfully over the ruts and bumps of the red earth beside the wash. With one final heave of mighty tires, the Hummer bounced onto the main roadbed. We drove down the narrow road toward I-17 and home in Mingus.

"The little kid, the woman—they okay?" I asked.

"They're just fine, thanks to you."

"That's nice."

I drifted off into a troubled, shock-filled doze. I was dimly aware of passing through Cottonwood and felt the upward whine of the engine as Rory navigated the hairpin turns on the road to Mingus.

"We're here." Rory nudged me upright.

I stumbled up the stairs to my studio apartment, Rory close behind me. Without asking, he started the shower and dug around in my dresser while I undressed.

"You got some pajamas in here?" He rummaged a little further and pulled out my flannel ones with the Wonder-Woman insignia. "These'll do."

"Need to get your body temperature back up," he muttered and pushed me into the steaming water.

I stood in the shower braced with both hands against the wall, letting the water run through my hair, down my back, sluicing away the mud, grit, and terror of the flood waters. Only when the shower turned cold, did I get out.

A towel and the pajamas were waiting for me. I put them on with stress-stiffened fingers. Rory had turned down my bed and I dropped onto the cool sheets, bone-weary.

Behind me in the bathroom, the water throbbed a steady rhythm while Rory took a shower in the cold water. Then there was silence as he toweled off.

Through a haze of exhaustion, I heard him calling HT.

"Yeah, she's okay. We're both fine. You keep Reckless. Bring the dog by in the morning? I'll watch her tonight."

***

The next morning, a beam of sun pierced my consciousness. Whispered conversations on the landing below alerted me that company was coming. I scooted up in bed and stuffed the still-warm pillow lying next to me behind my head along with my own.

There was the stolid clump of feet as Isabel climbed up the interior stairs to the apartment and then Reckless bounded on the bed, pressing a cold nose in my ear. He wriggled close to me. I pulled the sheet higher around my shoulders as my grandfather followed his housekeeper to the top of the stairs.

"Peg, are you okay?" he asked.

"We were so worried about you," Isabel chimed in.

HT pulled a chair over to the bed and sat down. His big hands engulfed mine. "You could have drowned."

I looked around the room blearily. My damp clothes made an untidy pile in a corner, accompanied by Rory's underwear and socks wadded into muddy balls. I stole a look at Rory over HT's shoulder. He was dressed in a mud-stained T-shirt and damp blue jeans. Bare feet.

What had he worn to sleep in? The obvious answer came to me, and I blushed. It wasn't as though I'd done anything wrong. In fact, I didn't think I could have, as tired as I was. But the thought of a naked adult male recently present in my bed, being observed by the housekeeper and my grandfather? Embarrassing.

"We won't stay," HT said. "Just wanted to bring Reckless over and make sure you were doing better. You're in good hands here."

He clapped Rory on the shoulder and the two shook hands. Then HT and Isabel left as abruptly as they came.

"Rory," I stammered. "Thank you for everything."

"That's what friends are for." He looked as awkward as I felt and made preparations to follow HT.

"Wait. Stay for breakfast, anyway."

He didn't need a second invitation.

"Coffee, first? I'll make fresh."

We moved to the couch waiting for the coffee to finish. I drew an old afghan around me and we talked about how unexpected the flash flood was, and how dumb people can be when facing life-threatening danger.

"Why did she stay there in that flooding car, for heaven's sake?" I asked.

"Probably uploading pictures to Instagram."

"Never want to go through something like that again." I shuddered.

"I never want to see you in water like that again. You could have died!"

Rory's eyes stared into mine.

Then he slowly peeled off his damp T-shirt and jeans and let me to the bed. I unbuttoned the top of my fleece pajamas.

The coffee could wait.

CHAPTER TWENTY-TWO

When I woke for the second time, it was about noon. I was alone.

Rory had returned to his home in Prescott. He'd made some vague noises about getting together soon, and so did I. But I couldn't help wondering if we would. Ours was an uncertain relationship at best.

After a sleepy cup of coffee, I dressed in casuals, snapped a leash on Reckless, and walked up the hill to the sheriff's station. Even though it was Sunday, Shepherd was there, eating his lunch. He set his sandwich down and peered over his reading glasses at my blue jeans and tank top.

"Look what the mutt drug in."

Reckless bounded over to give him a coonhound hello, and Shepherd fielded him back into play with an expert knee to the dog's chest.

"Time you trained that dog. He's a menace."

"You volunteering?" Shepherd had trained K-9s for the county for years. Even won some blue ribbons for some of his dogs.

"Not likely. He's a lost cause." Shepherd eyed the dog for a moment and then looked up at me. "Heard about your rescue operation yesterday. I thought you'd be home recovering, not here at the station."

"I wanted to call to my colleague back in Tennessee. Thought I'd do it on the sheriff's nickel." I explained to Shepherd the suspicions I had about Fancy Morgan's past.

"Lots of people are evasive about where they come from," Shepherd said.

"Maybe so, but I want to check it out."

"That a woman's intuition thing?"

Interesting, I thought, that when *men* "played their hunches," it was considered an enviable skill. Maybe I was just being too sensitive.

Reckless took the opportunity to grab the rest of Shepherd's sandwich and dived behind me, a piece of lettuce stuck to one lip.

"Damn! That was the last of my tuna fish."

"Ah, your gut didn't need it," I said. "What's the latest on Gil Streicker?"

My partner rocked back his chair. "We got the final word on his cause of death. Smoke in his lungs, substantial amount of arsenic in his system, plus a contusion on the back of his head. Looks like somebody knocked him unconscious."

"Then we've got a murder on our hands," I said. Finally, we could crank this investigation into high gear.

But with the passing time the evidence had grown cold. There wasn't much, if anything, left. This family, divided in so many ways, had shown a sudden unity of purpose in obliterating evidence.

Shepherd was undeterred. "What do we know so far?"

"Maybe follow the money? We have a hunch Gil Streicker squirreled away a lot of cash—way more than he'd make as ranch manager."

"So blackmail or possibly drug running?" Shepherd asked.

"I'd like to pin the death on Heinrich on general principles— that old bastard. But he's getting infirm—might not have the physical strength to do the deed."

"So what about Raven LightDancer?" I asked. "He's using an assumed name. That might mean he'd lose his job if his employer found out. And there are some rumors he's the drug connection on the ranch. Or, if it's prescription drugs, Marguerite's husband, Dr. Theo, might be involved."

Shepherd circled back to the blackmail angle. "Ray Morales might have a motive for paying up. His niece, Alana, is not a U.S. citizen."

"She's here illegally?"

The Verde Valley had, town by town, established its own way of dealing with people illegally immigrated from Mexico and parts farther south. Such individuals often took jobs no one else wanted here in the valley: Washing dishes in the restaurants, backbreaking yard work for rich second-homers in Sedona, making the beds in tourist hotels. Often it was a case of don't ask, don't tell.

Shepherd fidgeted in his seat, his reputation as a hard-nosed law enforcer suddenly in question with the knowledge he'd just shared. "She's a hard worker. Keeps her head down. 'Most everyone knows about her status. Now you do, too."

Alana seemed a long shot to me; the family seemed more likely suspects. "What about passion?" I asked. "Marguerite and her daughter were in love with the same man. Maybe Marguerite decided it was better to kill Gil Streicker than to share him."

"Or cast a wider net," Shepherd said. "Consider the Battles, sister and brother. Serena's got a fiery temper. She might have lost it one too many times over that water rights issue."

I nodded. "Or if Hank got in trouble again, Serena wouldn't hesitate to kill to save him—she's a real momma bear."

The front door banged as Ben, our assistant-on-sabbatical, entered the building with a stack of books under one arm. He wore a crow feather in his windblown black hair. It looked like the Native American side of him was ascendant this morning.

Ben sat down at the computer in the foyer and turned it on. "Got to finish my paper for entomology."

His motion caused the feather to drift to the desk and Reckless grabbed for it. Boy and dog tussled for a moment and then Reckless dropped to the floor, panting and happy. Ben refixed his badge of honor more firmly behind his ear.

"When are you *balagaanas*, you white people, going to fix the budget so I can come back to work? I need a car to court my new girlfriend."

"Soon," I said. "How are you doing out at the Spine Ranch?"

"I got the problem straightened out for Marguerite," Ben said with satisfaction. "All I did was unplug the computer and plug it back in. Works about half the time. She thinks I'm a genius." He grinned at me.

"Find out anything about the financial dealings at the ranch?" I asked.

"Other than Heinrich Spine is about to declare bankruptcy?"

"How'd you discover that?" Shepherd asked him. "Hack into the computer?"

"Didn't have to," Ben said. "Amanda told me everything. She's worried. If the ranch doesn't acquire additional water rights, they'll be forced to sell off the far pastures. Without those, their horse operation couldn't exist. It's already in the red."

"If they were about to lose the ranch, maybe the barn was burned down for the insurance proceeds. It could be Gil was just in the wrong place at the wrong time." I sighed. "I can't believe Amanda had anything to do with Gil's death, though. She's not the type."

"Don't let your heart get the best of you. *Everybody* is the type, given enough provocation," Shepherd said.

"Okay, then," I countered. "What about this? The husband would be another likely candidate, if Gil was involved with both his wife and his daughter."

"Why don't you go see him, Peg?"

"You want to come?"

He hesitated. "Got matters to attend to here."

It sounded as though Shepherd's Porsche obsession had surfaced again.

"Shepherd..."

He raised a hand to ward off my objections.

"Don't, Peg. Not your concern. Keep digging on this Streicker thing. I'll help as I can. We'll get something nailed down, soon."

I clamped my mouth shut. Shepherd's business might be his own, but what he did or *didn't* do at work directly affected my job security, too.

Ben chose that moment to toss a handful of chips out of Shepherd's half-eaten bag to Reckless. Most fell on the floor, and the dog dived to scoop them up.

"Don't feed that damn animal the rest of my lunch!"

Time to leave before I was minus a dog. I collared the mutt and we left.

***

Later that afternoon, I went for a drive. When I reached the

166

highway exit for the Middle Verde, the talk of death was still on my mind. I turned right and stopped at the nursery. They had the last of the spring plants on sale. I spent a dollar on a small geranium, bright with pink blossoms. Maybe it would cheer up my place.

Then, since I was in the neighborhood, I drove to Janet Miller's place. The woman looked terrible at the garden party. Figured I'd stop in for a moment and see how she was doing.

The small residence huddled under the shade of the big trees.

Janet Miller's little girl played in the shade of a cottonwood tree. A small corral built of twigs corralled a herd of plastic horses. The little girl talked to herself as she played, pretending each horse could speak.

"Hi, Holly. Your momma home?"

She looked up with a scared expression. "Momma told me to go play. She's sick."

I walked up the steps and knocked on the front door. "Mrs. Miller, it's Pegasus Quincy. I need to talk to you."

There was a long pause, and then the door opened slowly. She looked even worse than she had at the party. Her hair was straw texture, unkempt. Her face was drawn and blotchy-red. She wore down-at-the heel slippers and an old housecoat which she clutched to her chest

"Now's not a good time," she croaked. "Come back later."

Normally I would have acceded to her wishes, but something made me push a little. "Sorry, I need to talk to you now."

"Is it about Johnny's death?" She mustered some energy. "Come in."

The living room was a mess, unlike the neat-as-a-pin house I had first visited. There were clothes strewn about. An empty pizza carton sat on one end table, buzzing with flies.

"Just a minute. Let me put on some clothes," she mumbled.

She disappeared into the bedroom and the shower started.

This place needed some work. I folded the clothes, took the dirty dishes out to the kitchen, and dumped the pizza carton in the trashcan outside the back door. I thought for a moment and then walked out to my car. There, I retrieved the little geranium plant and set it on the coffee table.

"What about some coffee, Mrs. Miller?" I hollered at the

bedroom door.

There was a muffled response from the bedroom that I took for a yes, so I made a pot. The carafe was half-full by the time she reappeared, and I interrupted the brew cycle to pour her a cup.

Janet Miller had put on a pair of jeans and a T-shirt. It looked like one of her son's with a picture of *The Growler's World Tour* on the front. But she'd brushed her hair and put on some lipstick. Good.

We sat at the kitchen table.

"How are you doing?" I asked.

"One day seems to blend into another. Oh, I take care of Holly—she's all I've got left—but the rest?" She looked around the house and made a helpless gesture.

"It must be difficult."

"It doesn't seem real. I keep expecting Johnny to walk in that door, hair in his eyes. He'd stand in front of the open refrigerator, chugging milk out of the carton. I yelled at him for doing that. If only..." Her lower lip started to quiver and her voice broke.

It was the downside of being a family liaison officer. I witnessed a lot of pain that I couldn't take away. This room radiated with it. I could tell Mrs. Miller it would get easier with time, and it would, but nothing would bring back her dead child.

So I did the best I could. I patted her hand and gave her a box of Kleenex and listened. I laughed with her at the reminiscences and reaffirmed that she'd done the best she could, that she'd raised a good son.

When I sensed she had finally calmed a little, I stood to leave. I dug in my purse for one of the counselor's cards I kept there. The therapist had helped me through my own nightmares following the killing a man. Perhaps she could assist this woman as well.

Janet Miller dropped the card on a table. Her lips set in a hard line. "I will never forgive that man, that Gil Streicker, for giving my Johnny drugs. He got what he deserved." She sobbed loudly for a moment, then dabbed angrily at her tears. With an effort, she quieted her emotions.

She reached out her hand. "Thank you for making the effort to come out here on your day off. This meant a lot to me."

As I pulled out of her driveway, I heard her calling to her daughter. Perhaps the little girl could pull her out of this deep slump.

But Janet was a tormented woman who needed help.

I pulled off before I reached the highway and called Myra Bank's office. I left a voicemail for the attorney telling her of my visit to the Miller household and recommending she get her sister into counseling as soon as possible. No break of confidentiality there. I wasn't a priest or a doctor. Just a family liaison officer, wishing I could do more.

My phone beeped. I answered, thinking perhaps Myra had gotten my message already. But it was Bettina Schwartz, the realtor. There were complications with renting the cabin in Desolation Gulch.

Bettina told me the owner wouldn't sign the lease without meeting me first. "She lives in Silver Maples Retirement Home in Cottonwood..."

"And?"

"Well, if you aren't doing anything, she's free this afternoon."

Like I needed to check my social calendar. "Be there in about a half hour," I said.

***

A grove of huge sycamore trees, their leaves shimmering in the summer heat, surrounded the retirement complex. I stopped at the office to get directions to Dorothy Harper's apartment.

"You can't miss Dot's apartment. The door has a big Halloween pumpkin decoration hanging on it," the administrator said.

The door was ajar, and it sounded like Metallica was giving a concert inside. In addition to the pumpkin, a glittery Christmas star, and an Easter bunny decorated the door. I knocked and waited until the sound of footsteps neared.

Dot Harper was elf-size, under five feet tall, with shock-white hair piled on top of her head. She was wearing purple capris with a chartreuse top.

"Come in, come in. Ms. Schwartz told me you were coming. Let me turn this music down. It bothers the neighbors some, but they can't hear too good anyway. Here, sit, and let me take a look at you."

She swept a pile of magazines off a burgundy couch and pulled me down beside her. I looked into eyes that were sharp and alert.

"Call me Dot. And you are?"

"Peg. Peg Quincy."

169

"And you're here about my house in Desolation Gulch. You want to rent it, why?"

"It has potential. Needs some indoor plumbing, though." I said. Never act too interested when you are the buyer in a negotiation.

"Nonsense. I lived in it that way for fifty years." She pointed to a framed picture on the opposite wall. It showed the cabin with a couple standing on the front porch. Dot Harper and her husband?

I didn't relish the thought of making the trek to an outhouse in the middle of the night in my skivvies. "An inside privy would be nice." I made my tone a little wistful. Okay, a little pathetic.

"True. Fair enough. I'll see to it. Anything else?"

"Bettina said something about a tax issue?"

"I've been fighting with Elmer Ganzo down at the assessor's office. I had his father in my Latin class when he was a boy. He isn't any smarter than his father was." She reached behind her and pulled a wrinkled slip of paper off her desk.

She smoothed it out, handed it to me. "Mistake on the bill."

"The statement is computer generated," I said. "Computers don't make errors."

"This one did." She pointed with one precise finger. "See, right there."

She was right. Darned if the bill hadn't mis-added her payment. According to the computer-generated receipt, Dot still owed the assessor seven cents.

"Let me get this right," I said. "If I fix this tax bill for you, you'll rent me the house."

She held up a finger. "Of course, that also includes the attorney's fee to file the lien-removal paperwork. I'm not paying it. And anytime I talk to that lawyer woman, the clock is running. I do a better job handling my affairs than she does."

"And that lady attorney would be…let me guess, Myra Banks?"

"Yes!" Dot clapped her hands delightedly. "I knew I'd like you. Let me fix you some tea."

And she did. In the midst of the colorful chaos of her small apartment, I started to relax for the first time in weeks. In between sips of tea and nibbles of shortbread cookies, I told her about the foreclosure notice, and my job as a family liaison officer, and my dog Reckless.

"Redbone coonhound," she said. "Best dog on the planet. The breeder might be Cal Nettle?"

"He's gone now."

She nodded. "That's right. Seems to me your hound was involved in his death if I'm not mistaken. How's it feel to sleep with a criminal?"

I wasn't sure if Dot Harper was serious or not, so I laughed, just a little. "I'll bring him by to visit you one day."

"Good. I'd like that. Too quiet around here, by far."

"How old did you say you were?" I asked.

"I didn't." She pressed a hand to her chest. "In here, about seventeen or so, I guess. And that's all that matters."

As we sat in the sunlit room, she skillfully pulled the story from me of Shepherd's vendetta against the Porsche driver and the stalled Gil Streicker investigation.

I wasn't the only one getting her attention. Dot Harper's phone was busy as she dispensed advice, cleared up administrative problems at the front office, and rearranged a volunteer schedule for the retirement home's library.

We came to an agreement on particulars for the cabin and I promised to call attorney Myra Banks the next morning. I needed to move out of the apartment, and fast. Perhaps the bank wasn't serious about the eviction notice, but I didn't plan to be around to find out.

It was almost sundown when I pulled into the driveway. I climbed the stairs to the apartment and ducked past the welcome ambush of dog kisses. I pulled on my running shoes and we headed for the hills for a hard workout.

Tomorrow, my work week would begin all over again.

CHAPTER TWENTY-THREE

When I walked to the station the next morning, traffic lights blinked impotently up and down Main Street. Traffic was already backing up as the tourists arrived in town.

Shepherd held a glass of water into the sunlight, rotating it my direction as I walked in.

"What's up out there?" I asked.

"Wonder why this water is so pure and drinkable, why it doesn't have any arsenic in it?" He gave the glass one last turn, sending reflections dancing on the white wall behind him.

"Deep wells on Black Mountain," I answered. "The water flows to Mingus via the old wooden sluices that the miners built a hundred years ago."

Shepherd looked grumpy, foiled at his shot of knowing superior knowledge.

"Well, maybe you don't know *this*. The overflow creek just caused a sinkhole on Hillside Road. And the crew repairing it didn't check for the underground cables..."

Ah, that was the reason for the traffic backup. Unfortunately, it was our problem as well as theirs. Shepherd and I flipped for who would go direct traffic, and I lost. Shepherd promised to relieve me in about three hours if the DOT people hadn't fixed the break in the electrical cable by then.

I put on a reflective vest—hot but worth it—and bright white gloves. I didn't want to become a statistic. People are so used to watching for green and red lights that they are blind to a figure standing in the middle of the road.

We'd only had a half day of traffic training at the police academy. It had been sandwiched in between field stripping a service weapon and Krav Maga training. Those had been a lot more fun.

I forced myself to remember what I'd learned about traffic management—management, they stressed, not control. The one good thing about the operation, however, was that I got to use a whistle and blow it *loud*. One long blast for stop, two short ones for go.

By the time I walked up the hill to the T-crossing, the light was totally dead. Not good news. A blinking red, folks understand: stop and look both ways. But no light at all? The aggressive drivers start edging out into the lanes, not waiting for their turns. Things can become ugly.

Traffic piled up in both directions, long lines of impatient drivers. The first thing was to make all lanes stop. I walked to the middle of the intersection and first made eye contact with the driver of a beige Ford. I pointed at him then held my palm flat in a stop gesture. He did. I rotated in a half-circle, stopping the other two lanes of traffic.

I let the cross traffic go first. Point, make eye contact, then move my hand in an arc. Nice definite signals with no room for error, sixty seconds each direction. I had a new respect for kindergarten teachers controlling unruly youngsters.

That's when I saw the red Porsche driver shifting through gears as he inched up the hill. Mirrored sunglasses, expensive driving gloves, staring straight ahead until he reached the front of the line. Without waiting for my signal he gunned it, squealing around the corner and up the hill. He swerved around a slow-moving Camry and fishtailed back into the lane. The sports car was pushing seventy when it vanished from view.

I strode to the side of the road and clicked my mic. "Shepherd, your guy just roared through here. Want to pursue him?"

"By the time I could get the squad car moving, the guy would be halfway to Prescott. Let him go." He sounded resigned.

That didn't sound like my partner. The legal department must have been talking to him again. Shepherd wanted to nail this guy, bad, but he also wanted to retire with a clean record. It seemed that he couldn't have both and the Porsche driver knew it.

Frustrated that the Porsche driver got away, I went back to directing traffic.

DOT got the light functional in about an hour and I hiked up the hill back to the station. But I couldn't let go of the image of that outlaw red Porsche. I understood Shepherd's anger because now I shared it.

Hot and sweaty, I barged through the front door and stripped off my reflective vest and gloves. "He's thumbing his nose at us!"

Shepherd held one hand level, pumping up and down. "Slow down, Peg. It'll all work out."

When? Impotence in twisted my stomach like a heavy metal blade.

***

At noon, I walked down to the apartment to let Reckless out. An immense crane blocked the parking area in front. A black wrecking ball hung ominously near my upstairs window.

The wrecking crew had arrived.

"Hey!" I shouted to the man in the cab. "What do you think you're doing? I *live* here."

"Not for long, lady. This structure is coming down." He sounded both gleeful and final.

I peered up at my apartment. The narrow building, constructed of timber, tilted forlornly down the hill. That didn't mean anything—the whole town continually shifted with the mining tunnels underneath. The structure could last another ten years. I'd be long gone by then.

The man called his supervisor on his cell phone. Some words were exchanged. Then the man climbed out of the cab and walked over to me. "You got the rest of today, lady. Tomorrow, at dawn, this building is history."

I climbed the stairs and opened the door to the apartment. Reckless bayed his joy at seeing me and dashed past to reach the side yard. What to do? How could I move in twelve hours?

I let Reckless back in and walked out on the balcony overlooking the main street into town. I'd spent many sleepless nights out here watching the moon rise over the Verde Valley, pondering work-related problems and personal issues. Now my refuge would be gone.

I'd delayed too long finding a new place to live. Reckless and I would be camping out under a bridge somewhere unless I came up with a plan. I considered the earlier offer from Rory, then shook my head. Too many complications there.

The house Bettina Swartz didn't like and I did, was a possibility, but not a done deal yet. That left my Plan B, or maybe it was Z at this point, my grandfather, HT. Bunking at his house wouldn't be a permanent situation, just until I could get the house deal worked out, I told myself.

Snapping a leash on Reckless, we hiked up the hill to HT's old house. I'd lived in the loft there once with Ben when I first came to town. I could stay there again. But I felt like a failure, moving back in with family because I had no other option.

HT was out in the garden watering Isabel's roses when I arrived to explain the situation. He responded without hesitation. "Can't say I'm sorry you have to move. I saw that left front corner sagging on that building. You're welcome here. Be good to have young blood around the house. You can borrow the old truck to move—that'll be handy for shifting boxes." He tossed me the keys.

I left the pup with HT and walked up to the sheriff's station to finish my shift and get some house-moving sympathy from Shepherd.

"Can't help you move, much as I'd like to," he said. "Stairs give me trouble with this old injury." He touched his calf.

Shepherd had caught his leg in a bear trap—the scar was ugly and a reminder of tough times.

"What about Ben? He's got young muscles."

Ben answered on the second ring and agreed to come over at the end of the workday. He said he'd bring his girlfriend—they both needed money. He even offered to drop by the Spirit Bar to pick up some empty packing boxes from his uncle.

The immediate crisis averted, I put my mind to business. I called Lucy Zielinski, Raven LightDancer's mother and alibi. She agreed to meet with me at her home, and I headed out her way.

***

When Rory had mentioned that the Zelinskis were Gypsies, I pictured English horse-drawn caravan wagons with a goat or two tied to the back.

Instead, the Zielinski house was a modest Spanish adobe, with braided strings of blood-red chili *ristas* hung on either side of a carved oak door. A Costas hummingbird buzzed a magenta butterfly bush at the corner of the house. Flat sandstone pieces served as a sidewalk, and a jar of sun tea gleamed in the afternoon sun.

I pulled a primitive string door knocker and a bell trilled in the room beyond. Lucy Zielinski opened the door. She was small-framed, with black, frizzy hair hanging almost to her waist.

She grasped my hand in both of hers. "Hello. I was expecting you. Come in."

My eyes adjusted to the dim cool of the adobe interior. The room had no harsh corners, as the plaster curved softly between the walls and the ceiling. Bright Mexican serapes covered the futon couch and two stretched-leather *epiquale* chairs sat in front of it.

A tabby cat squeezed between my legs and hopped up on the futon. She stretched out full length, blinking huge yellow eyes. That left the pig-leather chairs for Lucy and me. I sat in one, feeling the leather give and creak around me. The woman looked at me closely with dark eyes under thick brows.

"You want to know about my son Marty."

"He said that he was here with you the night that Gil Streicker died."

"All day, actually." Her answer came easily, almost rehearsed. "Marty came about ten that morning to help with the cooking and slept here that night. We drank, we ate, we danced. He didn't leave until noon the next day."

"Can anyone else corroborate this?"

"We had a gathering of the Family, twenty or thirty people. There are more Romani in Arizona than you would expect. Marty interacted with most of the people here."

She gave me a direct stare. "My son is many things, Ms. Quincy, but he is not a murderer."

If she were telling the truth, that would cross Raven LightDancer or Marty Zielinski, whatever he called himself, off my list of suspects. Part of me felt relief. In spite of his history, the man was a good cook. It would be a shame to waste that mango-salsa talent behind bars.

On the other hand, the Romani were a close-knit clan, not unlike my own extended family back in Tennessee. And families stick together.

"I'll need a list of contact numbers."

"That I can provide you, but it will take a while. Some people do not wish to speak to the law, you understand."

In a sudden movement, Lucy reached out her hands and captured my own. She turned them palm upward and studied each hand carefully. The jewels in her rings captured a shaft of sunlight from the window. She dropped the right hand, touched the left palm.

"Your dominant hand?"

I nodded.

"Tell me what you see," she commanded.

"Hands, fingers." I wasn't sure what she was getting at. I was surprised at the level of unease her cool touch produced in me.

"Ah, but look deeper. Things are not always as they seem. For example, this…" She touched the top line with a ring-encrusted finger. "See, there?"

Her fingernail flicked the palm, and I jerked reflexively.

"Your heart line is long, signifying satisfaction, but it is forked at the end."

"What's that mean?"

She smiled, her face lighting up. "A significant love relationship late in life, after you thought you were finished."

Great! I had to wait until I was fifty to find love?

She traced a second line. "Your head line traces almost to the end of the palm, meaning you use logical focused thinking. Am I right?"

Okay, she had me there.

"Most cops do," I said defensively. "Doesn't prove anything."

Her voice sharpened like a fine-edged blade. "I am not out to *prove* anything. I only reflect what I see."

She examined my palm again, her fingertip touching a third spot. "Here, your lifeline is long, signifying much creativity which you have not yet explored."

I'd never considered myself a painter if that's what she meant by creativity. But what about music? I'd always wanted to take up the drums. Or bagpipes, maybe. They'd sound cool echoing down the mountain from my new home if I could ever untangle the lien laws.

Lucy's words interrupted my daydreams as her hand tightened about my wrist. "But here, this fourth line is the most interesting of all. Not all people have this." Her voice purred.

I peered at where she was pointing—a deep line that cut across the other three.

"That is your life destiny line," she said, "your fate line. Yours represents a self-made person, not easily swayed by the winds of time. It is difficult for you to change, once you set on a course. You need to learn to be more flexible."

This lady got way too close to the truth with her statements. Was I that easy a cold read? I pulled my hand from her grasp. It burned and yet was numb. I shook it to regain feeling.

"You expected the tall, dark stranger? Maybe winning the lottery?" Her voice held derision. "Pah! Life success comes to those who work for it, as I have, as Marty has. Never forget that, Ms. Pegasus Quincy."

Lucy snatched up a shawl and covered her hair, leaving only her large, mysterious eyes and hoop earrings visible. "But I can also entertain. I am Roma. Call me, next party you have. And leave my Marty alone. He has nothing to do with this murder."

Lucy gave me one final word of advice. "Go see Dr. Theodore Riordan. He can give you the information you need." Holding her cat with one hand, she walked with me to my car and then returned to her house.

Although my purpose in coming was to clarify Raven's alibi, her reading of my palm intrigued me. It seemed so complex and yet so simple. Maybe there were things beyond my ken. I shook my head a little to clear the cobwebs.

I could just hear Shepherd's reaction to this: "You did *what?*"

But he'd not argue with one statement she made. Things are not always as they seem on the surface. Dr. Theo was on my list anyway. I called him and arranged a meeting for the next afternoon. I wanted to check out Fancy's insinuations about drug use.

***

I returned to my apartment and changed into civvies. With hands on my hips, I surveyed my meager belongings: Clothes, plus linens and dishes. Too many books. Dog food for Reckless.

I wondered what would happen to the stray cat I'd been feeding on the balcony. Would she find another soft touch? Maybe she'd find her way to HT's house—I'd heard feral cats had a wide territory. I hauled up the empty boxes Ben had left on the front doorstep and started packing.

Several hours later, he arrived. His noisy energy was a good antidote for the blue funk I'd settled into. He and the new girlfriend pounded up and down the stairs loading stuff in the pickup.

Ben paused at the sled. "What's this? You taking up a new sport?"

"Some stuff I'm holding for a friend. Take it, too."

Ben nodded and the sled and box of picture books disappeared down the steps with the rest of my stuff. The old pickup motor made an uneven put-put as they chugged up the hill to HT's house.

I was alone, except for dust mites filtering down through the high window. Tomorrow this apartment would not exist. I wondered if I even needed to return the key. What was the use of a key to a building that wasn't there? I tossed the key on the table and left.

I pulled in behind the old pickup with my Jetta and followed Ben up the stairs with the last load. Ben palmed the two twenties I offered with the dexterity of a headwaiter, and my movers were off with a roar of his Ducati.

As I entered the loft, the box of Gil Streicker's possessions slid out of my hands and collapsed in a cardboard-weakened heap on the floor. Picture books and Happy Meal toys scattered across the floor.

I was too tired to care. I shoved the plastic pieces and books to one side, grabbed a towel and change of clothes, and headed down the hall to the shower. I stood in the steam and washed the dust of moving out of my hair. Then I put on a clean pair of jeans and T-shirt and headed down to the kitchen, hungry.

HT's housekeeper Isabel arrived like a silent shadow, her graying hair in a thick braid down her back.

"Where's my grandfather?" I asked.

"Asleep." She crossed her arms over her skinny chest. "We need to talk."

I grabbed a plate of leftover fried chicken from the refrigerator and slammed the door with my hip. I carried the platter to the kitchen table, hooked my calf around the leg of a chair, and selected a drumstick.

"Talk." I took a bite.

"How long you going to be here?"

"What?"

"How much you pay your grandfather to stay? Food's extra."

I stared at her. Then, I pulled a paper napkin from the table holder and lowered the drumstick onto it.

"HT can't afford for you to stay here free. You and that big dog."

Who was this housekeeper, usurping the role of my grandmother, now long dead? I counterattacked. "What about you, Isabel? You pay rent to stay here, be HT's housekeeper?"

"I pay. You pay." Her tone was definite, each word set like a boulder in a frozen field.

I wiggled inside, uncomfortable. What did Robert Frost say about family, that the door was always open? This one seemed to be closing fast.

"I'll pay," I said. "Not going to be here long anyway."

She gave me another disapproving look and disappeared.

The taste of chicken caught in my throat. I tossed the drumstick in the trash and put the rest back in the refrigerator. I'd grab a bite at the Flatiron Café later.

I felt the empty space in my back pocket where I'd kept the twenties I paid Ben. Maybe I shouldn't have been so generous. It looked as though I might need the money to feed me and Reckless since I was expected to pay rent here.

I'd talk to HT, get something settled between us. No need for Isabel to be so snippy. *She* wasn't family.

I trudged upstairs, needing to establish my right to be here. First, I opened the small window to put more air into the low-ceilinged space. I've never liked tight places—maybe because of my height. Good thing I never wanted to be a cave dweller.

I shoved cartons into a rough line against the wall of the loft, sneezing at the dust that action kicked up. I bent to push the sled against the wall so I wouldn't stumble over it in the morning. When

I straightened to my full height, my head banged the ceiling. Damn! It felt more like a cave already.

I re-taped the box from Gil's storage shed and piled the plastic toys into it. I dumped in the last handful of picture books and shifted things around so that I could close the top again. Then I stopped.

In the physical shuffling of box contents, the pages of one of the books had crumpled. I pulled it out to smooth the pages and found two stuck together. Carefully I pried them apart, trying not to tear the pages. They had formed a rough pocket, and inside was a folded piece of paper. I pulled it out and smoothed it.

The paper looked like a diagram, a map of some sort. The rectangle was divided into six squares on one side, and six on the other with a narrow center bar dividing them. One of the twelve squares had an X drawn in it. I turned the paper one way and then the other.

If Gil Streicker had drawn it, this could be a diagram of the stable at the Spine Ranch! He wouldn't need a simple diagram like this. *Unless* he had a premonition that his own life was in danger. Was this a treasure map left for his little girl Veronica?

I checked my watch. Much as I liked skulking about in the dark, it was almost one in the morning. If Gil's map had waited this long, another five hours wouldn't matter. I'd drop by the Spine Ranch and talk to Amanda in the morning. No way was I convincing Black Onyx to move so I could examine his stall without her help.

181

CHAPTER TWENTY-FOUR

When I arrived at the ranch the next morning, the horses bunched under a large cottonwood in the pasture, their tails waving in a slight breeze. A ranch dog came barking to my Jetta, gave one more woof for good measure and retreated to the far yard.

I knocked on the front door and Fancy answered it.

"Hello?" Her mouth had a sullen downward twist.

"Is the family up yet?" I asked.

"Marguerite has a headache. Heinrich's asleep. You'll find Amanda in the barn."

Not waiting for my response, she shut the unwelcoming door in my face. The sound of her sensible shoes echoed for a moment behind it, and then she was gone.

To the barn, then. The earthy smell of manure drifted from the dimness where Amanda was mucking out the stalls. She had tucked her straight hair under a sweat-stained cowboy hat and wore rubber boots that came up to her knees. The stable was quiet, all the horses out in the pasture.

A large muck bin, bungeed to a hand truck, sat in front of one empty stall. I sneezed as hay from a forkful hit the bottom of the big plastic container. The girl was intent on her actions, unaware that I was there. She hummed in that off-key way people do when listening to music only they can hear.

I touched her shoulder. "Amanda, I need to talk to you."

She jerked, startled, and pulled out her earbuds.

"I didn't hear you come in." She leaned the pick-rake against the wall and stepped around the muck bucket.

"I'd shake hands, but..." She waved her gloved hands in the air.

I didn't argue with her. No telling what yucky stuff lived in that debris she was shoveling.

I pulled the diagram from my pocket. Amanda shucked the gloves and studied the diagram.

"The picture would fit. Five stalls on a side, plus the tack room and the office. This square with an X could be one of the middle stalls. You think something was hidden there? You can't hide a horse—they're too big." She chuckled at her own joke.

I hate it when people do that.

"The new barn was built on the foundation of the old one," I said. "Have you seen anything like a trapdoor in the floor?"

Amanda shook her head. "I was still recovering from the shock of Gil's death, so I wasn't paying attention. Raven was down here a lot. Maybe he saw something."

"And Raven is where this morning?"

"Visiting his mother."

That meant I couldn't talk to him this trip. My list of people to re-interview was getting smaller and smaller.

I returned to my original mission. "Any chance we could take a look at that stall, since you're cleaning them, anyway?"

Amanda looked doubtful.

"It's not that simple. We put down wood chips and sawdust we get from the Camp Verde sawmill. But under that is the rubber pad the horses stand on."

She raked back some chips and showed me a thick rubber mat that looked like the flooring in the gym I never attended.

I bought a membership when I first moved to the Verde Valley and had visited twice. Once to pick up the free towel they offered, and once on my way to get coffee when I stopped to pick up a schedule of classes—figured one of these days I'd try some TRX or maybe do some CrossFit stuff. One of these days.

"It would all have to come up." Amanda frowned.

Undeterred, I pursued my plan. "Can't we just rake all the stuffing out into the aisle? Then you can help me pull up the mat in the center stall."

Amanda was incensed. "Those chips are expensive! Who's going to pay for that?"

I could just see Shepherd's face when he saw a line item for horse litter in the investigation budget.

"Hey, it'll be fun. I'll help you put it back." I hoped I sounded convincing.

"Even if we do it, there's another problem."

"Which is?"

She grabbed the diagram and turned it one way. "Depending on which way you turn it, this could be this stall..." She reversed the paper. "Or this one." She gestured toward the stall on the other side of the aisle.

"So we try both. Which first?"

"Well, if it's a choice between Black Onyx and Panther Baby, you don't want to muck out Onyx's stall. He does his thing and then tap dances all over it, spreading the joy. Panther Baby is our neat horse. Let's start there."

She looked doubtfully at my shoes. "There's an extra pair of rubber boots in the tack room. Bring another muck rake, too."

I shook my head as I donned the boots. This had to fit under that category in my job description called "other duties as assigned." I deserved hazardous duty pay.

I was awkward with the rake and Amanda repositioned my hands.

"Keep your fork low and jiggle it a little. That'll let the chips sift out. And pick up that matted hay, too. It's been contaminated, stomped on."

"Here, watch me." She tossed the shavings and their contents up against the stall wall in an easy underhanded motion, so certain items rolled to the bottom of the hill of shavings. Then she scooped a forkful of the heavier stuff and heaved it into the bungeed container.

I tried again, but in Amanda's judgment, I gathered too much bedding with my pitchfork full.

"Haven't you been around horses before? This isn't hard. Just concentrate."

Finally, she admitted defeat and handed me a water bucket to clean instead. "Scrub brush is in the tack room, water faucet outside.

Think you can handle that?"

Whew! The bucket smelled like an algae-slimed fish tank. I took the handle gingerly in my fingers and walked toward the tack room to dump it in the sink.

Then I took the bucket and the scrub brush into the sunshine and scrubbed at the bits of hay and clumps of grain. I rinsed the bucket, refilled it, and lugged it back to Amanda. She took it without comment and hung it on the stall hook.

Amanda was fast. The muck bin was soon full. She rolled the hand truck to the outside to where a dumpster stood. Together we grabbed the rope handles of the container and heaved the muck into the dumpster.

"Gil used to move this dumpster with the forklift when it got full. Now I don't know who will do it. I know horses, but equipment?" Amanda had tears in her eyes, and they weren't from the acrid ammonia smell that clung to the container.

She returned to the barn and I followed. She picked up a broom and swept the remaining wood chips into the aisle, leaving the black flooring mat. If what we searched for wasn't here, that meant tackling Black Onyx's stall across the aisle. No telling what we'd find over there. I kept my fingers crossed.

Together we heaved the horse mat to a vertical position and peered at the cement flooring underneath. In the center of the floor was a flanged metal door, about two by three feet. Together we opened the door and laid it flat on the cement. I peered into the blackness.

A large metal safe box filled the cavity. Together we hauled it out. A metal padlock dangled from the latch. I pulled out the key I'd gotten in Gil Streicker's safe deposit box. It fit smoothly into the lock and I clicked it open.

I gestured to Amanda. "You want to do the honors?"

She raised the lid with hesitant fingers. A torn corner of a hundred dollar bill and two paper currency bind strips lay on the bottom of the box. That was all.

"There was money here?" Amanda asked.

"*Lots* of money it looks like. Our suspicion is that Gil might have been a drug dealer or possibly a blackmailer."

"That's ridiculous." Amanda's face reddened and she clenched her fists.

"If Gil had lots of money, he wouldn't *need* to deal in drugs. He's not the type, anyway." She dismissed my assertions with a weird sort of logic.

"Whatever." Nothing would shake her faith in the dead man, even though the key from Gil's safe deposit box fit the padlock. But the next question was, however he had acquired it, if this had been Gil Streicker's stash, who had the money now?

Amanda and I replaced the empty cash box in the hole and closed the metal door covering. Together we heaved the rubber mat back over the hole. Amanda raked chips back into the stall with jerky, vigorous actions, and I returned to the tack room.

I hung my rake on the wall and deposited two smelly rubber boots under it. A farmer smell hung to the air, speaking of old barns and satisfied livestock with clean stalls.

I said goodbye to Amanda. Next on my agenda was Dr. Theo, Marguerite's estranged husband. I wondered if the good doctor would mind my stench and didn't much care. If he had murdered Gil Streicker, he deserved no better.

Nevertheless, I opened the windows to air out the car. No need to breathe in the aroma myself.

CHAPTER TWENTY-FIVE

The afternoon steamed with humidity, and the thunderheads were already building when I drove over the bridge at Red Tank Draw on my way to Dr. Theo's trailer.

Little over twenty-four hours after the flash flood, the waters had receded. Now only muddy red banks and braids of tire tracks marked where the torrent of water roared through.

I slowed as I crossed the bridge. At a far bend of the wash, the silhouette of the blue Toyota rose from a swale of mud. They'd bring a crane down to extract it soon. The car was totaled, but at least the passengers survived. I wondered if the little girl would remember this experience in her young life. Long enough to hesitate at water running over a road, I hoped, when she was old enough to drive.

When I reached Dr. Theo's trailer, I yanked the parking brake on the Jetta and opened the door. The creek level was back to normal, the stream clear again. A Costa's hummingbird swooped over the water to catch a gnat, its violet throat flashing in the sun. The cicadas' racket lent counterpoint to the water's run.

Dr. Theo was creek side, a bamboo pole in his hand, a red-and-white plastic bobber bouncing in the current. He waved.

"They biting?" I asked.

He laughed. "Not with this fishing get-up. The guys at the sporting goods shop said I'd need a fly rod to catch the rainbows, but this is how I learned to fish. I'll stick with my own way."

He pulled the bobber from the creek and wrapped the line

around the pole. Then he stuck the end in the soft mud and walked over to me. "What can I do for you, Miss Peg?"

"Got some more questions, Dr. Theo."

"Sure, no problem. Calls for some iced tea, do you think? Wait here."

In a few moments, he emerged from his trailer, bearing two frosted glasses of tea.

"Let's sit in the chairs under the sycamore. Love those big green leaves in summer."

Dr. Theo kicked off his sandals and wriggled his toes in the rain-freshened meadow grass.

I hated to break into his peaceful mood, but no way to come at it except directly. "Someone at the ranch says you're addicted to oxycodone," I said.

"Figured that would come out, sooner or later." He pulled a brown plastic prescription bottle from his shirt pocket.

"Every morning I wake up and wish this pill bottle was filled to the top. I'd take every last pill."

He shook it like a reformed cigarette smoker with an empty pack. No rattle.

The closest I'd come to addiction was biting my fingernails. I did that until I was twelve, then quit. And I still go back to it when I get under stress. But drugs? Never took that route. My mother called me a strange duck. Called me worse when I refused to buy her the booze that supported her own lifestyle.

"What do you know about oxycodone addiction?" Dr. Theo asked.

"Enlighten me."

"Believe it or not, back in my day I was quite a skier. One winter I had a bad fall and self-prescribed the Oxy to cut the pain. It felt so good I kept writing scripts for more. Someone reported me to the Medical Board and they put me on suspension. I lost the practice, all of our savings, too. We had to start over out here." Tears started at the corners of his eyes.

"I can't blame Marguerite for deciding to leave me. I've done terrible things in support of that habit." He stopped speaking, his face in a twisted expression.

He set the tea glass down with a jolt and some of the liquid spilled on the table. He scooped the liquid off with an abrupt gesture.

"Oh, you can have me tested. I'm clean—haven't used for over a year." His voice held both regret and pride.

"Did Gil Streicker ever mention drugs?" I asked.

He nodded. "Maybe a dealer can sense a victim, a potential user. He came to me once, offered to set me up if I was interested. *Sure* I was interested—not a day goes by I don't crave the stuff. But pay for it with what?"

It answered one question for me but raised another. I chose my words carefully. "Where were you the night Gil Streicker died?"

He hesitated, then said, "Right here, where I am every night."

"Anybody can verify that?"

"I was alone, as I am most nights." His eyes blinked rapidly.

Was this also a lie? I pushed a little. "Think back. Are you *sure* you weren't at the ranch, maybe for a few moments that night? Someone I talked to…"

I let my voice drift off, hoping he'd pick up the narrative. He did, but not in the way I had expected.

"No, no one could have seen me because…"

"Because what?" My voice hardened. "Dr. Theo, where were you the night that Gil Streicker died?"

"I *knew* somebody would find out, sooner or later." He wiped sweat from his forehead with one big hand and huffed a breath.

"Okay, here's what happened, God's truth. Fancy Morgan told me how Gil had treated Marguerite and how he was after Amanda, too. I couldn't let that happen. I had to *do* something."

"Yeah?"

"Gil had to be stopped. I called him and told him I'd changed my mind, wanted to buy some drugs after all. I asked him to meet me at the barn."

"That's when you killed him!"

Dr. Theo shook his head. "I just wanted to talk some sense into Streicker, tell him to stay away from my family. But he was already dead when I got to the barn."

"Are you sure?"

He snorted. "I'm a doctor. I can tell if a man is dead or not."

"What happened then?"

"I panicked. I thought if somebody saw me, I'd be blamed for the man's murder. To make it seem like an accident, I nicked the wires, got a spark, and added some hay. It wasn't hard."

"But the horses?"

"It was a warm summer night. Most were out in the pasture. I opened the stall doors for the others. And then I ran. I'm a coward, Peg. Always have been."

He wouldn't meet my eyes. "Marguerite was right to leave me. I'm a loser. She deserves better."

"What'd you use to cut the wire at the barn?"

"Scalpel."

"You still have it?"

Dr. Theo nodded and pulled a slim metal instrument in a leather sleeve out of his pants pocket. He offered it to me.

"Can I get it back? Means a lot to me, reminds me of better days."

"It's *evidence* right now." I stuck it in my pocket for safekeeping. "Burning the barn was a stupid thing to do. You could be charged with obstructing justice or insurance fraud. And that's just for starters."

"I'm sorry, I just didn't think."

"Do you know that because of your actions, you could be charged with Gil Streicker's *murder*?"

Dr. Theo put his head in his hands and cried with harsh, racking sobs.

I ignored his reactions and went for the information I needed. "Tell me the rest. What else happened?"

"The ranch was quiet. Amanda and Marguerite had gone to the movies in town. They asked me to come along. Now I wish I had." He clenched one fist and pounded it into his other palm.

I sensed both truth and falsehood in his statement. "You see anyone else there when you set fire to the barn?"

"No!"

His curt denial was strong, perhaps too emphatic. Who was Dr. Theo protecting? Was it Amanda? Or Marguerite?

"Wait," he said slowly, "there *was* someone…"

"What'd they look like?"

"Couldn't tell. They ran behind the barn as I got close. I just caught a glimpse."

He had replaced his vehement denial with a deliberately vague statement. That was convenient.

"Male or female?"

"It was too dark to tell."

I had the sense Dr. Theo was about to shut down on me, that I'd get no more today. But it was a start.

"You stay close," I ordered. "We'll need to talk to you again."

He shrugged. "Where else would I go? Everything precious to me is right here in the Verde Valley."

On the way back to my office, I thought about what Dr. Theo had said, and what he had not said. Did he speak the truth about Gil being dead when he got there? Or had he set a fire to finish killing a man who was still alive?

And more importantly, did I have enough to charge him? Not yet, but he knew more than he was telling. I'd be back.

When I returned to the station, I told Shepherd about Dr. Theo's confession.

"You think he did it?" I asked.

"Too soon to tell. Send the scalpel to forensics for evaluation and let's keep digging. We'll either get enough to bring him in, or find out who he saw out there. We're getting close."

CHAPTER TWENTY-SIX

The next morning, Shepherd called the Spine Ranch and set up a meeting with Heinrich Spine. My partner suggested I ride along and interview Ray Morales at the same time. That suited me. Much as I tried to keep an open mind, I liked Ray. I'd just as soon cross him off the suspect list.

Our police SUV was in for service, so we drove my Jetta to the sheriff's department carpool in Camp Verde to pick up a patrol car.

The head mechanic met us at the door. "Sorry. Everything is out. You shoulda come by earlier this morning."

Shepherd waited, silently staring at the man. Shepherd was good at these mind games.

The mechanic fidgeted. Finally, "You going to be gone long?"

Shepherd shook his head back and forth. Just once, like checking for traffic. Said nothing.

"Okay, I shouldn't do this, but seeing as how it's you, Shepherd...the sheriff's new car arrived this morning. Just finished checking it out. Sweet honey of a drive. I can let you have it for a coupla hours, but you gotta return it by shift's end. If it's not here when the sheriff comes back from Phoenix tomorrow, my job is on the line."

We walked to the end of the garage lot, and Shepherd tossed the keys to me. "Time you got in some road work."

The patrol car was a big-boned Crown Vic. It had a souped-up engine geared for high speeds, an alternator that cranked out 130 amps to handle the lights and siren, and the latest of techno gear. Eighty-nine total miles on the odometer instead of the two-hundred-thousand on my twelve-year-old Jetta. I breathed in the new-car smell as I settled on the leather seat.

The engine purred as I backed the car out of the garage, the sunlight glinting off the newly polished windshield. We headed down the access road and stopped at the intersection leading to Highway-260.

We still had an hour or two before our appointment at the Spine Ranch. "Which way?" I asked.

"Ladies' choice."

Shepherd liked to brag he knew every pothole and broken curb in his district. A good cop did that, drove the same roads hundreds of times, alert and watching for nuances that made the difference at high speeds.

I was technically a rookie with less than a year under my belt. Maybe it was time to start building that fundamental knowledge that I couldn't find in any textbook.

I considered my options. Left would take us back toward Cottonwood on a sometimes-divided road with a staid 55 mile per hour speed limit. There was always the potential for picking up a few traffic tickets, because most drivers exceeded that low driving speed.

Right led to Interstate-17 and from there another cross-road decision point: north or south. South led to Copper Canyon, a ten-mile stretch filled with curves and steep uphill climbs. They'd just opened a new lane for slow-moving trucks—been working on it for a year now, moved tons of rock.

On the other hand, if I turned north at I-17, I'd enter a straight stretch of four-lane road running across the valley before heading up the hill to Flagstaff.

When we reached the Interstate, I headed north. Traffic was light, unlike the weekends when lanes would clog with vacationers from Phoenix and locals anxious to get home to a cold beer and a lazy sprawl in front of the TV.

I goosed the engine a little and the speedometer jumped to 85. They'd resurfaced this section of road in anticipation of the bad weather to come, and tracking remained steady. The road curved out in front of us like a river to nowhere. I tapped the accelerator, and the car accelerated to 97 easily. Still a lot of room under the pedal.

"Sweet." Shepherd leaned back, stretched out his long legs. "Let her out, see what she can do."

I rose to the invitation like a shark smelling blood in shallow waters. The car leaped ahead, hitting 110. The mesquite and chaparral on the hillsides smeared into a gray-green blur. How fast would this baby go? I increased the pressure on my foot and the needle nosed over to 125. Still steady.

My vision narrowed, encompassing only the road before me, black and smooth. Signposts zipped by, and my heart pounded. My lips lifted in a silly grin, and I smashed the pedal to the floor. The speedometer hit 140 and hung there for a moment, the needle jittering. Could I get more?

Shepherd reached over and hit the lights and siren, and the pulsating lights and noise entered my brain, rattling back and forth. I couldn't breathe. I didn't *need* to breathe.

150…Time slowed. I was all-powerful, invincible.

I barely heard Shepherd's growly voice beside me.

"Ease her off a little," he said. "Getting light in the rear end. Feel the suspension float?"

I felt disappointment in my heart. Too soon. This car was flying, and I wanted to fly with her.

"Slow down!" Shepherd's flat tone of command broke through my road haze.

Reluctantly I raised my toe. The car bucked, crossing the heat grooves that the semis had worn into the roadbed, gearing down for the higher elevations ahead.

The car moaned in frustration as I pulled it down to highway speed. I signaled for the exit to Oak Creek Canyon.

I gulped, filling air-starved lungs, as I halted at the underpass stop sign.

Colors swirled around me like a rainbow on steroids. Every nerve crackled with the need to challenge the universe. I wanted to do it again! To take that mother of roller coasters by the throat and ride forever.

Shepherd grunted and motioned for me to make a U-turn under the freeway and stop when I reached the freeway access road facing south once more. I crossed under and stopped the car as he had directed.

I'd trained on the police academy driving course with helmets and yellow foam neck guards, but this was the *real thing*. I turned to Shepherd with a wide grin, expecting him to share my excitement.

His returning expression was pensive. "What do you feel?"

Why'd he ask that? I felt everything. I was a god!

"Describe that car parked in front of us," he directed.

"A gray—no, beige—Honda. Two—no, three passengers."

It was hard to concentrate. My sweaty hands clenched the steering wheel and thigh muscles cramped against the fabric of my uniform. I started to shake, just a little.

"Take your pulse."

I put my fingers on my wrist, started counting, one-two...my heart pounded out of my chest...seventeen, eighteen. I lost count, had to start again. "One twenty."

My pulse should be half that. What the hell was going on?

"Breathe," Shepherd said.

Irritated, I slowed the air rushing in and out of my nostrils. The world stopped whipping around me in a dizzy spin.

"Welcome to a Cop High," Shepherd said. "Nothing like it, especially the first time." He smiled as though remembering. "When you're in that zone, it can seem like you've got total focus, total concentration. But don't be misled. Mistakes get made there, big ones. Cops who lead with their emotions get killed."

I swallowed once, hard, and tucked his words away for future reflection.

Shepherd unbuckled his seat belt and opened the door. "Time for me to take a turn. Let's go write some tickets."

***

Later that afternoon Shepherd and I headed over to the Spine Ranch. Shepherd planned to interview Heinrich Spine, and I was going to recheck Ray Morales's alibi.

As we passed through Camp Verde, I asked Shepherd to stop at the post office so I could pick up some stamps. I'd tried calling my mother back in Tennessee, but in her dementia, she didn't seem to remember. Letters were something tangible to hold on to, a reminder that she still had a daughter. At least I hoped that was how it worked.

There was a demonstration going on in the parking lot, half a dozen people waving signs and walking around. One young man with a clipboard accosted me as I walked out of the building with my stamps. "Want to sign our petition?"

I looked over at his paper with interest. As a newly registered voter, now an official resident of Arizona, I could sign. But then I'm always a sucker for public action. I'm the one that buys the tickets for the local 4-H group fair and the boxes of Girl Scout cookies in front of Safeway. How can you resist those thin mints?

This petition was a recall for one of the county commissioners. "What'd he do?" I asked.

The young man was indignant. "He voted to approve Prescott's steal of the Verde River water."

Now I understood. It was a hot topic here in the Verde Valley. The headwaters of the Verde River began with a series of springs on the rim of the valley. Prescott, located on that same high plateau, was rapidly outstripping its own water supply and was buying up land that had more. If they succeeded in buying the land that held the springs, they'd have more water, but Verde River that flowed through this valley would dry up.

I tried to imagine our green valley without water and couldn't. As I scribbled my name at the bottom of the list of signatures, I thought about the recent cloudburst in Red Tank Draw and the fight Serena and Heinrich were locked into. Water—too much or too little—was the perennial problem of our high desert.

"What was that all about?" Shepherd asked as I got back in the car.

"Water. You want to sign the petition?"

"Already did. They got me in Mingus."

I didn't have to ask which side of the controversy Shepherd was on. We were all in the same boat on this one.

The Spine Ranch was next. Soon we passed under the hanging sign for the ranch. With one skillful twist of the wheel, Shepherd parked the vehicle inches from the barn. Clouds of dust billowed over us as he jerked on the parking brake. The man could drive. But that also meant we'd need to sluice off the dust before we returned the sheriff's new patrol car to the garage.

Shepherd walked toward the main house to meet with Dr. Spine, and I headed toward the barn. There I found Ray Morales sitting on an overturned five-gallon bucket. Pieces of black leather bridle harness covered a white sheet spread on the cement floor.

"What're you doing?" I asked.

"Getting the horse barn ready for Heinrich. He's got business people coming in to look at the ranch. Onyx always draws a crowd and I want him to look pretty."

What business people? Was Dr. Spine considering a sale of the property? He'd mentioned the Nature Conservancy—Was this yet another change of plans?

"Come sit a spell," Ray invited, as he dissembled a bridle and carefully examined the metal fittings for wear. He unbuckled the straps and tugged carefully on each one. Then examined the stitching on each side. He looked at me from under the brim of his green John Deere cap.

"Do this on a regular basis," he said, "and a broken bridle won't surprise you when you're at a full gallop."

My only experience with horses had been riding once or twice at the local stable back in Tennessee. There, the groom held the horse steady while I stepped onto the mounting block and climbed on for an hour's ride. This up-close-and-personal view was new to me.

Ray must have sensed my inexperience. "Ever polished your shoes?"

I nodded. What rookie cop hadn't spent the night before inspection putting a high shine on those black brogans?

"This is the same thing." He pointed to the dissembled leather pieces spread out on the sheet. "Pick one. I've cleaned them already with saddle soap. Be careful not to get polish on the horse side of the straps."

He handed me a small dish of water and a twist can of black Kiwi shoe polish.

I picked up a strap of leather, supple after Ray's ministrations. I dabbed the polish on a rag and rubbed it on the strap. "Why no polish on the inside?"

"Not so bad on our black horses, but get that dark polish smeared on a light-colored horse and you'll not forget. Anyway, it

197

irritates their skin, sometimes."

It was an unusual position for a interview, sitting here on an overturned bucket, but I figured I'd go for it. I cleared my throat. "Ray, they've declared Gil's death suspicious, so I'm checking with everyone. Where were you the night he died?"

Ray pulled the bridle bit out of a pail where it had been soaking. He flicked off a bit of encrusted matter and examined the metal. Then he gave me a keen stare. "At home. In bed with my wife. That's Rosa, works for Heinrich Spine. You might have met her?"

My mind flashed to the middle-aged woman who had comforted Amanda. "You live here at the ranch?"

"In that small casita over there." He gestured vaguely.

"Hear anything unusual the night the stable burned?"

He shook his head. "We'd been having a party for her niece, so maybe a bit too much to drink. Alana's going back home to Mexico." There was hesitancy in his soft voice.

I remembered Shepherd's comments. "She's an illegal alien?"

Ray rubbed harder on the metal. "Alana's a *person*, not a bug-eyed monster from Mars or something."

I raised my hands in surrender. "Hey, I'm not an immigration officer. Just asking."

He sighed. "She's going back to Hermosillo for her mother's funeral. We all chipped in for her trip. She's crossed the border to the States twice before, but I worry about her returning. My wife says it isn't safe for any of us. She wants me to liquidate our possessions and move to the high plateau of Mexico, the Mesa del Norte, where we're from."

"Will you?"

"When it next comes time to renew my visa? Maybe so. I've lived in Arizona all my life, but there are times when I don't feel welcome. I worry that your patrol officers might stop me. That's not right, to think somebody's a criminal because of how they look."

Racial profiling. It was awkward talking to somebody on the other side of that line who had experienced the bias. And it brought another fact into play. Ray Morales lived in Arizona legally but his niece did not. Would that fact be grounds for blackmail? Somehow I didn't see this soft-spoken man as a killer. But even if he was innocent, he might know someone who was not.

"Who might have wanted to harm Gil?" I asked. Always good to get another perspective. Triangulation, Shepherd called it.

"Streicker was good with horses. And women liked him."

"Any of the ladies here likely suspects?"

"Amanda? No." He thought for a moment. "Her mother? Not so sure. That woman is too stressed out. She needs to calm down, my Rosa says."

"What about Raven LightDancer? I hear he's the drug-connection here on the ranch." I picked up another piece of leather and applied more polish.

"Who told you that—Amanda? *Gil* was the dealer on the ranch, not Raven. Streicker sold the workers that poison and then there was no money to feed their families. I argued with him about it. He refused to listen."

"Argued, how?"

Ray chuckled. "I know where you're going. Not like that. I didn't hurt the man."

He finished buckling the bridle throat piece and hung the harness on a nearby hook to dry. "Can't let leather stay wet. It'll mildew and be ruined. You have to take care of precious things."

I wondered if he was referring to the leather in front of him or to other important items—like his job at the ranch, or protecting one of his extended family. I sighed. Ray wasn't off the suspect list, not by a long shot.

"Good to talk to you, Officer Quincy." He stood and held out a hand. "Stay out of cow pastures, now." He winked.

Would that escapade continue to haunt me? Not exactly what I wanted to be known for. I gave the fenced area a cautionary look as I returned to the squad car, but the Brahma bull who had given me chase was somewhere else tending to cattle business. Good thing. I might have challenged him for best two out of three.

Shepherd was already in the squad car, the engine idling. His fingers tapped the dash as I opened the door to a blast of air-conditioning.

"Saw you in there with Ray. What'd he have to say?" he asked.

I told him about Gil being the ranch supplier of drugs, not Raven LightDancer.

"Not surprised," Shepherd grunted. "Although Raven has his

own share of law-breaking activities."

"Ray's niece is going back to Mexico," I said, mentioning Ray's concerns. "You ever pull anyone over because of appearance?"

"Once or twice, when they fit the description."

I pushed a little. "And your view of our neighbors to the south?"

Shepherd shifted uneasily in the seat as he pulled onto the paved road leading back to the highway. "Two sides to every story. A friend of mine has a ranch south of Tucson. Says he spends days repairing that border fence, rounding up loose cattle. The *coyotes*, those guides, rip holes in it to get their 'clients' through and leave trash littering the place."

For Shepherd, the law was black or white, no room for question. Maybe seeing the human side of things was my weakness as a family liaison officer.

"What'd you find up at the Big House?" I asked.

Shepherd seemed relieved to leave a sensitive topic. "Well, Heinrich confirmed that since Gil's no longer in the picture, he may revise his will. Says he'll cut out the Nature Conservancy; give the ranch to Marguerite and her family after all. He uses that document like a goddam ping-pong ball to keep his heirs in line. What makes a man do something like that?"

I didn't have an answer. Gil Streicker had wanted that power himself, and that desire got him killed.

CHAPTER TWENTY-SEVEN

After lunch, we switched drivers. Shepherd was quiet, not talking much. He'd direct me to pull over one vehicle, then ignore the next. We wrote a few warning citations, and the quiet afternoon dragged on.

I was about to suggest we head back to the office when a car entered the freeway at the Middle Verde entrance. Gunned it up to speed in sixty seconds. A red car. A red Porsche.

"Got him," Shepherd said with satisfaction.

I eased into traffic and stayed two cars back of the Porsche. The traffic automatically slowed, as drivers became aware of our presence.

Shepherd watched our speedometer carefully, until I reached one mile over the speed limit. "Hold it there," he ordered.

It only took a few minutes before the Porsche impatiently pulled away from the line of cars.

"Now," Shepherd said.

I eased out of the traffic and clicked on the light bar. I blipped the siren when I was directly behind the Porsche.

The driver's head jerked up at the noise, and he looked in his rearview mirror. His hand hit the steering wheel in frustration. His turn signal blinked right and he slowed to the side of the road. We pulled to a stop behind him.

"Call in the plate," Shepherd said.

I did. It was Shepherd's nemesis, all right. But no wants, no warrants. His attorney must have been busy clearing all those old tickets. We sat there for a minute.

"You or me?" I asked.

Without responding, Shepherd opened his door and stood there for a moment. Then he straightened his shoulders and walked purposefully toward the sports car. I remained in the idling patrol car on high alert.

The Porsche driver rolled down his window, and there was a conversation between him and Shepherd. The driver reached into his glove box for his registration. I thought that it would be it, a routine rolling violation, just like he had gotten in the past. The ticket would reside in the glove box with the others his attorney eventually paid.

There was a roar in front of me. Shepherd jumped back and the Porsche accelerated onto the road, back-end fishtailing. A hand poked out the window and raised with a one-fingered salute. Shepherd ran back to the patrol car. I was rolling, before he slammed the door, before he even buckled up.

"I'll handle communications, Peg. You concentrate on stopping that son of a bitch."

We roared past the RV trailer park and pecan orchards on I-17. The patrol car humped a little on the bridge sections as we crossed the Verde River hurtling toward Copper Canyon. The squad car's speed hit a hundred when we passed under the Camp Verde overpass, but the Porsche still accelerated away.

Time slowed, but my focus was ice cold. This was no practice run. Our own lives, and others, depended on how well I drove.

"All units. In pursuit of a red Porsche going south on I-17, passing Camp Verde exit. Suspect drugs involved." Shepherd's voice was matter of fact as he broadcast our position.

The Porsche roared up the hill, sped by a white Cadillac and a pickup towing a horse trailer. A moment later we did the same.

The traffic grew heavier, as cars slowed for the grade. Copper Canyon loomed before us, that ten-mile length of straight up that the semi-drivers hated. Sometimes there'd be a conga line of five or six trucks struggling to maintain speed.

We flew past the slower traffic, siren blaring. Once, I had to slow once for some idiot on a cell phone who wouldn't pull over. I changed the siren tone to a warble, stayed a foot off his bumper. He looked back with a startled glance and quickly jerked to the right.

The delay cost precious seconds, and the Porsche edged ahead. Were we going to lose him? Then one semi ahead of us pulled out to pass another, creating a rolling roadblock. Traffic slowed to a 40 mph crawl waiting for the truck to gain momentum to pass completely. I pulled directly behind the Porsche, following slowly off his vehicle frame.

We had him!

The Porsche swerved into the breakdown lane, and passed the trucks on the *right*, two tires canted off the pavement. With a quick jerk of the wheel, I followed, concentrating on nothing but the vehicle in front of me.

The patrol car danced through the narrow opening between the semis and the rock wall, kicking up a rock that clunked against the oil pan. Brush scraped against the side of the car, the metal shrieking in protest.

"Easy, Peg," Shepherd cautioned.

Adrenaline flooded my system as the squad car bounded back into the paved lane ahead of the trucks. The traffic thinned, stopping to the side of the road. We gained on the Porsche.

"Good time to do a PIT maneuver," Shepherd said.

A PIT, the Pursuit Intervention Technique whereby the pursued car was deliberately put into a spin. I swung left and pulled parallel to the Porsche, matching its speed. Inside the car, the man clenched the wheel with driving gloves, his red face determined. Then that vision faded. I pulled back until my right front tire was positioned behind the driver's side rear tire.

The low-centered Porsche would be a challenge to spin. I'd have one chance, no time for hesitation. I took a breath, then yanked the patrol car sharply right, slewing into the Porsche, pushing it into a spin. I hit the brakes. The car in front of us spun in a half-circle skid, coming to rest at the side of the road, facing us.

"He's a good driver," Shepherd admitted reluctantly. "Came out of that spin like a pro."

The two cars faced nose to nose. My breathing slowed as I waited. I started to click off my seat belt to apprehend the man.

Shepherd touched my arm. "Wait." He rolled down the window and directed our public address system at the car facing us.

"Out of the car and on the ground. Now!"

The man stuck his head out the window and screamed curses at us.

Then he backed up twenty yards, spewing gravel. He slammed the Porsche into first and zoomed past us. He ricocheted off my driver's side fender and sped down the hill.

I swung the patrol car in a tight U-turn to pursue him. Both of us now drove the wrong way on the divided freeway lane, speeding rapidly downhill.

Oncoming traffic swerved desperately toward the side of the road, but one big RV, determined to keep speed, plowed forward, passing the line of cars that had stopped. The Porsche driver did not deviate, but drove straight toward the bulky vehicle in a weird game of chicken. I caught my breath. Was he going to deliberately ram the vehicle, making it a suicide by auto?

At the last moment, the Porsche driver swerved sharply right onto a crossover lane toward the other section of the freeway. I followed, skidding a bit as I reentered the downhill lane toward Camp Verde, ramming back up to speed.

A runaway truck lane appeared between the divided lanes of the freeway, an uphill grade of choppy road designed to halt semi-trucks whose brakes had failed. I maneuvered to the right of the Porsche, hoping to nudge the car into its snare of deep gravel. Instead, the driver hit a burst of speed and zipped past it.

The Porsche roared past the General Crook exit and accelerated once again. I matched him, the squad car cruising at an easy hundred-ten. The Camp Verde overpass loomed ahead. Its freeway exit ramp sloped upwards to meet the Highway-260 cross-traffic.

There, a stream of traffic halted at the red-lighted intersection, while straight ahead of us on the freeway flashing red and blue lights stretched across the road, signaling a blockade was in place.

The driver faced a decision point. He'd slow to take Camp Verde exit. Or he'd try to ram the blockade. My bet was on the exit.

Shepherd had the same thought. He thumbed the mic. "Magnum spikes requested, northbound Camp Verde exit."

The Porsche driver veered onto the exit. He downshifted as he neared the traffic congestion, his gears screaming and tires smoking. A patrolman darted into traffic and with an underhanded toss, slung the spike strips in front of the Porsche.

The car swerved left and I thought he'd miss the spikes. Then there was a muffled thump and the car jerked. Another strip was tossed in front of the slowing car.

"That'll stop him," I said.

"Maybe not."

Crippled as the car was, the man still pushed forward, passing on the outside of the stalled traffic. He ran on flats, then on rims alone. Sparks shot from all four rims.

From the left, traffic from Highway-260 was still moving over the freeway, with exit traffic stopped perpendicular at the red light.

Porsche man's vision was blocked. He couldn't see what was coming as he crept past the stopped traffic on the far side of the exit road.

But the situation was sickeningly clear to me.

A construction rig passed over the freeway, its semi bed heavy with a full load of concrete highway dividers. Rather than slowing, the truck accelerated through the cross-street green light. Perhaps he hoped to make it through before the light changed.

Normally we gave such vehicles a pass because it was almost impossible for the awkward trucks to brake with the immense weight of the cement load behind them.

For a moment, I thought the Porsche would make it through the intersection ahead of the truck. But he'd taken one too many chances. The truck plowed into the side of the car, spinning the Porsche around. The car paralleled close to the truck and stalled.

The truck driver slammed on panicked brakes. Slowly the truck tilted as the weight of the cement dividers shifted. Chains holding the load exploded apart. Then the full weight of its cargo slid down on the Porsche with a muffled thump.

The Porsche exploded in flames, and a fireball seared the skies.

The truck driver pulled himself through the passenger side door of the truck and rolled away from the crash. Bystanders pulled him to safety as the truck engine caught fire, its pyre of flames adding to the chaos.

Fire engine sirens screamed. The emergency crews reached the intersection and unloaded hoses. Streams of water sizzled and exploded as they hit the twisted metal, sending black clouds of oily smoke roiling upward. In spite of their efforts, the car's driver never had a chance, trapped by the cement dividers.

I sat in the front seat of the patrol car, numb and shaking. "Why didn't he stop, Shepherd? Why didn't he just *stop*?" Tears blurred my eyes.

"High on something. Panicked. It happens." Shepherd shook his head. "You did what you had to do, Peg."

We opened the doors and got out. My legs were wobbly and I leaned against the side of the Sheriff's new car for a moment. I wiped at a smear of red paint on the crushed fender.

We joined a knot of patrol officers by the side of the road.

One touched my shoulder. "Nice job. Textbook pursuit."

Another patrolman shook Shepherd's hand. "Got the bastard. You going to let Serena know?"

"Serena?" I asked, not comprehending.

"Serena Battle." The cop gestured toward the wreckage. "That's the guy what turned her brother into a vegetable."

CHAPTER TWENTY-EIGHT

The next morning I woke before dawn with a Charley horse in my calf. I jumped out of bed, hopping in agony until the cramp released. Did I need more magnesium in my diet? With a jolt, the day before came back to me. I was flooded with the memory of the car chase and the shock of the man's death.

When the throbbing subsided in my screaming muscles, I went for a run with Reckless up in the hills above Mingus. The dog bayed his pleasure at the morning, running ahead a quarter mile, then circling back to check on me. I ran harder, hoping to dispel the images flashing through my mind. Added was the guilt that I'd somehow been responsible for the accident.

At the top of the mining pit, I took a breather and looked down over the valley and across the next ridge. At this elevation, the mountain rocks were cool to the touch, but by mid-day, they'd be hot enough to scorch my fingers. The red rocks of Sedona gleamed in the rising sun across the valley, and the San Francisco Peaks, still snow-capped, edged the horizon line.

I didn't know if I was more upset with Shepherd for his obsession with the Porsche driver or with me for my part in the pursuit that led to the man's death. Either way, there was no going back, only forward.

The pup and I made a big loop past Gold King Mine and the Audrey mining shaft headframe. A Plexiglas shield covered a mineshaft over 1900 feet deep. Part of me wanted to descend into that blackness to blot out my own troubled thoughts.

Reckless and I cut across through Beale and Dias streets below Mingus, breathing easy now on the home stretch. The dog automatically turned right, toward the apartment I had been renting, now a snaggle-toothed silhouette open to the blue sky. I whistled him back.

I had one final dark thought. That could have been *my* mangled body underneath those cement pylons. Did I really want to stay in this cop business? The accident yesterday took more of a toll than I realized.

I reached HT's house and filled an outside water dish for Reckless. He lapped the water with enthusiasm and whipped that coonhound tail around to show his gratitude. I leaned over, hands on my knees to stretch out my back, and then did leg stretches against the porch steps to forestall another Charley horse, since this one had gone to pasture.

When I went into the kitchen, the sound of Isabel's shower drummed a tattoo on the ceiling of the thin-walled house. Another reason to move. Living in the loft, I heard the whole household, and I am sure they heard me as well. Including my big-footed dog. No wonder Isabel was anxious for us to leave!

I hadn't heard from Myra Banks yet on the Zoning commission ruling, and I couldn't stay at HT's much longer. Isabel was giving me pointed looks. I'd check in with Myra later this morning. When did attorneys get to the office? She probably kept bankers hours.

After breakfast, I uniformed up and hiked the hill to the station, not sure what the day would bring.

Ben waved at me as I walked in. Shepherd and I were surrogate parents to the young Navajo-Italian genius. When his folks died in an auto crash he'd been sent to live with his uncle, Armor Brancussi. But Armor had no idea how to handle Ben's wild mood swings. The kid often ended up cadging dinner from Isabel, or engaging Shepherd in long philosophical arguments. Sometimes we talked, too.

He shoved a thick batch of paper under my nose. "Aced the exam," he said proudly. "Ready for internship this fall. Plant those grapes! Lift that fertilizer." He did a celebratory dance around the foyer.

"Heard you had an awesome time yesterday," Ben said. "Chased that criminal up and down Copper Canyon. Must have been really something. Wish I'd seen that crash."

A shiver went down my back. "No, you don't, Ben."

Shepherd shot him a look and shook his head.

Ben looked from one of us to the other. "Well anyway, Peg, glad you're back in one piece. Just wanted to stop by and…" His sentence trailed off as he gave me another look and disappeared out the door.

"Trip to make this morning," Shepherd said. "We're heading out to Serena Battle's place."

Shepherd had picked up the patrol SUV from the repair shop, and I drove the switchbacks from Mingus to the valley floor. The heavy reassuring transmission and solid handling of the SUV settled me after the wild ride yesterday.

"How'd the sheriff take the damage to his new patrol car?" I asked.

"Not happy. I may get demoted."

"Why?"

"I was the senior officer in charge. My call, to pursue the vehicle."

I shifted the SUV into low for the final hairpin. "Did you set that Porsche driver up? Did you *know* he'd be there?" My tone came out harsher than intended.

"No, I didn't…not, exactly." My partner sighed deeply. "He usually made a drug run about that time of afternoon down to Phoenix. I was just going to warn him off, let him still know I was around. Didn't figure he'd run."

There was a moment of uneasy silence.

"Peg, it was an accident, brought on by that man's speeding. You didn't cause it, and you need to let it go. Put it to rest."

"Easy to say."

"Yes," he said slowly. "Easy to say."

And that was the end of it. I drove across the valley with only the occasional police radio traffic for company as we headed to the Battles' farm.

Hank was in the yard raking when the high-clearance SUV bounced down the rutted hill to the farm. Rows of heirloom tomato vines peered over six-foot rounds of hog wire fencing. Next to them was a fragrant plot of basil and another of blooming lavender. A truck garden like this took hard physical labor by both Serena and her brother.

Shepherd opened his door and hailed Hank. The man jerked up with an uneasy look in his eyes. He rammed his pink felt hat down over his ears and jogged towards his trailer in the crazy uneven gait that his accident had caused.

"Want to come with me to the house?" Shepherd asked.

My face grew rigid. "This one's your show."

Shepherd mounted the porch steps and knocked on the door. Serena opened it and Shepherd went inside. The telling didn't take long. Soon Shepherd reappeared on the porch. He gave Serena a long hug, patted her back and descended the steps to the SUV.

Did the chase and subsequent death solve anything? Hank was still disabled. That wouldn't change, ever. Perhaps the news brought Serena some closure. I could hold onto that, anyway.

The woman took one step toward Hank's trailer, hesitated. Then she turned and disappeared into the house.

"Serena says hi," Shepherd said, buckling his seat belt. "Hank's getting worse. She may have to institutionalize him."

He sighed. "We did what we could."

"Did what we could," I echoed hollowly. "One more criminal off the street." But somehow it didn't make me feel any better.

A half-hour later, we were back at the station. I opened the door to find my grandfather and his friend Armor deep in conversation.

"Hi Peg," HT said." You just missed Isabel. She brought this plate of brownies. Want some?"

Comfort food. I snagged a piece and a napkin to hold it.

Armor reached a big paw across the table. "Want to congratulate you, Peg. Making this valley safe for law-abiding people. Tell us about it."

People were *happy* that I'd been the cause of a man's death? I looked at the two men who were eager to share the victory lap with me. I struggled to give them what they asked for.

"It wasn't much. Initiated pursuit when a man ran a routine traffic stop. Up and down the mountain once. You know how it ended." My voice sounded dull, even to me.

Shepherd gave me a sympathetic look. "Don't be so modest. This guy took off, Peg right on his tail going a hundred and ten miles an hour, did this textbook PIT maneuver, spun that Porsche a 360..."

His voice was enthusiastic and his hands made swooping motions to describe the action. His audience listened appreciatively as he spun the tale.

While the three shared the story, I excused myself and went to the bathroom, the bile rising in my throat. Maybe with time I could accept congratulations for what happened. Not yet.

To my relief, when I returned to the lunchroom, talk had shifted from the accident to car talk. I made my excuses and left the three comparing carburetors and spark plug brands for HT's old pickup.

I decided to pay a visit to Myra Banks. Perhaps the trip would provide a distraction from yesterday's events.

CHAPTER TWENTY-NINE

Myra Banks operated her law business out of a small storefront on Main Street in Cottonwood. The original owner had designed each office as a small house representative of one he had lived in.

Myra's office was a New England saltbox painted in southwest colors of turquoise and mauve. It fitted her, somehow.

She was on the phone when I entered and she beckoned me to sit. Her voice was clipped and strident. "Just tell him that he needs to pay his attorney's bills or get new legal representation." She slammed the phone down, muttering. "If that son of a bitch can afford a 'round-the-world cruise, he can afford to pay me."

I smiled. Nice to see someone else on the receiving end of her sharp tongue. "Anybody I know, Myra?"

Her mouth snapped shut. "Never mind. Attorney-client privilege. Nothing to do with you."

She shifted to client-procurement mode. "And what can I do for *you*, Peg Quincy? Ready to sue the sheriff's department for harassment yet?"

"Not a chance. But I know who to use if I ever decide to." I smiled back at her.

That social rite concluded, I spread the sheaf of papers I'd collected from Dot Harper on her desk.

"I want to rent a house, and I understand you're the key to making that happen."

Myra put on a pair of black-rimmed cheaters and examined one paper, then the next. "Dot Harper, my favorite older-lady client. How's she doing over at the retirement home?"

"Just about got the place totally organized. You'd be proud." I gestured at the papers. "She says the state real estate department made a mistake on her bill."

"They did. But the tax department won't admit it. Says it's a rounding error. Dorothy won't buy that one. She wants to know where the rounding goes—says it should be designated for at-risk kids to learn math skills."

"I'm inclined to agree with her," I said. "But does that mean they can condemn her property for non-payment of taxes?"

Myra twiddled a pencil. I used to do that in grade school. If I did it fast enough, the pencil looked like it bent in the middle.

Myra's pencil looked pretzel-shaped by the time she paused. "No, I can fix that..."

"Good. Then I want to rent the house."

"You want to rent *that*?" Myra laughed derisively.

"What's the matter with it?" I protested. "Good view, plenty of elbow room."

Myra tapped her teeth with the eraser end of the pencil. Then she came to a decision. "We might get it through the zoning board with a variance—assert that you were a workman hired to make necessary improvements. Wouldn't hurt if you lived there while you did them. Let me talk to Elmer down at the Zoning Board. He owes me one."

I imagined everyone in the valley with the exception of Shepherd owed Myra for one reason or another. She was the original Godmother of the Verde Valley. I looked at her. The zoning-variance sounded like Myra's usual over-the-top legal paperwork. Wondered what she was charging Dot Harper.

"No! It's not what you think. I do Dot's work pro-bono. She loves to ruffle feathers as much as I do. Thank goodness, she's one of a kind. I'd go broke otherwise."

There was one other small matter. "Uh, about the plumbing..."

"Look, you wanted this house knowing it had no inside plumbing. And now you want some?" Myra asked.

"Dot *said* you'd fix it..."

Myra sighed. "All right. Time she installed that bathroom

anyway. With her approval, we should get a crew out there next week to start laying the inside line." She reached into a file cabinet and pulled out a standard lease for me to sign.

I read it carefully. The "no pets" clause shone like a beacon. I pushed it back across the desk. "My dog Reckless comes with me."

Myra muttered under her breath and then scratched out the clause with a hasty pen. "What can a red mutt hurt in that wreck of a place?"

"And..."

"Yes?" At this point, Myra looked down her glasses at me. Nothing like one strong-willed woman matched against another.

"The road. Can you get someone to run a blade over it?"

"I'll try. But no guarantees. It'll probably just flood out again," she warned.

Fair enough. I figured I'd squeezed this particular lemon dry of all the juice I was going to. I signed the lease with a flourish and handed over the deposit and first month's rent. It flattened my bank account, but I could mooch off HT for a little while longer. I ignored a mental vision of his guardian angel, Isabel. I'd pay him back. Soon.

Myra stood, probably wanting to dismiss me so she could do some real work. "Do consider suing the sheriff's office," she said. "I'll do that one on contingency—won't cost you a cent up front. Got a few scores to settle over there."

Suddenly it clicked. If I sued the department, my primary complainant would be Shepherd, my supervisor. I'd be pitting my boss against this female bulldog. Why did they hate each other so much?

On impulse, I sat back down again. "Okay, Myra. Spill it. What's this feud between you and Shepherd?"

She stopped, startled, and then gave a full-throated laugh. "You caught me, Peg. You'd make a good interrogator. Want some coffee? This story will take a while."

Over a mug of black coffee, she began. Told me how Shepherd's obsession with work had driven a wedge in his marriage years ago.

"You know how that can be," Myra said.

I nodded. The divorce rate was astronomical among cops. "But how did you come into it?"

Myra took a sip of coffee. Shook her head and added some more cream from a pitcher in the small refrigerator next to her desk.

"I didn't know him personally at that point, but our paths crossed from time to time in court. One day after a hearing, I was driving back from Prescott. Had a flat. I'd never fixed a tire before, but I was game. Checked out the owner's manual, assembled the machinery, thought I had the car braced, but—"

"—it slipped off the jack," I finished for her. "What then?"

"I stood there in heels and trial skirt; the rain pouring down. And then Shepherd's car slid in behind mine, as easy as could be. He had that tire changed in seven minutes flat."

I smiled. Cars were a strong point for Shepherd. He could drive and fix anything wearing four wheels. "And then?"

"Well..." Myra got a little flustered. "He invited me out for coffee and I accepted. One thing led to another and we became lovers."

"And that broke up Shepherd's marriage?"

"Well, it didn't help it."

"I'm not passing judgment," I said. "These things happen. But you seem like bitter enemies now, not friends."

She sighed. "That's the rest of the story. When Shepherd told his wife about me, she threatened to leave him if he didn't break it off. And I unwisely pleaded with him to stay with me anyway.

"Shepherd hates conflict, I should have remembered that. Caught in the middle, he chose her. He laughed in my face, said I wasn't worth one hair of her precious head. But then his wife decided to file for divorce anyway. She came to me, asked me to represent her."

Myra shrugged. "I was angry, hurt..."

"So you took him to the cleaners."

"Absolutely!" She brightened. "Best legal work of my career. Never trust men, Peg. We ladies have to stick together and help each other. So now you know the rest of the story."

We shook hands on the rental agreement and Myra gave me the key. I stood to leave.

She put a hand on my arm. "I took my sister to her first appointment with the counselor, Dr. Westcott. Thank you. Janet likes her. I do, too. It was a good recommendation."

I made light of it. "Just part of the service of your friendly sheriff's office."

Myra didn't want to leave it there. "No. It's more than that. You have a talent for caring about people like Janet. My sister told me about your gift of that pink geranium. She was planning to kill herself that night. Your visit might have saved her life." Unlike Myra's usual brittle legal veneer, her tone was honest, almost vulnerable. "If ever I can return the favor, Peg..."

Although I hadn't intended to profit by my actions, maybe I was collecting a few future paybacks myself. Just call me Godmother-in-Training.

We said goodbye and I headed out to my car. On the way, I checked my watch. An hour had passed while I was with Myra. Wondered what her normal billing rate was for filing legal documents like a lien release. Maybe I could get a loan from Ben to pay the bill—I knew he had extra cash. I'd paid him some.

I sat in Myra's parking lot letting the Jetta idle for a moment. So, a new house for Reckless and me. It didn't make up entirely for the events of yesterday, but some sun appeared in my dark world.

I debated calling Ben to help move from HT's to my new house, but the enterprising college student wouldn't work for free on this second move. Couldn't blame him. On the other hand, I had another bird I could flush. I even had him on speed dial.

Rory answered the phone with a "Hi, Peg." He sounded tentative.

Maybe I was, too. We'd slept together and parted without words. Fear of commitment—we both held that conviction in high esteem. On the other hand, we were friends, so I explained the situation.

"I've got a Late Night Commitment," Rory said. His tone added the capitals. "But I may be able to spare a few hours. I'll meet you at HT's house after work, say about 5:30 or so. Lots of room in the Hummer, shouldn't take more than a trip or two."

Part of me questioned exactly what or who the L.N.C. was, but I needed his strong shoulders for the move.

"Great! I'll provide the beer," I said. I had enough money for that, anyway.

I shifted the Jetta into drive and pulled out of the parking lot.

My cell rang again. I braked to the side of the road and dug the phone out of my purse. I covered one ear to hear over the road noise.

"Hello," I said. "Hello?"

The reception was bad, kept breaking up, but a woman's voice rose through the static. "Please come. It's...something's..."

"Who is this?"

"Please hurry. Hein...Heinrich..." Then the connection closed.

I looked at the caller ID. "Restricted."

That figured. But the Heinrich part was clear enough. Was it Marguerite, calling numbers at random with her latest crisis?

Then I remembered Myra's words. I cared about people, right? Even those, like Marguerite, that affected me like the screech of fingernails on a blackboard. I could swing by the Spine Ranch, check it out before I needed to meet Rory at HT's house for the move. Plenty of time.

***

The grounds were quiet as I drove under the Spine Ranch sign. It was just after two in the afternoon, and most of the household would be resting. At least I hope so. Fancy opened the door and peered at me with her usual sour expression.

"What do you want this time?"

How did I turn into persona non grata in her eyes? She'd seemed so human when we were in her iris garden.

"I received a phone call from Marguerite," I said. "Something about Heinrich and needing help."

Fancy stood stolidly in the doorway. "Heinrich is upstairs, asleep. Marguerite is in the kitchen." Her smile turned knowing in a mean sort of way. "Perhaps it *is* best if you come in."

She opened the door the bare minimum for entrance, let me in, and pushed it closed. I followed her tap-tapping heels on the marble tiles toward the large kitchen.

Marguerite greeted me with wails of anguish. Encrusted pots overflowed the sink, dirty dishes covered the counter, and vile-smelling odors rose from a big pot on the range.

"Where's Raven?" I asked.

Marguerite shrieked again and dropped a heavy cast iron pan she was pulling from the oven. Meat and juices splattered over a floor already tacky with debris. The woman stood shaking burned fingers, weeping.

I reached around her and turned on the cold water in the sink. "Put your fingers under the water. They'll feel better." I handed her a towel. "Where's the first aid kit?"

"I don't know." She sniffled. "Raven always took care of that."

I poked around in the cabinets and found it. I rummaged through the contents to find some burn ointment. "Here, let me put some on your burns."

"No. Don't touch me. It's all your fault that he's gone."

"Then you do it." I set the tube of ointment on the counter.

She dabbed it on her burned fingers, trying not to mar her manicure. Fancy leaned against the door jam, smirking.

"Let's try again," I said. "Where's Raven LightDancer?"

"He quit!" Marguerite said. "He couldn't work any longer in that atmosphere of suspicion and mistrust you created. He said it ruined his creativity. First Gil, now Raven. We were doing just fine before you arrived. It's all your fault!"

I couldn't help wondering if they were doing "just fine" with a barn that burned for no good reason with a murdered man inside it. Didn't sound like just fine to me.

"Did you call me on the phone?" I asked.

Marguerite looked at me as though I'd grown a third eyeball. "Why would I do that? Haven't you done enough damage already?" She threw her hands in the air. "Who's going to fix my dinner?"

"How about fixing it yourself?"

Marguerite put a hand to her forehead. "I think I'm getting sick."

"In that case, I'll be on my way," I said cheerfully.

"Wait." She looked doubtfully at the stacks of cutlery on the counter. "Could you wash up the dishes? I'll pay you."

"Not a chance."

Marguerite stared in dismay at the mess.

One of the ranch dogs poked his nose in the kitchen doorway, apparently attracted by the enticing smells and commotion. He grabbed the roast that Marguerite had dropped on the floor and dragged the meat into a corner, creating another well-defined smear on the kitchen floor.

Time to leave. When I entered the hallway to the front of the house, Fancy had disappeared. Apparently, her genes didn't include the dish-washing one, either.

Behind me in the kitchen, there was a yelp, followed by a door slam. I wonder if Marguerite let the poor dog keep the bone at least.

With Marguerite occupied and Fancy absent, I sauntered through the house unsupervised. I passed by the entrance to the chemistry lab and tried the handle. Locked. I peered through the wire-re-enforced window on the door. The room was dim, with faint light glinting off the test tubes and glass beakers.

I gave the space a closer look. A larger crack of light seeped around the edge of the far outside door. Was it ajar? Wouldn't hurt to check.

I'd close it like a good neighbor before the javalinas got in and ruined all of Heinrich's experiments. And maybe poke around a little, while I was at it.

I shut the front door quietly behind me and moved to the side of the house.

CHAPTER THIRTY

A moment later, I entered Heinrich Spine's laboratory. Leaving the outside door cracked to air the thick atmosphere, I switched on the overhead lights.

Someone had been here since my last visit. Heinrich's papers were stacked in disorganized piles, and dust smeared the black counters. Maybe they hadn't found what I was looking for, either.

I started with the upper cabinets, opening doors, shifting bottles around to check the back corners. Heinrich labeled all the bottles with German precision, and the cabinets contained enough junk for a chemistry garage sale. It *all* looked suspicious.

I was searching for the thirty-third element on the Periodic Table. I knew that because my high school chemistry teacher decreed the entire class had to memorize the elements before anybody could pass. I'd get up to number 32 and balk. My lab partner would hiss in my ear. "33...33...Arsenic, you blockhead!" So what's the number of the periodic element I can now recite in my sleep? Arsenic, of course.

I squatted to inspect the bottom cabinets. Hidden in the far reaches of the last lower cabinet, I spotted a thick glass bottle of a dusty blue. I pulled a paper towel off the roll on the counter, wrapped the bottle, and pulled it out. The worn label, written in a spidery hand, read, "*As*, No. 33."

I'd found the missing arsenic. Either Heinrich hadn't located it after my visit, or someone had returned it after he'd been here. If so, there might be fingerprints. I set the bottle carefully on the counter. Was there more? I got on my knees to search the next lower cabinet.

A gust of wind slammed the propped door shut with a loud bang. The air immediately got heavier, and I rushed to the exit. I turned the handle, but it wouldn't budge.

Jammed.

I shoved a shoulder against it, but nothing happened.

What about the inside door? I walked to the other side of the room and checked. It was securely fastened with a key lock, no thumb latch. I was trapped! My heart fluttered and my vision narrowed. With effort, I took a few deep breaths that seemed to help.

The hunt for evidence was abandoned as I stood in the small, dark room. There was an odd whistling sound. Had that been there before?

Using my ears as a Doppler beacon, I scanned the room hunting a source. Stacks of paper and bottles lined the counter, in addition to test tubes and beakers. But none of those would make a sound like that. Six Bunsen burners connected to the gas outlets on the wall...My head swiveled for a closer look. *Not* connected.

The tubes piled in a coil like a den of unhappy snakes and poisonous vapor seeped into the room. Vapor with the rotten egg odor of natural gas.

My head spun, and my vision tunneled. I grabbed my phone out of my pocket to call for help. No bars. The heavy adobe walls of the house must be blocking the signal.

I hammered on the interior house door and stopped to listen. There were no footsteps, no calls of alarm. No one had heard me. I raced to the other side of the room and pounded on the door to the outside. Then I screamed until my voice was harsh and kicked futilely at the door.

The walls pulsated, malevolently drawing closer as my panic increased. How long could I hold out? I sunk to my knees, trying to breathe shallowly as lights danced before my eyes.

Then the outside door crashed open. Ray Morales's form was silhouetted in the doorway. He held a crowbar over his head. Was he the killer, coming to finish what he'd started? I ducked reflexively.

Ray dropped the bar and rushed into the room. I scuttled away from him like a hermit crab from a predator.

"No, Peg, it's okay. I want to help!"

Ray pulled me to my feet and staggered under a firefighter's lift to carry me outside. He lowered me to the stone bench and took off his straw hat, waving it in front of my face.

I braced my hands on the bench and straightened into an upright position. Sunlight eased my body tension. I gulped huge mouthfuls of fresh air. Slowly the stranglehold of panic eased. The old stone bench beneath me felt solid, reassuring. Overhead, a thrasher sang in an acacia tree. My breathing slowed.

"What happened?" Ray asked. "I heard shouting and ran to help." His brown eyes were concerned.

"The door slammed behind me." I started to rise. "I have to go back in there."

"Are you crazy?" Ray pushed me down. "Sit here for a moment while I locate the shutoff valve for the gas." He disappeared around the corner of the house.

I shook my head to clear the fumes. What happened wasn't an accident. This was a deadly message that I was getting too close. I shifted back into cop mode. Everyone became an enemy until proven innocent, including Ray.

How did he happen to be so near when I called for help? Did niece Alana return to Mexico because Gil was threatening to expose her? Ray could have killed Gil Streicker to protect her. Maybe Ray lied about no arsenic in the barn. He didn't look like a killer, but you couldn't trust anyone when—

Stop it! I halted my paranoid thinking with effort. This man rescued me, for Pete's sake.

The arsenic bottle was critical. If the surface held fingerprints, they'd be a clue to the person who used it last. Putting a handkerchief over my nose and holding my breath, I lurched into the lab.

Swaying on unsteady feet, I approached the counter where I'd abandoned the glass bottle in my panicked need to escape. The counter was empty. The bottle had vanished.

There was noise at the outside door and I whirled. Marguerite stood there staring at me.

"Well, come out here," she ordered. "I'm certainly not going into that smelly room."

She touched the shattered door frame gingerly with a red lacquered nail as I moved past her into the yard.

"You broke this door, Peg Quincy," she said. "Heinrich will be furious."

I almost died, and she was worried about what she'd tell her father? I'd had enough of these crazy people for one afternoon. Someone in this household had swiped that bottle of arsenic, and I'd find out who soon enough.

"Send the bill to the sheriff's office," I muttered and left.

***

For an hour I drove the back roads aimlessly, a rooster tail of dust following me like a shroud. I had no destination—I just knew I needed time and space away from the dysfunction of the Spine Ranch. Gradually my head cleared and the toxic exposure subsided to a throbbing headache behind my left temple.

I stopped at the top of a hill for good reception and checked my cell phone messages. The most recent one was from the sheriff's headquarters, sent minutes ago.

I patched through to our dispatcher Melda. "What's up?"

"We need an officer out at Montezuma's Well. Standard fender bender."

Taking names and writing reports would be a good distraction right now.

I claimed the call. "Estimated time of arrival, five minutes."

When I pulled into the parking lot, the cause of the accident was clear. A pickup truck backing out of his parking space had rammed into the side of a mega-RV pulling into the lot. Both drivers were out of their vehicles and circling like professional wrestlers looking for the first takedown.

"Back up, both of you," I said, inserting myself between them.

Technically, the pickup guy deserved a ticket, but they were both at fault. The pickup driver should have been checking his rearview mirror, but the RV guy had pulled in too fast and wasn't watching for backup lights.

"Anyone injured?"

The RV guy said he was fine, and that, of course, they'd exchanged information.

Of course. Nevertheless, tension crackled in the air like lightning before a storm. Time to separate potential combatants. The pickup driver wasn't leaving until the RV moved, anyway, so I directed him to wait by his vehicle while I scribbled an accident report.

Then, I pulled the RV driver aside to hear his tale first. I listened patiently to why *he* was in the right, recited my standard speech about being a courteous, defensive driver. I handed him a copy of the accident report. "I'm not going to cite you, but be more careful in the future. Have a good day."

Shepherd would have approved of my cool cop stance.

The RV pulled away from the pickup with a crunch of splintered metal and disappeared down the road in a cloud of diesel fumes. Pickup guy was next.

He started swearing as soon as I approached.

I cut him short. "Sir, you should have been checking that rearview mirror the *whole time* you were backing up. An RV's a big target to miss."

He muttered a bit, unwilling to accept his share of the blame.

Okay by me. His choice, to ruin a good afternoon with bad temper. I gave him a copy of the accident report, offered the same olive branch of no citation, and the same cautionary warning about defensive driving.

The pickup driver shoved the warning notice in his shirt pocket, turned without a word and got back in his vehicle. But I noticed he checked both ways and backed up at a sedate pace. Didn't hit the gas until he was well down the road, away from the parking lot and possible cop pursuit.

I'd seen another driver react the same way not too long ago. A driver that had died. I put that memory out of my mind with difficulty. I couldn't fix the past. I couldn't even change the future if I saw it coming.

I purchased a bottle of water at the ranger station and hiked up to the top of the ridge that lipped Montezuma's Well. A catclaw acacia provided shade and an errant breeze hit my face. I took a slug of water and watched a small lizard do pushups on the pockmarked limestone ledge.

Today at the Spine Ranch, I'd poked my nose where it didn't

belong and caught it in a twisting, painful trap. I'd given in to my need for closure, trespassing and causing the destruction of property. I'd be more cautious in future dealings with the Spine household.

I rose and followed a marked trail around the rim of the crater until it descended to Wet Beaver Creek, some 500 feet below. The running water splashed over rocks, tossing sparkles into the air. In the deep shade of the sycamore and ash trees near the water, the air turned moist, some twenty degrees cooler than on top of the hillside.

A small irrigation ditch paralleled the path, finding its way down to the creek. The sides of the ditch were moss-encrusted, deepening the water's color. I traced the origin of the ditch to the rock face of the hill surrounding Montezuma's Well. There, a spume of water exploded from the center of the rock. Yellow columbines and wild fern crowded its edges, creating an unexpected oasis in the desert heat.

A park ranger rose from a stone wall where she'd been sitting. "Hello. You get those folks sorted out in the parking lot?"

"You the one called it in?"

She nodded. "Most complaints we can field, but when tempers flare we're under orders to bring in the heavy guns." She smiled. "That's you."

"Peaceful here, though," I observed. "Where's the water coming from? An artesian spring?"

"That's the drainage from Montezuma Well. Underwater springs fill the pond and this natural passage siphons the overflow into Wet Beaver Creek. The Yavapai Apaches call this the place of broken water."

"Fits," I said.

"Time I hike back to the station," the ranger said. "We're about to close for the day. Thanks for handling that trouble." Her footsteps echoed for a moment against the rock walls and then faded.

Three mallard ducks circled in an eddy of the creek, as a red-winged dragonfly kissed the back of my hand and then vanished. A black-and-white Phoebe hovered over the water, then returned to the same rock perch in a characteristic back-and-forth pattern. In a way, my life with its chaos and conflict echoed that pendulum of existence.

The quiet here was almost hypnotic, lulling me into a sense of peace that I couldn't afford. I rose to my feet and dusted off my back. Then I hitched my belt gear into place to start the short, steep climb to the top of the crater to return to the parking lot.

As I reached the top of the crater hill, a bullet whined, ricocheting off the rock ledge. Then a sycamore branch above me cracked, broken leaves raining down in a green shower.

I dropped to the ground and drew my weapon. Someone was shooting live ammo, and I was the target!

CHAPTER THIRTY-ONE

I was on my own. Likely the ranger was already on her way home by now. And this area was a no-cell-tower zone, one of many that dotted the valley. No way to call in reinforcements. The pavement of the path dug into my knee. I shifted to get more comfortable.

Another shot rang out. A rock chip splintered out of the boulder next to my head, cutting into my forehead like a razor's edge. Blood streamed down my face, and I wiped at it to clear my vision.

Scrabbling on hands and knees, I crept behind a boulder. Not total cover, but the rock concealed most of me. I shuffled my legs back and forth to camouflage them under twigs and dry leaves. No sense in presenting any larger target than I had to.

A fly crawled across my sweaty forearm and I brushed it away. The head wound continued to bleed, patterning the rocks with red. I pressed my sleeve to the wound to staunch the flow. I'd need to attend to it soon. Already the first sting had grown to a throbbing beat.

Then, above me on the trail, gravel clattered down like hail hitting a slate roof. Was the shooter leaving? I rose cautiously, tired of waiting.

Another shot whined close to my head. I ducked and returned the fire, aiming high as a warning. "Police officer," I shouted. "Throw down your weapon."

Instead, a person rose to their feet on the hill, a rifle in hand. Then the human silhouette disappeared beyond the edge of the crater heading toward the now-closed ranger station.

I gave chase, but the person loped in an awkward gait and made the parking lot before I could stop him. As the person reached the two lone cars, his body caught in an errant beam of light from the setting sun. Khaki pants, blue plaid shirt, and on his head a hat—a pink hat just like Hank Battle wore.

The person jumped into his vehicle, backed up with an uneven squeal of tires and disappeared down the access road. I slowed my plunge downhill to an unsteady walk. I'd lost him for now, but I knew where he lived. He'd be heading home to Serena.

I stopped at my car and pulled a first aid kit and a spare shirt out of the trunk. Then I staggered to the women's restroom and pushed open the door. Other than a black widow spider camped in one corner, I was alone. Just as well, because I didn't want to be scaring the tourists. I must look like a war refugee.

I stripped off my bloodstained uniform shirt and the T-shirt underneath. Balling the T-shirt into a washcloth, I held it under the dripping water faucet. The cold water stung as I washed the blood away and I held the bloody cloth under the water to rinse it.

To the side of the sink was a hand-lettered sign: "Non-potable water. Contains arsenic." Great. I could choose between death by lockjaw infection or death by poison.

I peered into the wavy metal mirror over the sink and touched my forehead. I'd need stitches, probably. It would make an interesting conversation starter on future dates— if I made it that far.

I disinfected the slash wound as best I could and pressed a gauze pad against it. The cotton immediately turned bright red. Swearing, I dug two more pads out of the first aid kit to replace the sopping one. I pressed tight. That seemed to help. Then I ripped a piece of adhesive tape from the roll and wrapped it around my head over the gauze pads. The adhesive would be a bugger to get out of my hair, but at least it held the bandage firm.

I put on the extra shirt and dumped all the bloody rags in the trash. Then I walked back to my car and loaded the first aid kit back in the trunk. I'd have to call the ranger in the morning and tell her what happened. After the altercation following the parking-lot accident, I didn't want her worried about fights at Montezuma's Well. I still had the injured body, somewhat intact.

The patrol car hit sixty on the dirt road to the Battle's farm, skimming the tops of the washboards. When the rear wheel fishtailed dangerously near the side of the road, I slowed reluctantly. No point in totaling the car. I knew my destination and who would be waiting for me when I got there.

***

My head ached under the primitive bandage I'd fashioned, and I was out of patience. I screeched to a halt in front of Serena Battle's porch, sending a cloud of dust billowing against the side of the house.

No sign of activity at Hank's trailer, so I pounded up the house front steps and hammered on the door. It was time Serena realized that Hank was not just brain-injured; he was dangerous.

"Open up."

I didn't add "in the name of the law" even though I felt like it. Somebody needed to be held accountable, and if it wasn't Hank then it damn well could be his sister.

"Open up!" I shouted again.

The door opened and Serena looked out, puzzled. "What's wrong? What happened to your head?"

Her words poured cold water on my rage. The only danger prowling about was my own temper.

"I need to talk to your brother."

"Hank's asleep."

"Let me in."

She braced against the door, responding with stubbornness. "I can't do that."

"Then you come out here."

She stepped out the door and touched my arm. "Sit over here on this bench, and tell me why you're here."

"Hank just shot at me, minutes ago at Montezuma's Well. I have to arrest him."

Serena looked at me blankly. "He couldn't have done that. He's been here all afternoon."

"I don't believe you."

"Someone stole Hank's favorite hat, the pink one, down at the grocery store. He was inconsolable. I tried to talk to him, reason with him, but you know how he can get." In the filtered light on the porch, she touched a growing bruise on her arm.

We were *both* battle veterans at this point. But that didn't mean Hank hadn't assaulted me. Such an attack seemed likely, even.

Serena shook her head. "You don't understand. I finally quieted him down and fixed him some root beer—that's his favorite. I promised him I'd go help him look for his hat when he was finished."

"And?" I wasn't seeing the connection.

"I slipped a sedative into the drink. Here, see."

She rose and opened the door. Hank lay on the sofa, snoring noisily. An empty soda bottle was tipped over nearby.

She spoke softly. "Peg, he *couldn't* have been the one who shot at you. He's been there for hours, just like that. I've been sitting here waiting for him to wake up. When he does, I've arranged to take him to a locked facility for evaluation." The tears streamed down her cheeks.

I hugged her and we both cried some. I'd been wrong, and I acknowledged that to Serena. Then I said my goodbyes and walked to my car.

Serena faced a life decision ahead, dealing with Hank's disability. But if her brother hadn't shot at me, *who had*?

***

As I returned to my car, my cell rang. It was Ned Jamison, my buddy in Tennessee.

"Peg, where have you been? I've left word all over for you to call me."

Probably lost in the batch of unreturned messages on my cell, forgotten when I dealt with the accident at Montezuma's Well. At least he was persistent.

"Think I've found something." His voice pitched higher with excitement.

"Wait a minute while I get something to write on." I dug in the glovebox for a notebook. "Go ahead."

"Something stuck in my mind when you asked for help. I had to go digging in some dusty local papers but…"

"Spill it!"

"Okay, your Fancy Morgan is likely a person called Frances Morgenstern. There was a big flap in a small town near Manchester, Tennessee about five years ago. That's the place where the Bates

Casket Company has its headquarters.

"Frances lived with her aging parents. First, the mother died of heart complications. Then the father had a stroke that left him paralyzed on one side. Frances cared for him, too, round the clock for three years until he died. The County Coroner put his cause of death as heart attack. Saw no need to go further than that. The old man had lived past his prime."

"So?" It was a tragic story, but not unknown, as ailing parents leaned on family members for final care.

"Well Frances asked for the old man to be cremated, but the funeral home made a mistake and buried him instead. The daughter was livid. She demanded that they dig him up and do it right. Made a little too much noise about it, and the sheriff got curious. He ordered a stay on the cremation, asked for an autopsy. Turned out the old man was poisoned. Probably the mother, too, only that body *had* been cremated and the ashes scattered in parts unknown."

"And the poison they found in the old man?" I asked, even though I already knew the answer.

"Arsenic."

"Did they arrest Frances?"

"No. By then she'd disappeared. They put out an all-points alert, but she just vanished. Not heard from since."

Until now, I thought. "One final question, Ned. Did you call a place called Spine Ranch looking for me?"

"Yeah. Your assistant, one—" There was a rattle of paper as he searched his notes. "—Ben Yazzie told me that's where you were. I left a voice mail to have you call me."

And the Tennessee area code would have been on the caller ID for Fancy to see and intercept.

"When did you call?" I asked.

"As soon as I fired up the computer, about ten our time this morning."

Which had to be eight by Fancy's watch. She'd lured me out to the ranch, been there waiting for me all the time. When Ray rescued me at the chemistry lab, she tried again at Montezuma's Well. I had a good idea who had stolen Hank Battle's hat.

Ned must have noted my silence. "Did I do something wrong? Sorry, Peg, if I blew your cover."

"Don't worry about it. I'll take it from here."

I rang off and sat for a moment. Then I cranked the engine and drove to the main road, accelerating each mile. I clenched the steering wheel with both hands and pushed the pedal to the floor.

Would I reach the Spine Ranch before Frances Morgenstern vanished once again?

CHAPTER THIRTY-TWO

It was near dusk when I approached the Spine mansion. Only one car was in the parking area as I pulled up. I walked over to the vehicle and touched the hood. Still warm. I paused there a moment.

The front door was ajar as I approached. I shoved it open and stood for a moment in the foyer, letting my eyes adjust to the dim light. The living room curtains were drawn, but on a side table was a spot of pink—the hat that Hank had lost. I'd come to the right place.

"I thought you'd be along, sooner or later. Come right in, Peg Quincy."

Fancy Morgan sat in a side chair, a rifle in her hands. "Unholster your gun and lay it on the floor."

I listened for a moment. The house was silent with no evidence of anyone near. I did as she asked.

"Now slide it over here. Slowly. And your cell phone. Now!"

I did.

"Won't do you any good to go grabbing for the house phone. I disconnected it. Sit there on the couch while I decide what to do."

"I know who you are, Frances."

Her grip tightened on the rifle. "That's who I *was*. I left that place years ago."

"After you killed your parents?"

She shrugged. "They were close to dead, anyway. I just helped the process along."

"And Gil Streicker?"

"Stupid man. Found out about my old life, wanted to blackmail me." She laughed a short barking laugh. "Where would I find that kind of money? But Gil wouldn't listen. He never listened."

"You didn't have to kill him."

"I didn't plan to, at first. Then I followed him to the barn the night of the fire, discovered *his* secret. That money was my ticket to a new beginning. Now I won't have to take orders from anyone ever again." Her grip on the rifle was unwavering. "See how things work out, Peg? All for the good."

"What's good about murder and theft?"

Fancy's eyes turned distant. She'd already stepped over that invisible line between sanity and madness.

The ticking of the wall clock echoed in the empty house. Could I stall her until I alerted someone else?

Almost as though she could read my mind, Fancy continued. "Amanda is in town with Rosa. I gave them a long list of supplies that I said we needed. They won't be returning for hours."

"And Marguerite?"

"Indisposed. She likes to mix pills and booze. See, I know *her* secrets, too."

I took a deep breath, steadying myself for action.

"Think. Who's left?" Fancy said.

"Heinrich."

She nodded slowly. "That's right, Heinrich. Right now he's up in his room. He struggled a little when I gave him the medicine, just like my father did. If you listen, you can hear him struggling to breathe."

She cocked her head. "But I'll give you a choice..."

"Yes?" I had a feeling it wasn't going to be a good one.

"You can cross that floor, try to reach me before I shoot you. You won't make it. I'm a good shot, close range."

"Or?"

"Or you can dash upstairs to try to rescue that miserable old man, and I walk out this door. Your choice, Peg. Me or him?" She smiled bitterly. "Better decide soon. I don't know how long that bastard can survive without help."

There was only one option for me. I took it.

Before I was halfway up the steps to Heinrich's room, the front door slammed behind Fancy.

I raced down the hall to the old man's bedroom. He was still breathing, but his lips were blue. I put my head on his chest. A steady pulse. Perhaps we still had a chance.

I dashed across the hall to Marguerite's room. She lay passed out on the bed, a damp washcloth across her forehead.

"Marguerite!" I shook her, but she just moaned and turned the other direction. An empty glass sat on the bedside table. I picked it up and sniffed. Bourbon fumes. Fancy had been right about that.

Where was Marguerite's purse? I pawed through a pile of clothing on a wingback chair at the foot of the bed. There, I found a large Coach bag and dumped its contents on the floor. I spread them about frantically until I found the black rectangle I had been searching for.

"Medical emergency at the Spine Ranch," I told the 911 operator and gave the address. "A poisoning. Bring a heavy metal antidote for arsenic."

My second call was to Shepherd. It was high time he got back in the game.

Then, I strolled out to the front parking lot. Fancy wasn't going anywhere, with the distributor cap on her old car disconnected.

***

The driver's side door was half-open when I reached the car. Fancy cranked the starter, repeatedly. The hollow clicking mocked her.

"Car problems?"

"You!" She levered the rifle in my direction.

"Hear the sirens? They're almost here."

I held up my hands. "Fancy, killing me won't prove anything. You still have a chance."

She lowered the rifle, sobbing. "Nothing ever goes right for me. Not ever!"

Part of me felt sorry for her. Her life hadn't been an easy one, and Heinrich Spine was one miserable bastard. Didn't give her the right to attempt to kill him, though. Or her parents, either, for that matter.

I pried the rifle out of her limp fingers and set it out of reach.

235

Then I helped her out of the car and handcuffed her. No Las Vegas trip for the lady this time around.

CHAPTER THIRTY-THREE

It was nearly a week later before the hospital decided to release Heinrich Spine after his close call. I drove over to the ward to debrief him before he left for the ranch. Dr. Theo and Amanda were coming out of his hospital room. Amanda seemed excited as she held onto her father's arm.

"Peg, guess what! I'm going to veterinary school. My dad finally convinced me that's what I need to do. I'm studying for the entrance exams—he's going to help me. It's what Gil would have wanted me to do."

Her face shadowed at the name and then cleared. "Dad and I came down to give Heinrich the news."

She looked young and excited, and was no longer slouching.

"The vet school is gaining a great candidate," I said. "How's your grandfather doing?"

Dr. Theo spoke up. "He's going to recover, thanks to your intervention, Peg. Any word on Fancy Morgan?"

"She's considered a flight risk, so they're holding her without bail while Arizona and Tennessee fight over who gets to try her for murder first."

"I should have realized what she was up to," Dr. Theo said. "I feel so stupid."

"Don't. No one saw. I'm glad that Heinrich is recovering. He's lucky to have his family to look after him."

Dr. Theo nodded toward Heinrich's room. "Marguerite is in

with him. Go say hello. They'll be glad to see you."

Marguerite adjusted Heinrich's pillow as I walked in the door. He swatted at her hand.

"Go away. I can do it. Don't need your help."

"What about some orange juice? It's got plenty of Vitamin C." Marguerite's voice was brittle and appeasing at the same time.

Heinrich looked up at me. "You! Where's Fancy? She knows what I like."

"Father, you know Fancy tried to kill you. Officer Quincy, here, saved your life."

The old man peered at me closely. "That so? Guess you think I owe you a thank you."

I waited, but one didn't seem to be forthcoming. "Could I talk to you in private, Dr. Spine?"

"Marguerite. Out." He pointed toward the door.

She threw me a glare, stalked into the hall, and slammed the door behind her.

"I have a favor to ask you," I said. "Would you rethink your position on the water issue? Hank Battle has been institutionalized, and his sister is going to need money to pay for his care."

"What's that to me? I don't run a charity. She want to sell? Ready to admit she's wrong? Too late."

He waved a bony finger in my face. "I don't need that worthless desert land she owns. I've got all the water I need."

"*Her* water." I held my temper with difficulty.

"Not until she proves it in court. And she doesn't have money for that." His eyes held a crafty gleam.

"Then you won't reconsider?"

"Not on your life. What's mine is mine."

His eyes shifted to the door. "Marguerite? I need you! Come in here." His voice was needy and shrill.

I didn't envy his daughter's role, now that Fancy was gone.

I stepped out into the hall and gestured to Marguerite. "He's asking for you."

When the door closed after her, I stepped farther down the hall and made one last call. The attorney answered on the first ring.

"Hello, Myra," I said. "Remember when you said you owed me a favor? Well, I've got a legal case that should interest you..." Then

I explained the situation.

Myra laughed and agreed to set up a meeting with Serena Battle.

"It sounds like exactly the sort of case I like. I'll take it on contingency. We ought to nail Heinrich Spine for plenty."

Knowing Myra, I figured that's exactly what she'd do.

***

That left me with a few other issues to put in order.

When I'd stood Rory up the night Fancy was arrested, he'd ignored my messages for days. I moved into my new house by myself, thinking how much easier it would have been with his help. I'd wondered if offering to wash the Hummer might help. Maybe not, this time.

He finally called, and we mended fences after a fashion. We left the relationship on hold. That's the way it needed to be right now. Best to stay sort-of friends—It was safer that way.

Amanda located Veronica Streicker's address, and I packed up the picture books to send to the little girl as a remembrance of her father, Gil. I hesitated about what to say. Finally, I wrote, "Your dad was a good man. He died taking care of those he loved."

I left it at that.

After the trial, that little girl would be coming into a good college fund when the bag of cash Fancy had stolen was released from evidence.

I hung the sled in my new garage to remind me that winter would be coming after this summer heat. If it ever snowed in the Verde Valley, I'd use it. In the meantime, it was a good reminder to be more flexible. As the soothsayer, Lucy Zielinski, had suggested, things were not always what they seemed.

Shepherd? He's getting ready for retirement, for real this time. Going to become a private investigator. He says there's a place for me there, anytime I want to quit this cop business.

One of these days, I might just do that.

AUTHOR NOTE TO READERS

I hope that you have had as much enjoyment reading this novel as I have had sharing it with you.

Although I've set this story in the fictitious town of Mingus, the mining region of central Arizona is still alive and thriving, and the historical setting that I've provided is accurate. The Copper Canyon grade and sudden flash floods are just as treacherous as described!

Reviews: Because an Indie novelist survives through word-of-mouth recommendations, if you enjoyed *Fire in Broken Water,* let others know about it. Tell your friends and neighbors! And please, if you will, consider posting an online review at Amazon.

Where to contact me: Please visit my website at www.LakotaGrace.com to get news of upcoming novels, to read my blog, or to give me feedback on my work.

Visit me online at my Amazon author page, my website, or on Facebook and GoodReads at Lakota Grace, Author.

I'd love to hear from you!

ABOUT THE AUTHOR

Lakota Grace has called the American Southwest home for most of her life. She has a doctorate in counseling psychology and has written stories since age five.

Lakota has an abiding love for the high desert plateau and the abundance of life it supports. Quail and red-tail hawks visit her feeders; bobcats and coyotes wander by. She maintains a cautious co-existence with the scorpions and javelinas who visit her backyard.

Most of all, she enjoys getting up before dawn, watching the sun hit the red rocks, and sharpening her pencil for yet another writing session.